"A splendid, gripping story, a mystery, deftly told and with
a fine sense of both Ireland and Newfoundland ....
Nora is a character to love and Matthew Molloy is a magnificent
creation, a maddening, intriguing fella to the end."

—*John Doyle*, author of *A Great Feast of Light* and *The World is a Ball*

"History again comes alive in Kate Evans' debut novel
Where Old Ghosts Meet, *a touching and tender tale of one
woman's efforts to uncover her family's history. Evans has
succeeded in not only giving a voice to the past of her two homelands
and its peoples, but to do so in one that is distinctly her own.*"

—*Stephen Clare*, Atlantic Books Today

"[A] *touching tale of a young woman's quest for understanding
and forgiveness.* Where Old Ghosts Meet *is a story of redemption.
It's about making an effort to find a way to open our hearts, pardon
past grievances in our families, move forward into a more
peaceful state of mind, and finally free ourselves in the end.*"

—*Sharon Greer*, Celtic Connection

"Where Old Ghosts Meet *is romantic, that is to say, mysterious and
excited about love, without ever becoming over-sentimental. Evans'
writing is fluid, carrying readers along for the ride, and her use of the
Newfoundland accents and turns of phrase give the story personality.*"

—*Melanie Grondin*, Rover Arts

"Where Old Ghosts Meet *is a novel of secrets, mystery, and
redemption. Evans captures the atmosphere of place — particularly
Shoal Cove — well. Her characters are intriguing.*"

—*Sharon Hunt*, The Chronicle Herald

KATE EVANS

WHERE

OLD

Ghosts

MEET

A Novel

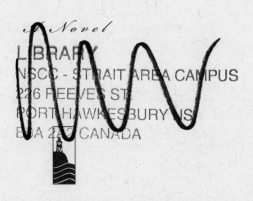

BREAKWATER BOOKS
WWW.BREAKWATERBOOKS.COM

LIBRARY AND ARCHIVES CANADA CATALOGUING IN PUBLICATION

Evans, Kate, 1943-
Where old ghosts meet / Kate Evans.
ISBN 978-1-55081-327-2
I. Title.
PS8609.V338W54 2010   C813'.6   C2010-903557-7

© 2010 Kate Evans

REPRINTED IN 2011

PRINTED IN CANADA.

We acknowledge the financial support of The Canada Council for the Arts, the Government of Canada through the Canada Book Fund and the Government of Newfoundland and Labrador through the department of Tourism, Culture and Recreation for our publishing activities.

 Canada Council for the Arts / Conseil des Arts du Canada   Canada   Newfoundland Labrador

Printed on Silva Enviro which contains 100% recycled post-consumer fibre, is EcoLogo, Processed Chlorine Free and manufactured using biogas energy.

     BIO GAS  FSC www.fsc.org RECYCLED Paper made from recycled material FSC® C021757

For Tony

On a quiet street where old ghosts meet I see her walking now...

FROM "ON RAGLAN ROAD," PATRICK KAVANAGH

1

The dank smell of autumn filled the air. Crusty leaves like tiny field mice scurried fretfully across the lawn and settled in dark corners. Pale and tired, Nora Molloy closed the front door on the last of the stragglers and switched off the porch light. The house on Hawthorn Road settled into a quiet lull and seemed to breathe a long sigh of relief. Nora shivered and went to join her sister Maureen in the sitting room of the family home.

"That was a grand send-off for the Da," Maureen said, intent on stoking the fire and banking the coals with hard dry turf. A single flame leaped upwards as the sods came to life. Maureen stood back, admired her handywork and then collapsed into the big armchair. "Now, I'm not sure that he'd have approved of a shindig." She turned to smile at her sister. "But it's too late for that."

"Now don't start on the Da, God rest him. He wasn't so bad." Nora kicked off her high-heeled shoes and threw her sister an irritated look that quickly changed to a grin when she spotted the devilment in her sister's eye. "And by the way, it wasn't a shindig. It was a ..."

"Call it what you like, he wouldn't have approved anyway."

They hadn't been together for almost two years, not since their mother's funeral in '68. Those had been days fraught with tension, reflecting nothing of their mother's life: her warmth, her interests, and her love of company. Nora remembered how she had wanted to pick armfuls of fresh flowers from her mother's precious garden and fill the little church where she lay with their colour and fragrance. It would have been so right, what she would have loved. But, "no," her father had pronounced, "a couple of small bouquets would be sufficient," and that was that. It was shortly thereafter Nora decided to leave her father to his own devices and left home to go to Canada, to Montreal, where she still lived and worked as a teacher.

This time around things had been handled differently, resulting in the arrangements taking on a slight air of defiance. Following the funeral, Nora had organized a get-together to which relatives, friends and neighbours were invited. There was food for all and plenty of whiskey and stout to drink. It had been a grand time: a final salute to the family and the old neighbourhood. Nora couldn't help but feel a twinge of guilt. It was not what her father would have wanted but deep down she felt good and she had no regrets.

The sisters talked late into the night. With the house to themselves, they revelled in their newfound freedom, they laughed and cried, drinking hot whiskeys with cloves and lemon to fuel their spirits and telling stories of old times, stories of the Da and his many eccentricities.

"My God." Maureen sat forward in the big chair. "Do you remember the day he took the bread knife to the new sideboard because it was an inch too big for the alcove?"

"I thought Mammy would have a heart attack." Nora could hardly get the words out with the laughter. "And the day he headed out to the back garden with a brush and a gallon of bright green paint, hell-bent on painting the concrete wall around the garden. He was going to 'expand his boundaries,' so he said."

"I think there might be a ripple of lunacy in the lot of us, not enough to count, mind you, but enough to make us difficult." Maureen settled back in her chair satisfied that she had just made a critical statement.

"You speak for yourself. I'm sound as a bell." Sparks flew as Nora threw another sod on the fire. The yarns became more outrageous, and the louder the laughter, the better was the telling so that in the end it was hard to distinguish truth from fiction. But the stories were there nonetheless, both real and imagined, stories that had never before found voice under their own roof, stories that sometimes brought the unexpected sting of tears. Of course the old story of the Da's da, and his disappearance so long ago, surfaced and the same questions about his mother, their grandmother, and her total absence from their lives were asked. But there were no answers. It was all a mystery and neither one of the sisters seemed to care that much anymore.

Eventually Maureen went off to bed but Nora lingered behind, reluctant to let the night end and simply feeling the need to be alone. Being an emigrant made things different. Maureen would go back home to her family in Dublin and she, Nora, would return to Montreal to her job and her small rented apartment, and from then on she would be a visitor to Ireland, staying with Maureen or whoever could accommodate her at the time. This was the end of home as she had known it, she thought as she glanced around the room. The Molloys, the model church-going family, law abiding, talented and successful, were moving on and with them all the inner tensions and uncertainties created, in large part, by a father who frequently distanced himself from those he loved and who believed, with an unfailing conviction, that he alone knew what was best for everyone. Tomorrow she would speak with Maureen about selling the house and furniture. There were a few items she would keep:

books, family papers, photographs, small treasures wrapped in tissue paper. There was little else.

Nora went to the kitchen, made cocoa and wandered back into the sitting room, clutching the hot mug, absorbing its comforting warmth. She surveyed the room and decided to empty the ashtrays but otherwise to ignore the mess. The cardboard box containing her father's papers sat in a corner. She had taken it from behind the wardrobe in her father's bedroom a few days before, looking for her father's birth certificate, and had then put it aside. Nora pulled the box towards her and found a comfortable spot on the floor in front of the fire and began to sift through the contents. Her father had been a meticulous record keeper. Old receipts and bills from years back, guarantees, certificates of births, marriage and deaths, all kinds of old documents, were neatly filed. That was his way. There was a slight catch in Nora's throat as she unfolded the faded hire purchase agreement for her mother's first Hoover washing machine. It was dated July 14, 1959. Nora remembered well the day it arrived and how her mother's eyes had sparkled, lighting up a face grey with exhaustion.

She picked up a thick wad of faded newspaper cuttings tied together with a brown string and carefully unfolded one, then another and another. Many of the articles had minutely scripted annotations and comments written in ink in the margins. She read rapidly, skimming from one to the next until finally, feeling overwhelmed, she decided to set them aside for another time.

At the bottom of the box she found a plain sealed envelope. She hesitated for a moment then turned the envelope over and gently eased open the flap. The glue was dry and brittle and came apart easily. There were two envelopes inside, each one neatly slit across the top. She examined both carefully. One was yellow with age but otherwise looked untouched. The postage stamps were American, the postmark New York, and it was addressed to Mrs. Sadie Molloy, Ballyslish, Cullen, County Roscommon, Ireland. Cullen, she murmured under her breath: her father's hometown. She felt a dull tapping in her chest as she turned the letter over. Sadie Molloy? Was she his mother, her grandmother? On the back of the envelope was a note, written in her father's hand: *This letter was found amongst the effects of my late uncle, Mickey Dolan, who died September 17, 1960. At that time it was unopened and so I suspect, unread.*

The other envelope Nora had seen once before, many years ago. She hadn't thought about it in years.

The kitchen had been empty, her mother nowhere to be seen. Maureen's school bag had lain abandoned on the table. A letter with foreign stamps sat on the mantelpiece, propped against the clock. She took it down, examining every detail, and returned it to the exact spot where she had found it. Then she went into the back bedroom where she knew Maureen was waiting.

"It's from the Da's da," Nora announced without preamble, cutting her sister off before she could draw breath.

Sitting cross-legged on the bed, Maureen slowly unravelled herself and followed, with eagle eye, Nora's every move. "You mean the grandfather who's supposed to be in America?" she asked.

"Yes," said Nora, "the very one." She threw her sister one of her know-it-all looks. "And he's not in America, he's in Newfoundland, in Canada."

"And how in the name of God would you know that? Nobody knows anything about him."

"The postmark, stupid, the handwriting of an older person … I've just put two and two together, but I bet I'm right. Besides, who else would be writing to the Da from Newfoundland?"

"Where's that?"

"Somewhere in Canada."

"He must be a real oul' fella by now, seventy years old or more." Her eyes searched the room, darting hither and thither. "Wouldn't you wonder what he's like?" She shifted in the hollow nest of the bed, eyes dancing. "Maybe he's a cowboy or even a film star … like, like, Roy Rogers! He might even have a bundle of money stashed away somewhere and is looking for someone to leave it to."

Nora turned to face her sister. "Now you're talking. He just might. We could be rich, my girl, as of this very day!"

But Maureen wasn't listening. She had sprung to her feet on top of the sagging bed, her arms flung wide in a dramatic pose. "Maybe, like Oisín, he was carried away on a great white charger, by the beautiful Niamh, her golden hair flying in the wind." She flicked at her own blonde mane. The bed springs gave a sharp yelp as she struggled to keep her balance. "Gone, gone giddy gone! Off to Tír na nÓg to live forever in the land of eternal youth." She paused for effect.

Nora jumped in. "Yes, or maybe he's just an oul' reprobate looking for a place to hang his hat!"

Maureen was quiet for a while, then, with a sharp intake of breath, she gave a wild whoop of abandonment and began to sing in her best Yankee drawl: *My daddy he's a handsome devil / He wears a chain that's five miles long / And on every link a heart does dangle / For another maid he's loved and wronged.*

Then, excited and wild-eyed, she had turned to her sister. "Wouldn't it be a gas to track him down, Nora?"

Now, the question seemed to echo in the quiet peace of the sitting room. Nora smiled at the memory as she slipped the yellowed writing paper from the envelope. She began to read, skimming for information. Then she read again, slowly this time, unconsciously brushing the pages with fleeting images of people and places, the past whispering between words. *I have never been as a father to you, so I do not presume to call you son … Blood stranger … I have no excuses to offer for my actions in the past that I think can honestly serve any purpose at this time … There are reasons only the heart can understand*

and they too, sometimes, fall short. The fact is that I deserted you and your mother… attempts at making amends went unanswered. Nora's grip tightened on the other envelope. *My life has not been to my credit … of little worth … a drifter … seventy-one years old … My dearest wish, that before I die we could perhaps look upon one another … I cherish the notion that your children would care to sit with an old man who might have been a grandfather to them … I have in my possession … items of value … they are yours …*

Nora looked up from the letter. Deep in thought she moved towards the window and drew back the curtains. To the east, a streak of pearly grey light diluted the dark sky. She cried softly, aware now of the great silent void that had existed between him and his family and realizing too late how little they had understood of him and his odd ways. In the end, exposing this very private man's secrets had been so simple. The burden of his silence left her feeling sad and then angry. She made up her mind that the next day she would go to Cullen.

The downpour was relentless. Nora leaned forward, straining to keep her eye on the edge of the road, using the side of her hand to help clear the windshield. The finger sign-post pointed to the right: Cullen 2 miles. She was almost there. She wished that Maureen had come along with her but Maureen had "no interest in seeing the back end of Roscommon on a dirty day in October. However," she had hastened to add, "down the road, if you come across anything of interest, I'd like to know."

"Maureen would only be interested if there was drama or loot at the other end," Nora muttered aloud to herself. "Then she'd be aboard all fuss and business." Suddenly, as if someone had flipped a switch, the rain eased up and the last droplets hit the windshield with a loud splat. A bit of sunshine would help, she thought as she scanned the sky looking for a break in the clouds.

It was mid-morning as she drove into the small market town, but not too many people were about. "So this is Cullen." She repeated the name again, wishing it would strike a familiar chord but the sound died on her tongue. Nora knew nothing of this place. It didn't have an identity, not even in her imagination. Cullen, where her father had grown up and gone to school, where her grandmother had lived, had rarely been mentioned in the Molloy household. They had never set foot in the place, not even to visit their grandmother.

It was strange now to stand on the wet pavement in the main street, looking up and down, trying to get a sense of the place, knowing that she belonged here, yet feeling like a complete stranger. It was a drab, dirty little town. A few small shops with dusty, faded window displays stood on either side of the main street. There was a bank, several pubs, a large three-story house with "Hotel" painted in fancy letters on a grubby glass panel above the door. A solid brass doorknob and knocker gleamed bold and defiant on the green, chipped paintwork. Stepping carefully to avoid the filthy puddles, she passed close to a garage with a single petrol pump. The reek of oil hung on the damp air. She stopped to look around. A woman wearing a bib apron and carrying a shopping bag passed by, nodded and hurried on her way. A young man parked his bicycle by a lamp post and stared blankly at Nora. This was a town stuck in the past.

She walked on up the street towards the place where a tall steeple reached into the sky above the treetops. The church with its neatly trimmed lawn was set back from the road and was surrounded by black iron railings. A sign read, Saint Michael's Catholic Church. Next door was a simple but well-maintained school. It was Saturday so there was no sign of life. The gate was slightly ajar so she went through and entered the schoolyard. She tried to picture her father as a little boy running about, yelling and shouting with the other children but that scenario didn't seem to fit. She went to the window and peered through, cupping her hands about her eyes.

She fancied she could see him inside seated at a long wooden desk, up at the front of the class, head bent with pen in hand, carefully forming letters in his copybook. He would have been comfortable here, a good student. She left the schoolyard with a new spring in her step, determined to seek out the locals and talk to them. She glanced at her watch. It was lunch time, the shops would be closed, but Muldoon's, the pub down the street, would be open by now. As she walked back down the street her father was still on her mind. He would never have crossed the threshold of Muldoon's pub. No, he had been a teetotaller all his life and wore a Pioneer pin in his lapel, the symbol of total abstinence, for all to see. As she pushed open the door to the bar, she was wondering if Muldoon's had been around in her grandfather's day.

The heavy smell of stale tobacco and porter met her as she stepped inside. Heads turned, followed by a brief lull in the conversation. An L-shaped bar surrounded by several bar stools stood to one side, and on the other there was a small group of tables and chairs. The patrons, all men, were gathered around the bar, with the exception of one old man who sat alone at a table in the corner, nursing his pint. Nora walked to the bar and stood by an empty stool. Two young men to her left nodded in her direction.

The barmaid, a brisk middle-aged woman with a fresh face and a big generous smile, leaned into the bar and asked brightly, "What are ye having?"

"A glass of orange and a ham sandwich," Nora said, returning her welcoming smile.

"Grand." She disappeared into a back room.

Nora decided to take a stool at the bar rather than sit on her own at a table. Perched like a hen on a roost was a brave choice but one she had to make if she was to engage anyone in conversation. She looked around her as if a world of interest existed within the confines of this country pub. The conversation opener, she knew, would eventually come. She just had to wait. She shifted uncomfortably. Beside her a man in a dark unkempt suit and a peaked cap leaned against the bar, his back to Nora. She knew by the very set of him, the space he commanded, the look of his clothes, that he was a man of importance, a shopkeeper or a cattle dealer, perhaps. She also knew that despite his apparent indifference to her presence, he had taken stock of her, as she had of him and that he would want to know her business. She tried to ignore his bulk, which seemed altogether too close to her, but in spite of her best efforts, her eyes kept returning to the pink stubbly bulge above his shirt collar. Like a pig's rump, she thought, resisting an urge to reach over and touch the prickly lump with her fingertip.

The woman behind the bar appeared from the back room with two steaming plates of dinner: boiled bacon, cabbage, turnip, potatoes, and set them down in front of the two lads to her left.

"Begob, that'll put fuel in the old tank, boys." There was laughter. The shopkeeper had broken the ice. He turned slowly to face Nora, shoving his big hands deep into his trouser pockets and drawing himself up to his full height. "Y'er not from these parts now, are ye?"

The answer, she knew, had to be informative and forthright if she hoped to engage him in conversation.

"No, I'm not," she said. "I'm from Leitrim, but I live in Canada now, Montreal. I'm just home for a short stay."

"Ah, home from America, so that's it."

"No, Canada." She was glad to take a jab at the self-importance of the shopkeeper.

"And what would bring a girl like you to Cullen?" His eyes travelled the length of her.

"My father came from Cullen. His name was Molloy, Eamon Molloy. They owned a small farm around here years ago." Nora watched carefully.

The shopkeeper contemplated his boots for a minute, finally turned and spoke to the others. "Have ye ever heard tell of a fella from around here be the name of Molloy?"

There were mumbles. "No, never heard tell of that name. No, no Molloys around here, must be farther away towards Boyle they lived. There's Molloys over that way," one fellow offered.

Nora's sandwich arrived. They talked some more but she was getting nowhere with her inquiries.

The lunch-time crowd gradually got up and left and Nora, disappointed, gathered her belongings and headed back out to the street. Outside, she paused to consider her next move.

The door behind her opened and shut. The old man who had sat alone in the corner with his pint was standing beside her.

"Years ago, I knew the Molloys from below in Ballyslish."

Nora scrutinized the rough weather-beaten face with its dark eyes set deeply above a high arching nose. A bony hand reached up and made a slight adjustment to his tweed cap as if to set a thought process in motion. Then he put one foot ahead of the other and looked down the main street and off into the distance.

"The Molloys had a small far'um o' land maybe five or six mile out the road. Yer father lived there with the mother as a young ladeen. She was a Dolan from these parts. He went to school down below in the town. I was there meself then. He was a smart ladeen, yer father, got the scholarships and all, and went off to the secondary school, in spite of everything."

"What do you mean, everything?"

The man looked at her askance and set about adjusting his cap again.

"Do you mean the business with the father?" Nora urged.

"The father I didn't know at all. I think he went off to America and left them high and dry: all alone … the mother and the young fella, Eamon, yer father. That was how I heard it anyways, but I don't rightly know. We didn't see much of Eamon after he went off to the secondary school." He looked Nora over as if seeing her for the first time. The skinny tip of his tongue appeared and slicked his lower lip. "I thought he joined the priests but I suppose that couldn't be right."

"No," she said simply, "that's not altogether right. He did spend some time in the seminary but he left and later married. I'm his daughter. Nora is my name. I don't know yours."

"Packie Brennan." He shook her offered hand.

"My father died recently," Nora said, by way of keeping the conversation going.

"The Lord have mercy on him. It's comin' time for us all." He looked off into the distance again.

"Mr. Brennan." Nora felt strange asking this question: "What became of old Mrs. Molloy, his mother?"

He shifted position, again fingering his cap. "Well now, as far as I know, she lived below in Ballyslish for a whileen. During the Troubles, I remember hearing how the Black and Tans ransacked the house one night and then put a torch to it. The story goes she stood her ground, with the young fella by her side, until the flames was lickin' her ankles. After that, they had to move back in with the brother, Mickey Dolan. He lived farther up the way. An oul' bachelor he was and a miserable oul' crathur, to the day he died."

Mickey Dolan, she knew that name from the letter. Already she disliked its owner.

"I don't rightly know what became of the oul' woman after that."

"Do you know anyone who might know?"

"Arra, girleen, don't go worrying your head about things like that. It's a long time ago and there's not too many of us left."

"What about the house?"

"Ah, sure, tis all fallen down. The land belongs to the Farrels now. Twas only a small placeen. Yer father sold it after, I suppose."

"Can you tell me how to get there, Mr. Brennan?"

The ruins of the cottage lay in a little isolated hollow surrounded by trees and vegetation. At one time it must have been a comfortable location, but high in the treetops heavy growth had closed in, cutting off the sunlight, creating a dark, damp vault below. Thick ropes of ivy clawed their way up and around the tree trunks and into the branches, silently choking life from the trees. The creeper had also attacked the cottage, entering the house by the doors and windows, eating into the mortar and dragging the walls stone by stone to the ground. Nature had taken over from the fire and wiped out the past. There were no memories here, no stone boundaries to contain and define former times, just a tall gable end, standing on its own like a giant headstone, with no epitaph.

Nora sat huddled on a mossy mound, trying to capture the home that had once been there, but silence settled heavily on the clearing so that she barely heard the misty rain as it touched the leaves. One day, more than a half-century ago, her grandfather had walked away from this place, leaving behind his wife and little son. He had never returned. She had, at one time, on a memorial card, seen a picture of the woman he had deserted. It was a grainy kind of photo. Nora couldn't even recall the face. However, she did remember clearly one day when she was maybe nine or ten years old. Her father had appeared in the kitchen dressed in his best suit of clothes, carrying a small briefcase.

"I'll be back in a day or two." It was just a statement of fact and invited no comment. With that, he walked out of the kitchen, quietly closing the door behind him.

She had clutched her mother's hand tightly.

"What's wrong, Mammy?"

"Your father's mother died today. He's gone to the funeral."

"And are we not going?"

"No, child, we're not. Daddy wants to be alone today."

"But I could hold his hand, Mammy, and I promise I wouldn't say a word."

Her mother had drawn her close. "Maybe if you and I hold hands tightly, Daddy will feel that we are beside him."

Nora fingered the soft green moss on the rock. Her mother, she thought sadly, always the conciliator, always trying to make things right. Late afternoon was drawing in, slowly deepening the shadows in the hollow. Nora decided to go back to the car and head for home.

That night in the small bedroom that she and Maureen had shared all their lives, Nora's sleep was troubled and fretful. In her dreams she was in an empty room standing on a stepladder, scraping wallpaper. She held a large wet sponge which she passed slowly, ever so slowly, across the dry surface, watching the colours deepen and spread. Water ran down her arm, falling pat, pat, pat on the paper below. As she slipped the thin metal edge of the scraper beneath a puffy bulge, the paper came away in long damp swales and fell to the ground. Underneath, there was another layer of paper, and another. She remembered feeling tired and frustrated, wanting to give up, when suddenly, she sensed a presence hovering close beside her and a voice, soft but insistent, repeating over and over "good girl … good girl." There was yet another layer of paper: faded water lilies on a pale background. Beneath the water lilies was the bare wall.

2

In the small community of Shoal Cove, Newfoundland, Peg Barry moved quietly about her kitchen. Mornings were always the same: first a cup of tea with two spoons of sugar – that was the only time she took sugar in her tea – and then later on a bowl of hot porridge with a teaspoon of molasses, no milk. Her breakfast was almost ready. She was late today, had stayed longer than usual sitting outside her front door enjoying her tea with sugar in the early morning sunshine. To her mind it was the best time of the day: before the sun became too hot and too many people were about. When her food was ready she sat down to the table, dropping heavily into her chair with a little groan, glad to be off her feet. Before she ever got out of bed these days she could tell the weather by the ache in her bones. But she wasn't complaining, for otherwise she was in good health.

Peg's place was a small boxy house set a little way back from the road. It had neither character nor style, one of those modern homes built cheaply without a whole lot of thought. At this stage in her life she cared little about the outside appearance. Inside it was warm and comfortable, easy to care for and it suited her needs just fine; besides, from her window out back she had the finest view of the bay in the whole of the community. She had moved there from Berry Island a few years back, in '62, around the time that many of the island communities were being resettled. The government was encouraging people to move to the mainland where they said better services and more jobs were available. She had held on for several years after most of the inhabitants had gone, but finally the time came when she too made up her mind to leave.

Her nephew Pat had made all the arrangements. He had asked her to move into his place with Bride and the children but she was too independent for that. Pat understood Peg and her ways. He was her mainstay, as good as any son. What's more, he could turn his hand to any job she needed done. A few years ago, knowing her fondness for the view out back, Pat had replaced the little slider in the kitchen with the big picture window. She called it her window on the world: her own private world.

Now as she sat there sipping her second cup of tea, she lingered on those days she had spent on Berry Island. She recalled how, as a young boy, Pat would come by every day to see Aunt Peg. She loved to watch him come over the path, breaking into a run for the last few yards to the house. She'd have fresh-baked bread and molasses for him and a mug of tea or sometimes a piece of plate tart spread thick with berry jam. He'd sit to the table like a little man and tell her all the news and then be off to help at home. In many ways she still thought of Pat as a youngster, even though he must be close to fifty years old now with a slew of his own youngsters, but he never seemed to grow old in her mind.

She finished the last of her porridge and quickly ran her fingers over her chin and mouth to check for stray scraps. Satisfied, she eased herself up from the table and began to tidy up.

The screen door opened and banged shut and Pat's little daughter Hanna stood in the doorway holding a bunch of flowers. She held them out to Peg, not saying a word, just glowing with the pleasure of her giving. Peg reached for the posy, a big purple lupin banked with the delicate creaminess of Queen Anne's Lace, several stalks of grass, their smooth green heads standing stiffly to attention like the queen's own guard, and a few sprigs of pink clover and golden buttercups. Below the chubby fist, ragged stems and muddy roots hung in disarray, but the child saw nothing of this, only the delight in the old woman's eyes.

"Well, God love and bless you, my darling."

Peg could feel the soft little hands, hot with exertion, as her own crippled fingers struggled to hold the flowers together.

"Smell, Aunt Peg, smell."

Peg brought the flowers to her nose. "Is it any wonder the bees like to play about in the meadow all day?"

The child clapped excitedly. "And the butterflies," she insisted.

"Yes, my dear. We'll put them here in the yellow jug. That will be lovely."

They had just finished doing up the flowers when the doorbell rang.

"The fine weather's got everyone on the go today. Go see who's there, that's a good girl." Peg ushered the child towards the door. She ran off but she was back again in a second, looking uncertain and not saying a word.

"Well, who is it, child?"

"She wants you, Aunt Peg."

"Well, tell her come in."

She reached up, pushed a wisp of hair off her face and fiddled about with the loose knot of hair on the top of her head in a futile attempt to hold it firmly in place. A strange voice came from the porch. She dabbed at the bodice of her faded floral dress. That morning she had decided it wasn't dirty enough for washing. Now she wished she hadn't been so foolish, trying to get another day out of a dress.

"In there," she heard Hanna say.

A young woman stepped hesitantly into the kitchen. She was tall and thin with long bare legs and a very short skirt. Two purple daisies on gold chains dangled from her ears. She was a very modern-looking young woman, the kind you saw on the television these days.

For a moment the stranger stared blankly at Peg without speaking. Then, as if prodded by an invisible finger, she stepped forward and blurted out, "I'm Matt Molloy's granddaughter, Nora Molloy, from Ireland."

Reaching behind her, Peg grabbed the edge of the table and with an effort shifted her weight unsteadily. "Blessed God," she muttered under her breath. Her gaze until now had been direct and smiling but now it was alert and guarded.

The screen door banged shut. The child was gone.

Suddenly everything had changed for Peg Barry. Her day had hardly begun in earnest and already it was upside down. Matt's grandchild was here in her kitchen, standing not four feet away, tall and lanky, with bare legs and a head of dark curls on her just like his. Her mind was addled. For years she had hoped and prayed for this day, she and Matt both, and now inside of her, something was twisting about like a rope on a winch. She was speechless.

"You are Peg Barry who used to live on Berry Island?" Huge dark eyes, heavily outlined in black, focused on Peg.

Not his eyes. Peg had recovered some of her composure and was taking a long hard look at the stranger. The light from the window was full on her face. She had a good mouth, full and generous. You could tell a lot about a person by their mouth, she always thought. Peg took her time before speaking. "Yes, I'm Peg Barry. You've got the right one."

"The man at the store told me that you knew my grandfather. He said you were the one to talk to."

"You spoke to John Joe at the store?" There was an edge to her voice. Like a watchful bird ready for flight her eyes darted back and forth. "Might as well have put it on The Doyle Bulletin." She offered no explanation but it was clear to Nora that she had done the wrong thing.

"I had no real address, just Berry Island and Shoal Cove. I had to ask." The colour had begun to rise in Nora's cheeks. She toyed with the idea of turning around and simply walking out the door as the child had done and forgetting the whole business. What did it matter after all these years?

The old woman shifted her weight again, her hand clutching hard at the edge of the table. She winced, her forehead gathering up like a concertina, her eyebrows coming sharply together, but still she never took her eyes off Nora.

"I'm sorry. I shouldn't have barged in on you like this. I'll leave now." Nora made a move towards the door.

"How did you know about Berry Island?"

"A letter he wrote, years ago. My father kept it safe amongst his things."

"Did he now?" Peg's mouth clamped shut, the corners dropping to form small fleshy pockets close to her jawline. With a slight toss of her head she turned away. "I wouldn't have thought he'd care about the like of that."

Nora's eyebrows shot up. "I think he cared," she said, leaping to her father's defence. And then more hesitant. "He must have. He kept it, didn't he?"

Peg turned back, a sharp retort ready on the tip of her tongue, but in that brief moment before she spoke, she saw Matt in the young woman, something in the turn of her head, the uncertainty in her eyes. The words died on her lips. Without warning, the fear and apprehension that had gripped her like a tight corset began to fall away. She sighed deeply, a sigh of acceptance. "I wish with all my heart that Matt was here today to see his grandchild." Her words were only for herself and barely audible.

An uneasy silence settled on the room, like the empty feeling that hangs about after a lie has been told and then exposed.

"Come, my dear," she said finally. "If I seems a bit strange, don't pay no attention. It's just the shock is all."

She left the table and came towards Nora, rocking slightly from side to side on her painful knees. She clutched Nora's forearm for support but in the pressure of her fingertips there was also reassurance. Smiling now, she led Nora to the other side of the room where a big over-stuffed armchair and a wooden rocker stood on either side of a small television set.

"I calls this my throne," she said, relieving some of the tension as she lowered herself into the rocker. It's nice and high, easy to get into and easy to get out of. You can sit there." She indicated the armchair. "That's Matt's chair; he loved that chair, he did. When I moved here from the island, I brought it with me all the way; up front she was, in the bow of the skiff. I couldn't part with it. It's very old, used to be my father's chair."

The tip of her shoe touched the floor and her own chair rocked back and forth, making small clicking sounds on the vinyl floor. "There's a lot of memories with that chair."

"We had a couple of chairs at home very like this one." Nora ran her hand over the faded brocade, smoothing the threadbare arm. "They were set on either side of the fireplace and they too were old with a musty smell off them, not offensive, just a part of home." She sat back against the heavy horsehair cushioning, feeling how snugly it settled in around her back. "When we were children," she continued, "my sister and I would kneel together at one of those chairs when we'd be saying the family rosary. We'd search amongst the crevasses and down behind the springs, looking for pennies or any other treasures that might have fallen from pockets." Her hand slipped automatically into the gap between the seat and the arm of the old chair. "Between the Hail Marys we'd whisper and giggle, remembering all the bums that over the years had created the big hollow in the middle of the seat. When we got to naming names, things usually got out of hand and giggles became great snorts of laughter. My father would get mad then and separate us."

Peg laughed. "My dear, that's how it is with children. Much the same the world over, always up to some mischief." It was very quiet in the little kitchen.

"Matt liked to sit in that chair of a night when he read his books." Peg raised a finger to scratch at the hairline just above her left eye. "Sometimes he'd read to me. He'd say, 'Listen to this, Peg, listen to this.' He was a wonderful reader, your grandfather. The words would flow so beautiful. Sometimes I didn't understand right, what he was readin' to me, but it put me in mind of music. That was good enough for me most times." For a while she sat, eyes downcast, lost in thought.

Nora took the chance to study the face of the woman she had come to see. Her skin, pale and dull, hung in limp folds along her jawline. Her mouth had all but disappeared. Across her forehead and about her eyes there were deep careworn lines. Time had not been kind to this face.

"I've never had that chair cleaned, you know. All the dust of the island is still there and the dirt too, I'll allow." They both laughed softly. It was then Nora saw the bright mischievous twinkle that lit up a pair of lovely grey eyes and transformed the ravaged face to one full of life and humour.

Her eyes wandered from the woman to her surroundings. At a glance Nora could see that the room was a multi-purpose space. Across from where they sat, a small kitchen unit ran along one wall. By a large window on the back wall, there was an old wooden kitchen table surrounded by three old-fashioned chairs. There was clutter everywhere. Things were tucked into corners and piled on every available space. There were letters and brown business envelopes, newspapers piled on the floor, a bag of knitting on a wooden stand, several potted plants and, to her surprise, elegantly perched on the front window ledge, a fat marmalade-coloured cat. It blinked once, a long slow blink as if to acknowledge her presence, and then resumed its frank unperturbed stare.

"Do you have any pictures of my grandfather?" She dragged her eyes away from the cat.

Peg indicated the wall behind Nora, where a whole assortment of photographs all done up in frames hung between the two small front windows. Nora rose from her chair for a closer look. Some of the pictures were old and yellowed, some were new. There was a little girl in a long white communion dress, looking shy, a young man in a soldier's uniform, legs tightly bound from ankle to knee. A coloured portrait of a young woman in a nurse's uniform, holding a bunch of roses, stood out from the others. Then she saw him: a pallid serious face looking right at her. She waited for a rush of affection, a feeling of excitement, but there was nothing. She moved in closer for a better look. He was quite good looking, a strong jawline, a neat well-shaped blunt nose and, on top of all, a thick crop of dark curly hair brushed to one side and sticking up, looking remarkably like a whin bush that had been set in place forever by the prevailing wind. Her hand flew to her own hair. So, she had him to thank for her unruly mop.

"This has to be him," she said, pointing to the picture. "He's the image of my father, except for the hair."

Peg nodded.

"I was hoping he'd still be alive but I knew it was a long shot." She hesitated. "I'm glad that you are here, Peg. May I call you Peg?"

"Yes, my dear, you can indeed. Most people calls me Aunt Peg, but call me whatever you please."

Nora sat down.

Peg had stopped rocking and now leaned over to speak to Nora. "That letter you have that Matt wrote to your father…" She searched about, looking for the right words. "My dear, I have to tell you about that. It was me got him to write that letter. I didn't know for sure but I felt in my gut that it was the right thing to do. It was some hard for him, writing that. Said he didn't know what to say. A man that loved words so much didn't know what to say! I told him: Write what's in your heart, that's all you need do. You see, he knew a little bit about you all. There was someone lived in Boston who gave him a bit of news time to time. He knew there was grandchildren and he knew when she died, his wife, I mean, and where the family lived to. Just a few facts, far as I could make out, but that was all. Day in, day out, he watched for the mail, looking for a reply. Then, one day, there it was."

"There's a letter, come from Ireland, looks like." She was trying her best to stay calm but her heart was flapping like a sheet in a stiff breeze.

Matthew's shoulders tensed, his grip tightening on the newspaper in his hands, but otherwise he never moved.

Peg held out the thin greyish-white envelope edged with green and orange squares. "Here, Matt, take it. It's for you." She pushed the letter towards him, nodding encouragement.

After a moment he folded the newspaper carefully and set it to one side. She put the letter in front of him. She watched, as, like a dog sizing up a new bone, he regarded the rectangular envelope. He touched the stamps, running his finger corner to corner around the serrated edge. "Eire." He spoke the word on the stamp softly and a moment later picked up the letter and asked for a knife.

Peg hurried to the drawer and set a knife by his hand.

He turned the envelope over and then carefully slit it along the crease. The single sheet of thin transparent paper was folded neatly three ways from top to bottom. It crackled to the touch.

Peg moved away and busied herself at the fire, but a few minutes later when she glanced over her shoulder he was staring out the window. The single sheet of paper lay discarded on the tabletop.

"What does it say?" There was no need to ask who it was from.

He didn't answer right away but then, without even a glance at the paper, he spoke the contents in a dull monotone:

> *Dear Mr. Molloy,*
>
> *I regret to inform you, that at this time, I cannot see my way to issuing you an invitation to come to Ireland with a view to meeting with me, my wife and my children. As you have not seen fit to contact me over the past forty-six years and consequently know little about us, I think that this move would be inappropriate and an exercise in futility.*
>
> *Yours sincerely,*
> *Eamon Molloy*

"I don't want to say anything out of turn about your father, but that letter, well, the letter sounded just like something from a government official. I tried to console him, saying that one day maybe things would change. Now, can you believe it? After all these years, you've come. I was right. Now, I think we should have a cup of tea, girl, or maybe a bite to eat. It's getting on for lunch time."

3

Peg held the loaf of bread close to her chest, drawing the serrated blade back and forth with a well-practiced hand. Crumbs tumbled to the floor and onto the table but she took no notice. Balancing the thick slice of bread between the knife blade and her thumb, she passed the bread to Nora and then proceeded to cut a second slice for herself.

"I'll get the soup." Nora went to fetch the two steaming bowls.

"It's just a bit of pea soup I made yesterday." Peg brushed the crumbs off the table and sat down.

"It looks delicious. You still cook for yourself every day?"

"Yes, girl. I like everything fresh. Might as well boil up them newspapers," she nodded at the pile stacked at the end of the table, "as eat that old garbage you get to the store. Besides, I like to do a bit of cookin'. Gives me something to do."

The sun had edged its way around the corner of the house and fell diagonally across the table. Feeling the warmth on her shoulder and forearm, Nora looked up. "What a grand view you have from here."

"On a day like today everything looks grand, girl. But there's days I can't see beyond the rise out there, the fog is that thick. It's the same with the snow and sleet: everything blotted out, just like you've pulled down a blind. Can't see a blessed thing then. But it can shift about just like that and then the cliffs and the rocks come out of nowhere, right at you. It's all fine and grand so long as you're in here lookin' out, but if you're out there lookin' for a way in, it's not so grand then."

"Does the water freeze over in winter?"

"No, girl, not really. But time to time we get a skim of ice close to shore, and in the spring of the year the slob ice sometimes comes in the bay. The youngsters go pan hoppin' then. You know, jumpin' from one pan of ice to the other, playin' about. When we were to the island we seemed to get it worse. Winter months I remember lying in the bed, a gale blowin' outside. Nights like that you'd think the house would just take off with the lot of us still in our beds and be gone out to sea. Next mornin' when we'd wake, the spray off the water would be froze solid on the windows to the front of the house." She finished up her soup, wiping around the edges of her bowl with the last crust of bread.

"Matt never liked to be on the water," she said suddenly. "Made him sick to his stomach, but now he loved the sound and the smell of the sea." She dabbed at the corners of her mouth. "Of an evenin' he'd walk up over the hills and down in the coves. He paid no heed to the weather. He'd just sit for hours and watch the waves, and the tide and the kelp floatin' about on the rocks. Put him in mind of Ireland, he told me one time." She began to tease at the woolly fringe of her placemat, picking apart the matted strands with her thumbnail.

Nora watched and listened.

"June 10, 1920," Peg continued, feeling grateful for the silence and the lack of small talk. She turned to look out across the water to the horizon. "It was a beautiful day, the day he arrived on the island, not so hot as today, but sunny and bright." She smoothed the unruly fringe with her fingertips and pressed it flat to the table. "I was in the garden to the side of the house getting the ground ready to set out the cabbages. Tell truth I saw his shadow before I saw him. It was a long dark shadow with a hat and it fell right across where I was to. When I come about, the sun was in my eyes so I had a hard time to see who was there. 'That's heavy soil you have there, it needs to be worked.' Them's the first words he spoke to me. It seemed like he'd been close by, watchin' for a while and I didn't know. I was stunned for a minute but by and by I got a good look at him. First thing I noticed was the white shirt; all proper he was done up in a suit and a soft kind of hat. He looked for all the world like a priest except that the clothes were not real black, just dark. The only thing out of place was the suitcase in his hand."

Her eyes twinkled as she turned to Nora. "'Well,' I said to myself, 'God be praised, it's not every day a fine looking man in a nice shirt and suit shows up to my door.' He was too, a fine looking man," she added quickly. "Not a big man, but sort of regular size with a nice serious face. He was no youngster either; thirty-four years old he was then. 'Am I speaking with Mrs. Barry?' he says. 'Yes,' I said to him, 'I'm Peg Barry.'

"With that he set the suitcase on the ground by his feet, took off his hat and began to tell me he'd met Johnny, my husband, in London a few years earlier. Johnny was on leave and was headed back to the front the next day. Matt made him a promise he'd come and see me. Well, my dear, if he'd taken the spade from my hand and knocked me to the ground I wouldn't have been more shocked." She turned to explain, "Johnny, my husband, twenty-four years old he was when he marched off to war one day and never came back. Missing in action is what they wrote me. Gone, like last year's snow, disappeared into the ground in France. I never laid eyes on him no more." Her voice trailed off like a wisp of smoke.

She found a small smooth dent in the table and began to rub

gently with her forefinger. "I made supper for Matt that evening while he sat and talked to my father. Those days my father was poorly. He'd had a stroke the winter before and couldn't get about no more. His mind was the finest kind but he had a hard time talking. You had to listen close to know what he'd be trying to say. When the neighbours used to come and visit him, they'd talk like he wasn't there, like he was gone with the fairies or couldn't hear no more. Instead they'd go on to me with their old men's talk and foolish jabbering. To begin with, I tried to include my father in the talk and be interested in what they had to say but in the end I'd just say yes and no and wish them gone. But now Matt, he sat and talked to him and listened to what he had to say. He told him about London in war time and about Ireland and the troubles there. He took time with him, answered his questions, what he could understand of them, and never seemed to get crooked. At the time I thought how nice it was to hear again the sound of a man's voice about the place: a young man's voice. My father asked him to bide awhile with us and I was right delighted."

She took a deep breath and cleared her throat. "Later that night when my father got tired of all the talk, I saw him to bed in the front room: that was where he slept those days. It was easier for me. When I come back to the fire and sat down, it was a bit awkward between us, but after a bit I got around to speaking."

"About Johnny, a message written on a piece of paper … well, it doesn't put a man to rest, you know."

Matthew Molloy leaned forward in his chair, his elbows coming to rest on his knees, his hands clasped together. "I'm sorry," he said softly.

She leaned forward, alert, anxious not to miss a word. The back of his head was close to her face. There was a faint oily smell off his scalp. The hair was thick and coarse, cut close in at the back and sides. Her eyes followed the curve of his head up to the crown where tight curls twisted and turned into a thick clump. About his ears, tiny flecks of grey showed through. In that moment, she had an urge to reach out and touch those curls, to reassure herself that it was someone real who sat in the chair beside her, but even as the thought crossed her mind, his head came up, as if he had sensed what she was about to do.

She caught his eye, compelling him to look at her. "You know something, Mr. Molloy," she said. "People don't talk about Johnny no more, not even his own mother. Once the letter came that was it. It's like he never existed." His eyes dropped and he shifted in his chair, pulling back ever so slightly, but she paid no heed. "Sometimes I think I hear him laughin' below in the yard. I think he's goin' to walk in through the door or sneak up behind me like he used to, and frighten the livin' daylights out of me."

For a fleeting moment laughter seemed to fill the kitchen and then just as quickly it was gone, leaving behind an empty silence.

"How did you come to meet Johnny?" Her question, hard and precise, dragged them back to reality.

"I met him purely by chance." The answer was on the tip of his tongue, as if he had been anticipating the question. "It was a chilly evening in London, close to the end of October. I had things on my mind that night so I decided to take a walk down by the river near Victoria. The war was on everyone's mind, it was all people talked about. The streets were alive with men in uniform like Johnny. Some were injured, maimed, some laughing, excited and happy. The train stations were packed with soldiers leaving and returning from the front. It was a ghastly kind of excitement. Everywhere I turned, Lord Kitchener was staring out from a poster, pointing a finger, demanding: JOIN YOUR COUNTRY'S ARMY! It wasn't my country and I wanted no part of the war here or anywhere else. I made the decision that night to go to America."

He straightened up and leaned back in his chair. All the while he spoke, her eyes never left his face. Every word she took in like a clean breath of fresh air.

"Go on," she urged him.

"I was feeling a bit light-hearted and relieved at the thought of going to America and as I walked back along the embankment, I heard noise and laughter coming from a pub and I wandered in. The lads in there were mostly in uniform. I thought they were Irish fellows who had joined up. They sounded Irish, but they were Newfoundlanders: The Newfoundland Regiment. They were back in London for a refit before returning to France. It was your Johnny who spoke to me. We talked for a while. That day he'd been 'down to No. 58,' he said, to pick up his wages and letters, and now they were celebrating. He looked fit and well, no injuries that I could see."

He looked right at her then and she knew that he spoke the truth. She waited, not wishing to hurry him but eager for more.

"Johnny talked about Newfoundland and Berry Island," he continued, comfortable in his role as storyteller. "He was full of stories about fishin' and what he called swilin', that was, 'going to the ice,' he told me, 'after the seals.' He was a great man to talk. In fact, when he got going he sounded as if he came straight from Waterford in Ireland. When I told him that, he was delighted, said his great-grandfather came from there way back."

She could hardly believe what she was hearing: her Johnny, young, healthy, enjoying himself, and gettin' ready to march off to his death. "Yes," she said, "he was a great talker." Then, suddenly, frightened that their time that evening might pass with chit-chat and be gone forever, she summoned up the courage to ask the one question that had been in her mind all along. "Did he ... well, did he mention me?" The words sounded silly and girlish and were no sooner out of her mouth than she wished them back.

Without a second thought he answered. "Johnny told me that he had married the brightest star in the whole of Newfoundland."

The very idea of him saying such a thing to a stranger shocked her but deep down she was delighted. That was the Johnny she loved: he made her laugh and that made up for a lot of his faults. "You wouldn't want to pay no attention to him," she said, pushing aside her feelings. "He could charm the leg off an iron pot with his old palaver."

Matt began to rummage inside his pocket and produced a small package wrapped in brown paper. "He gave me this for you," he said, holding out the package. "I was to tell you that it was what all the girls in London were wearing."

Peg touched Nora's arm and got to her feet. "I've got something I want to show you." She shuffled off in the direction of her bedroom. A minute later she was back and placed a small package on the table. She sat down and slowly undid the string. The pale sheen of silk stockings, new and never worn, caught the light from the afternoon sun. Peg reached out to touch the silky folds. "I've never told that story to a living soul before today," she whispered.

4

When the dishes were done Peg removed her apron, hung it on a nail behind the back door and with a touch of apology said, "I need to take a little spell now. Come afternoon, I get tired. While I'm at that you could take a look at Matt's books; you'll want to see them."

"Books?" Nora had forgotten about the possessions. "Yes, of course. I'd like that."

"They're below in the back bedroom." Peg pointed to the end of the hallway before entering her own bedroom and closing the door behind her. She had in her quiet way brought the morning's activities to an end, but Nora, standing by the stove folding the damp dishtowel, knew it was not a signal that it was time for her to leave. There was a shared intimacy between them now which, like a bud in the spring of the year, was gradually unfolding.

The room at the end of the hallway was small and at first glance seemed to be used partly for storage; yet, it was bright and fresh smelling. A single metal-framed bed covered with a bright, multicoloured, knitted blanket stood in one corner of the room. Beside the bed several cardboard boxes piled one on top of the other served as a makeshift bedside table. A white crocheted doily with a green trim covered the top of the boxes. Nora moved across the room and stood by the small slider window that looked out to the back of the house. Beside the window there was what looked like a kitchen dresser with four shelves all neatly lined with books. It was a lovely piece of furniture, she thought, handmade, and old. Nora touched the smooth surface of the wood, admiring the simple lines and the honeyed warmth of the old pine. It should have held pretty dishes but it served its new purpose very well. Her hand dropped to one of the round wooden knobs on the drawers. Endless years of handling had left a shiny bright spot on the curved surface. She pulled gently and the drawer came smoothly towards her. It was full of papers, neatly bound into bundles with elastic bands. A slight push and the drawer slid back in place. A small wave of pleasure ran through her. She liked things that worked.

She turned her attention back to the books. Curious, anticipation mounting, she scanned the titles and the authors, her fingers running along the curve of the spines, pausing to smooth over a small tear on a faded dust jacket. They were in beautiful condition for the most part, finely bound and old. Were these the possessions he had mentioned in his letter? Peg must have brought them with her from the island. Nora looked out the little window to the vast expanse of ocean, imagining the scene: a boat piled high with the very necessities of life and a box, boxes of books belonging to a dead man.

She ran her fingers along the spines again, pausing here and there, finally choosing *Wordsworth's Poetical Works*: gold lettering on warm brown leather, the spine ornamented from top to bottom in golden filigree patterns. A touch on the tip and it came smoothly into her hand. It was exquisite, the cover soft and pliable, gilt-edged pages fanning delicately at her touch. Hanging from the bottom, a silky braided ribbon guided her to an opening: *How richly glows the water's breast / Before us tinged with evening hues, / While facing thus the crimson west, / The boat her silent course pursues!*

She fingered the ribbon, wondering if he had been the last person to read these lines and mark the page. She tried to picture him as she was now, standing there reading, book in hand. Would he have placed one foot ahead of the other as her father did, muttering to himself as he read? She began to turn the pages slowly, barely touching the thin sheets – "Lines Written Above Tintern Abbey." She read on, recalling her school days in dreary convent classrooms, knowing at the time that there was magic somewhere in those lines but unable or unwilling to rise beyond her hatred of school. Reluctantly, she closed the book and returned it to its place next to a faded clothbound volume entitled *A Treasury of the Theatre* and alongside *Chief European Dramatists*.

On the lower shelf *The Complete Works of William Shakespeare* caught her eye. It was unusual in that it was quite compact in size, maybe 5 x 7 inches. She slipped it from its place. Age and sunlight had left the spine discoloured and slightly worn but the front cover was the rich green of a Mediterranean olive. She touched the tooled calfskin, feeling the luxury of the soft padded leather. Here, in her hand was the weight of thousands of brilliantly chosen words bound in perfect balance and symmetry. She turned the book over and drew in a sharp breath in shock. An ugly black burn mark spread across the entire back cover. She touched a rough brittle spot along the rim at the corner. Then, concealed in the thickness of the book, she saw a small section of charred brown edges. She brought the book to her nose. The acrid smell of burning was long gone but the cruel evidence remained. Carefully she opened the book at the damaged section. A black jagged edge halfway down the pages marked where the creeping glow had run its course and been extinguished. She touched the scorched words with the pad of her finger as if, by some miracle, she could undo the harm. She was upset by her discovery. Why, she wasn't quite sure. She closed the book and turned it over, examined the cover closely, opened it again, searching for possible explanations. The end papers were the colour of thick cream and were finely marbled in green and gold. She turned the leaf. On the plain dedication page, neatly written in a fine hand, she read:

Matthew Molloy
From William Sommerton
With Congratulations
MDCCCXCVII

The ink had faded to a watery brown but the words were still quite legible. One thousand, eight, she began to decipher the roman numerals, pointing with her finger: one, eight, nine, seven. 1897. She checked again. Yes, she was right. She began to subtract … Seventy-three years ago, this book had been given to him by someone called William Sommerton. She repeated the name under her breath; not a common name in the west of Ireland. She looked again, closer: William Sommerton. She spoke the name again and again, hoping for some explanation to leap off the page.

A sharp meow by her feet made her jump. The cat stood there, its frank, inquisitive eyes fixed on her. She snapped the book shut and immediately returned it to its place on the shelf. The cat continued to stare. "Out," she whispered angrily, pointing in the direction of the door. "It is my business." Then, walking purposefully to the door, she held it wide open. Slowly the cat turned and with a self-satisfied swagger, made its exit. Nora closed the door tightly, making sure this time that the catch held. She had been invited to explore, she reassured herself, as she returned to the books, but put the Shakespeare back in its place.

On the lower shelf a small collection of Irish writers caught her attention. Yeats; *Sean O'Casey: Early Poems, Plays, Essays; The Playboy of the Western World: Poems and Translations* by J.M. Synge. The publisher was Cuala Press. These were treasured old copies. She drew *Poems and Translations* from the shelf. As she suspected it was a first edition. Given the time in which he lived and the look of the books, she surmised that there were likely many such books amongst the collection. Excited, she decided to pick out a random selection and take a closer look.

She settled herself on the bed in the corner of the room and spread the books on the coloured blanket. First she chose a small pocket-sized book. Tipping it towards the light she tried to read the title. Only the indentations remained on the blue baize cover, the colour on the lettering was all but gone. *De Profundis*. She picked out the letters and underneath, *Oscar Wilde*. Her hands dropped to her lap. To Nora, *De Profundis* meant All Souls Night, November 1, "Out of the depths…" dark frosty evenings in a tiny churchyard, the hymn of supplication for the souls in purgatory, sad and plaintive yearnings directed to God. In the front door of the church, icy holy water from the stone font hastily sprinkled before entering the dim interior. Inside, the heavy smell of incense, the flicker of lighted candles, covered heads bowed in prayer, secrets being shared with the Almighty. "Out of the depths to thee O Lord I cry," the choir would intone from the loft: "And let thy light shine on them saviour blest, / Grant to the poor souls everlasting rest." Out the back door into the cold night and the ritual began all over again.

The hymn ran relentlessly through her head as she sat cross-legged on the bed. In those days she knew little of death and dying, the one exception being Joe Healy, the quiet, gentle man who owned the huckster shop in the town and sold sweets and toffee to the children. No child left Joe Healy's shop empty-handed. There was always a free sweet to be had in exchange for a chat. Joe had dropped dead in his shop. Frantic with the very thought that he might be in purgatory for some unforgiven sin, Nora had prayed each November first for his deliverance from the fires of purgatory. *Grant to the poor souls everlasting rest.* Now, she was shocked at how vivid her memory of the old shopkeeper was and at how fervently she had believed in the power of her prayers.

She picked up the book again and began to leaf through the preface, stopping to read a pencilled line: *Still I believe that in the beginning God made a world for each separate man, and in that world, which is within us, one should seek to live.* Written in the margin alongside were the words, *and be connected. Should seek to live and be connected.* Was this what he meant?

She turned the page.

Epistola : In Carcere et Vinculis
H.M. Prison,
Reading

Dear Bosie,
After long and fruitless waiting I have determined to write to you myself . . .

There were pages and pages to this letter written by Wilde from prison to Bosie. She knew little of Oscar Wilde and his writings but was aware that he had gone to jail for his homosexual activities. She began to read, skipping ahead, not very interested in the piece until she came to a small section near the end that had a pencilled line in the margin. She read slowly now, feeling no need for haste: *Society, as we have constituted it, will have no place for me, has none to offer; but Nature, whose sweet rains fall on unjust and just alike, will have clefts in the rocks where I hide, and secret valleys in whose silence I may weep undisturbed. She will hang the night with stars so I may walk abroad in the darkness without stumbling, and send the wind over my footprints so that none may track me to my hurt: she will cleanse me in great waters, and with bitter herbs make me whole.*

Had he, she wondered, simply highlighted a beautiful passage with his pencil or did he too have his own private hurt? She closed the book and laid it on top of the boxes.

When she opened the slim copy of *The Playboy of the Western World*, the first thing she saw was the heavy black signature of J.M. Synge scrawled across the page. She could hardly believe it, a first edition with the signature of the man himself. This couldn't be right. She turned to the first page and began reading the opening lines of the play as if somehow that would convince her that what she was seeing was true. She read on and on as if in denial, taking in nothing of the text, just riding from page to page on a great wave of excitement.

There was a soft tap on the door and Peg stepped into the room. "You're enjoying yourself, by the look of it."

"Yes. Peg, this is quite an incredible collection of books. This one …" She held it up. "It's–

"Oh yes." Peg came forward. "I know that one. I've read it a few times in my day." She sat on the end of the bed. "We used read it together, from time to time: we both loved that play. He'd read the men's parts and I'd do the women. It was something to do on the long winter nights. We'd just read it over and over. I knew it by heart in the end, every bit of it: *And myself, a girl was tempted often to go sailing the seas 'till I'd marry a Jew-Man, with ten kegs of gold, and I not knowing at all there was the like of you drawing nearer, like the stars of God.*"

She laughed as she ran off the lines. "See, I haven't forgotten it. I still know it all. I liked that girl Pegeen; she was some bit of stuff. Same name as me." For a while she sounded as if she might go on but then stopped herself and said, "They are all yours, Nora, that's what he wanted. 'If anyone comes,' he said, 'they are to have them. It's a fine collection so be sure they go into the right hands and that they appreciate them.'"

She pointed to the boxes. "There's more there and more under the bed. I had nowhere else to put them all when I moved. There's stamps too, in one of them drawers I believe. Stamps he collected for years, special ones. Sinn Fein stamps, he called some of them from back in 1908. They were put on letters for propaganda not for real postage, so he said. There was another stamp for that. Beautiful they are with the lovely Celtic cross and the shamrock and the harp and the big Irish dog."

"The wolfhound," Nora prompted.

"Yes, that's it. My dear, there's all kinds there, real special ones from after the revolution and on up. I suppose they are worth something now. He's written down why they are special. There's pages of them: the ones he really liked, that is. There's ones too with pictures of some of those famous writers. It's all yours, Nora. He'd be some pleased, for I can see you'll appreciate them. But girl, you can come back to the books by and by. I thought we'd go outside for a spell, while the sun is there. It's lovely out back."

5

Nora stood on the edge of the bluff and followed the sweep of
the ocean to the horizon. She thought about the dark secrecy of
Matt Molloy. How could he have fitted in with this place? She
searched the landscape, the endless stretches of rocky cliff face, the
grey scrubby soil, the dense growth on the hillsides. Her eyes settled
on the community of Shoal Cove with its haphazard scattering of
houses built solidly into the dips and hollows of the land: simple
homes, some that looked boldly outward to face the sea, others that
turned their backs on the rigours of their environment. A dark
wooded headland circled the cove on one side and reached out into
the water like a long crocodile snout, flat and impassive. From the
north side of the road, Peg's house overlooked the community.

Nora's eyes came around to where Peg sat on her bench. On the
way outdoors Peg had taken a dilapidated straw hat from a nail
behind the back door and, making a half-hearted attempt at
adjusting the drooping flower on the brim, had popped it onto her
head, slipping a narrow elastic under her chin. Set against the sharp

white edges of the house and with the coloured cloth of her dress flapping gently against her knees, she looked a picture.

"I like your hat," Nora called out as she made her way back towards Peg.

Peg patted the bench, coaxing Nora to take a seat beside her. She touched the brim of the hat.

"Your grandfather gave me that; he ordered it one time from New York. It arrived on the steamer all done up in a fancy box. I remember taking off the lid and seeing it lying there so beautiful. I'd never seen the like in my life. You can imagine now, I was afraid to even touch the box, let alone the hat." She glanced at Nora to see if she understood.

In the bright sunlight she looked fragile: the skin around her eyes and on her cheekbones seemed blue, almost transparent, like thin rice paper.

"'It's for you,' he said to me, 'put it on.' I felt some foolish in my old working dress, my hair all over the place, my hands just out of the dishpan. But then, out of the corner of my eye, I took a look at him and he seemed right delighted. Well, I had to put it on now, didn't I? So, I wiped my hands on my apron and put the hat on my head. I was afraid to look at him, afraid he'd laugh right out at the sight of me." Her voice became quieter. "But he didn't. He just told me I was to look straight ahead and then he caught hold of the brim and shifted it a little to one side so it felt right comfortable, like it was a part of me. He was some pleased, I could tell. 'Have a look,' he said."

She paused, tapping her lips with the knuckle of her index finger as if to stop what she was about to say but a second later took it away. "Looking in my father's old shaving mirror above the wash basin … well, girl, all I can say is, I was transformed. I thought, Is that you, Peg Barry, widow, from Berry Island, Newfoundland? I was like a lady, all elegant and mysterious looking. In a foolish moment,

I imagined I was like those fancy women he knew in New York." She turned to Nora, momentarily looking embarrassed but then the twinkle appeared and lit up her face.

"'Now what am I supposed to do with the like of that?' I said to him. He just shrugged his shoulders. 'Wear it, I suppose.' Where? That is what I wanted to say but I held my tongue. Well, I never did wear it." She inclined her head towards Nora. "Not in public anyways, not for the longest while. But there was many a night afterwards when I'd be on my own, feeling a bit lonesome or maybe even a bit foolish, then I'd take out the hat and fool around with it. I'd pretend I was walking the streets of New York all swanky like or I'd be having tea at Government House in St. John's or fancy I was parading on the deck of some ocean liner. I could be anyone I liked then, anyone I pleased, and be far from Berry Island." There was a hint of defiance in her voice but she was chuckling softly to herself.

"So nobody knew about the hat except you and Matt?" Nora asked.

Peg shifted, straightened her back and folded her arms at her waist. "No, girl, not for the longest while, until one night I had the hat out and in walked my sister Ellen and that was the end of it. 'How can you hide such a beautiful thing? If you don't wear it then I will,' she said and wouldn't give up on it. Well, shortly after that it was Lady Day on the island. That was a day in July month when all hands took a holiday from work for a bit of sport and fun. Back then it was a big day. There were games for the children and for the adults who wanted to be children and then a soup supper and dance at night. Well, nothing would do Ellen but that I wear the hat to the festivities. I took it along in my hand just to keep her quiet. That day, I believe every woman on the island tried on the hat and some of the men too! Soon I was wearing the hat, setting it off to one side like Matt had shown me and feeling right proud of myself."

"Was Matt there to see you?"

The look on Peg's face made Nora realize her error. Peg's mouth had clamped shut tightly and her chin was now thrust forward, giving her a stubborn determined look.

When the silence became too much between them, it was Peg who broke the tension. "No, he was not. He was gone then. I was alone." Her head dropped and she began to stroke the thin cloth of her dress, making circular motions on her knee as if to soothe an ache.

From where she sat beside her, Nora could see only the top of the bowed head. In one spot the straw was worn right through. The flower on the brim had fallen forward and hung limp by a thread. She wished with all her heart that she hadn't been so thoughtless. She was trying to form an apology, to say she had meant no harm, when Peg lifted her head and took a deep breath. Her mouth was set in a determined line.

"It was all just a bit of fun to begin with and I paid no attention but about mid-afternoon a stiff breeze suddenly comes in off the water and took the hat right off my head. It took off across the meadow, jumpin' and kickin' about, pitchin' down for a spell here and there." She looked down at her hands again and began her little rubbing motion. "The children was all lined up to the side of the field for a race but when they saw the hat, they took off after it like a pack of dogs. It was the race of the day, many said after, with the mothers and fathers all riled up, shoutin' and bawlin', cheerin' the youngsters on:

"'After her, b'ys! That hat's got a mind all its own, I'll allow!'

"'Look at her go! She's caught a fair breeze; there'll be no stoppin' her now.'

"'I believe she's bound for New York!'

"'Be the lard jumpins, I wouldn't mind a spell there meself.'

"'Hang on to yer drawers, Jimmy Slade, you're not gettin' clear of yer missus that easy.'

"The laughin' and carryin' on seemed like nothing to begin with, just a bit of silly old foolishness, but by and by, I come to think they were all having a laugh at me and my situation. That was hard to swallow." She began to rub her knee again. After a moment she continued, "I put the hat away that night and never took it out again, not for the longest while. It just didn't feel so good no more. Tell truth, I hated it then. But you know, Nora, age brings its own rewards. What others say and think doesn't bother me no more. I've told Pat, my nephew, that this hat is to go to the grave with me. When I roll up, I don't want it kicked about at some church sale."

Nora watched a large ant creep across the toe of her shoe. She followed his journey for a little while until it disappeared into the grass. "Where is Pat now?" She reached for Peg's hand, anxious to reassure herself that Pat was still around to take care of her wish.

"Oh, he's here in Shoal Cove," she said, brightening up. "That was his little girl you saw this morning, brought me the flowers. Little darling she is. You'll meet Pat by and by. He'll be down later with a bit of fish for supper, especially now he knows I have a visitor. He'll be happy to meet you. Right from when he was a boy on the island, he and Matt were best kind, although they did have their differences later on. But he'll be glad you've come."

There was so much that Nora wanted to know, so many questions to ask. Up until today she had thought her grandfather had made his home in Newfoundland but now she was no longer sure. Silently she reminded herself to be patient.

"This morning's catch is nearly squared away and they've gone again for another load by the looks of it." Peg pointed up the beach where a small boat had pulled in earlier and a couple of women were working steadily at the fish.

"That must be hard work."

"My dear, that's nothing to what it used to be. The men would be gone to the fishing grounds long before daybreak. It was a day's work just gettin' there. The lines had to be baited, lowered in the water, hauled in, then baited again, and that went on all day long. Then they had the journey back and the weather most often wasn't like today. There'd be rain and wind and fog enough to scare the livin' daylights out of you. What you see there is just a small haul. The big stuff goes to the fish plant to Arnold's Cove now."

The smell of fish and the clatter of work drifted up from the beach and again Nora wondered about Matt Molloy with his books and his pencilled annotations.

"It must have been difficult for you. As a widow, I mean. Did you work?"

"Well, yes, it was difficult at times. When Johnny was alive, he wasn't much of a worker, but before he had the bad turn, my father was a great man to work and I was like him in that way. I could do all the women's kind of jobs and most of the men's as well but I was also a good hand to sew. When Johnny was lost, he had some wages coming to him that had never been collected and that was sent to me altogether. I had the idea to buy myself a sewing machine. So I ordered one from St. John's. When it arrived at the door I was full of nerves at the sight of it. Here I'd spent nearly all my bit of money on a machine that I didn't even know how to use. 'Never mind, girl,' my father said. 'It's like havin' your own boat, you'll always be able to make a livin'. You'll learn how to use it by and by.' Later on when Father couldn't work no more, I had the house and Father's boat, which I sold, and I had my small pension from the government for Johnny and my sewing machine. Well, girl, I made dresses and skirts and the like for different people. The money wasn't much but it bought seed and plants enough for the garden and a bit of flour and molasses and the like. Havin' a bit of cash was important for the likes of me because I couldn't get credit from the merchant against my

K A T E   E V A N S

51

catch because I didn't have such a thing."

She paused, looking out again over the water.

"I remember the day a woman brought me a length of beautiful corduroy. She wanted two pairs of pants made, one for her husband and one for her boy. Well, I was frightened to death the way I was going to spoil it. I could see how to do the legs and the front, but how to get around the backside, you know." She made a curving motion with her hand. "Well, it came to me to get my father's old overalls and rip them open to see how it was done. I lay it all on the floor and I could see how it was slack down below in the gusset and how it came in on the waist. There was no zippers in those days, just what we called a fly and that was no problem. My dear, they turned out wonderful! I put pockets and all in them. After that there was no stoppin' me. But you don't want to hear all this old foolishness, do you?"

"No, no, I'd love to hear more, but I'm concerned that you'll tire yourself out and that I won't know when it's time to go."

"You don't want to worry about that, my dear. I've had a lot of old stuff balled up inside of me for a long time, waitin' to be told to the right person. You're the right person, girl, I know that." Reaching over, she patted Nora's knee. There was urgency in her touch, a pressure that bid her to stay. "I want to tell you, if you have the time to listen."

The old woman's eyes darted back and forth, looking to pick up the threads of her story.

"That first time, when he come by, Matt stayed on a nice while with us. We had plenty of room in the house and we were glad of the company. He paid his board, so long as he had a bit of money. The way it was then, with my father sick and havin' to have everything done for him, it was good for me to have another pair of hands around. He took right over in the garden. The vegetables were good that year. At least I thought so. He just had a way with growing things. There was no end of trouble he'd go to. He'd watch over every plant, bringing them along 'til they came strong and healthy. But he wasn't happy with the result; the potatoes were small, the cabbages not right, the ground poor. I had to take them up myself and store them in the root cellar. I believe those vegetables would have rotted right there in the ground if it was up to Matt. It didn't seem to matter to him that he was helpin' provide food for us all."

She looked down at her hands where they lay lightly clasped in her lap. "Everything about him was different, and tell truth that's what I liked so much. He–"

"So this is where you're to!" A short, stocky, middle-aged man came through the back door. "I've brought some tongues for supper and laid them in the fridge."

"I told you he'd be down later. This is Pat, my nephew, my sister Ellen's boy. Looks after me, he does, like nobody else. Now Pat, come over here. You're in for a surprise when I tell you who this is. It's Matt's granddaughter Nora, come to see us, all the way from Ireland."

He came and stood by Peg. Nora noticed the pale, steady eyes, Peg's eyes. He stood motionless, his sturdy frame rooted to the ground, and regarded Nora with an easy confidence. When he was ready he stepped forward and offered his heavy square hand. There was no hostility in his look but he didn't say a word as he shook her hand. He turned to Peg. "Now you be careful and don't catch too much sun, there's a breeze up here but it's hot just the same. Do you want tea?"

"Oh, a cup of tea would be lovely, Pat. I'm thirsty and what about you, Nora, tea or something cold?"

"Thank you, tea would be great."

He nodded to her again and went into the house.

"Pat worries about me," Peg said.

"I can tell that. It's good to have someone to look out for you."

"Yes, girl, I know. I'm very lucky."

Nora glanced back towards the house. He was standing at the picture window watching them. She looked away.

A few minutes later he appeared with a tin tray loaded up with three steaming mugs of tea, a small can of Carnation milk, a bowl of sugar and a plate of biscuits.

He poured the milk from the can into one mug, stirred it vigorously and handed it to Peg.

"Milk and sugar?" he asked.

Nora hesitated. The thick sweet milk did not appeal to her. Her mother used to pour it over jelly when they were children.

"Just a little milk, thank you," she replied quickly.

He passed the mug. "Have a Jam Jam. Made right here in Newfoundland." The plate was thrust in front of her. It was a kind of challenge, like she had to have a biscuit whether she wanted one or not. His eyes said so.

The biscuits were round and soft, made like a sandwich with a chewy raspberry jam inside. They stuck to the roof of her mouth.

He sat on the grass by the tray and sipped his tea. "Wilf, up to the store, told me you were here. This is a bit of a surprise. You've come from Ireland, you say?" He looked straight at her.

"Well, not quite." She had managed to clear her mouth of the sticky mass and returned his gaze. "I live in Montreal now but I was home in Ireland this past spring, to my father's funeral. It was only then I found out about my grandfather's connection to Canada, well to Newfoundland."

They continued to regard each other. He had a wild look about him, nothing to do with his rough haircut or his work-stained overalls, but something in his physical presence said he was not to be trifled with.

"It's all right, Pat." Peg stepped in and relieved the momentary tension. "Nora and me, we've been talking a lot. She wants to know about her grandfather. It's only natural and I'm happy to tell her. So there's no need of you to go worrying."

"Well, so long as you're happy, I'll leave the two of you be. When are you off back?" he asked abruptly, turning to Nora.

"I need to be back in St. John's on Monday evening to catch a flight on Tuesday morning. I have a room at the hotel in Placentia tonight and then I'd like to drive around and see some of the villages before I go back."

His directness was beginning to unsettle Nora.

"There's no need of you goin' to that place in Placentia tonight, there's a bed here if you wants it. But it's up to you. Isn't that right, Pat?"

"I dunno, Aunt Peg, last time you offered one of them Molloys a bed for the night they ended up stayin' a while." Then, in one quick movement he was on his feet, winked playfully at Peg, nodded to Nora and was off, leaving behind his mug half full of tea.

Nora watched him disappear around the side of the house.

"Don't mind Pat. When there was anything to do with Matt, people were always a bit cautious. He never fitted in, see, and in a way it was his own doin'. He kept to hisself, but island people is curious about strangers. They wanted to know all about him, but he wasn't about to tell anyone. So don't pay no attention to Pat; he's the best kind." She could feel Nora's uncertainty and continued to try and reassure her. "Back then, see, a man's life was the fishery. That was it. Matt went out to the trawls only the once. It was my father's idea: a man should do a man's work, and to his mind, seeing to the garden and readin' books wasn't a man's work. But Matt hated the water, made him sick to his stomach. At the end of the day his hands were in tatters from haulin' the lines. With the men, not going back was a sign of weakness, and maybe they were right. I'm

K A T E   E V A N S

55

afraid Matt only did what he wanted to do, or what he was good at. Thing was, he was good at quite a few things, but he'd never push hisself forward or pick up for hisself."

She drained her mug and passed it to Nora to set on the tray. "I'll tell you now the kind he was. My father used go huntin' in the fall of the year so as we'd have plenty of bottled turrs and partridge stacked on the shelf through the winter. Come the fall we needed to stock up again. I knew how to shoot a gun because my father had taught me. One day late September that year, I took out my father's shotgun, cleaned it out like he showed me and decided to try my luck on the barrens. Matt asked to come with me, didn't trust me, I believe. I didn't do too good and wanted to go on home out of it, when he said, 'Here, let me have that.' I stayed well clear of him, but, my dear, I knew just looking at the set up of him, he knew what he was about. He was a fine shot, no doubt about it! That year he took birds enough for ourselves and enough that I could share with others in need. That got him the bit of respect with the men. Not that he seemed to notice. He'd just go about his business, read his books and do the garden. Sometimes when I was to the flakes workin' on the fish, he'd bide with Father and see to him and that was fine by me. It was only others thought it strange."

"So, was he happy here?"

"In those days we didn't think too much about being happy. Survivin' is all was on most people's minds. If there was food on the table and a roof over your head, that was reason enough to be happy. But yes, I suppose he was happy. He was good company for me anyways. He stayed on through the fall and winter and well into the spring of the following year. He had hauled kelp from the beach and had a stack piled five feet high to the back of the house ready for the garden. For sure I thought he was here to stay. To begin with I didn't notice how things had changed about the house, until one evening around supper time, Matt was off on his own walkin' the cliffs and I was fixin' a bit of supper over by the kitchen table. I was hot and tired and I'd had enough for one day."

"Buddy," the old man had suddenly begun to shout across the kitchen. "Buddy, now what's the story with him?" His words were a bit slurred but the meaning was clear. "Is he plannin' to stick around here for good or is he goin' on back to New York or Boston or wherever it is he's come from?"

"Buddy? And who might I ask is Buddy?"

"You knows damn well who I mean. Now what's the story?"

Sometimes, it made her heart turn right over when she'd look across and see the thin, frail, old man sitting passively in the chair by the range. His hair wanted combing, and he could do with a shave and, God in heaven, his nose was runnin' down in his mouth again! Why couldn't he at least do that for himself? In two steps she was by his chair, and with the corner of her apron pinched hard on the end of his nose. "Are you talkin' about Matt, Father? Because if you are, he's got work enough here. In case you haven't noticed, we've had vegetables, best kind all winter and if that's not enough, I'll have you know that if he didn't bide here with you all afternoon then I couldn't be down to the flakes, now, could I?"

His left hand lay lifeless on the arm of the chair. It should have been big and square with strong hard fingers. But the flesh was soft and flaccid, the skin pale and mottled. Only the hard yellow fingernails reflected the power that had once been in those hands.

"It isn't right, and you knows it. People is talkin', sayin' how Peg Barry's gone and found herself another no good wanderer who's never done a day's work in his life. I warned you before you got hitched up with that Johnny fella, how he was good for nothin' but enjoyin' hisself. Well, I'm not goin' supportin' another one the like of that in my house."

"Supportin'? You haven't done no supportin' around here lately, not to my knowledge. It's Matt an' me is doin' the supportin' these days, Father. We been managin' the best we can. And don't go tormentin' me no more about Johnny. We've been through all that before. Johnny's dead and gone, Father. He won't be back no more, so leave him be."

Milky white liquid seeped from the raw potato flesh and dripped steadily into the water.

"Well, girl, Johnny may not be back no more but be the looks of things he's sent you a fine replacement. If you don't watch out, Peggy Barry, you'll be left again, out on the bawn!"

"And what's that supposed to mean?"

"He's not our kind and you knows it. He's got plenty of oul' yap out of him and has the grand manners but he has no thought for you, Peg, and it's time you got clear of him. God damn it, he's just a no good oul'… angishore! Get clear of him, girl, before tis too late."

"Get clear of him? Father, if I didn't have that oul' angishore around here, I couldn't manage."

"Are ye blind, Peg girl? There's others only too happy to step up and be glad to marry you. There's Paddy Murray, used to come by regular before Buddy arrived. He's a good man to work."

The knife came down hard on the table, making the potatoes jump in the pan!

"Father, will you stop callin' him Buddy, talkin' about him like he's nothin'. His name is Matt Molloy, an' as for that Murray fella, I wouldn't have that oul' maumeen, supposin' he was the last man on the island or up and down the shore for that matter."

"You're not gettin' younger, girl." His good hand began tapping fretfully on the arm of the chair. "One of these days you'll wake up and you'll be all alone … out on the bawn …. alone, girl." The agitation had caused him to slide forward in his chair. Unable to

WHERE OLD *Ghosts* MEET

hold on, he slumped to the side, his lifeless arm hanging over the side like a silent pendulum.

She was by his side in an instant, adjusting his cushions, smoothing his straggly hair, stroking the stubbled cheek, whispering how sorry she was to have upset him and of course she understood and yes, she would think about what he said. She lifted the withered hand, kissed it gently and placed it on the arm of the chair. He closed his eyes then and slept.

6

"*Do* all fish have tongues?" Nora asked, looking on wide-eyed, as the plump greyish-white morsels were rolled in flour and then popped one by one into hot fat.

"I never thought about that before, but I suppose they do. Around here, we only have the cod tongues. They're some good, especially when they're done up in a bit of fat-back pork with a few scruncheons like this. We also have the cheeks. They're some good, too."

Nora winced. She'd rather not think about the cod's cheeks and tongue, but the crispy brown tidbits of salty pork skin that had been rendered down and set aside looked good. "You call these scruncheons?"

"Yes, it's just a bit of fat-back pork." Peg held up a thick lardy slab to demonstrate.

Nora reached for a scruncheon and popped it into her mouth. "Mmm." She licked the fat off her fingertips. "In Ireland we call this crackling. We have it with roast pork but it's fresh, not salty."

The fat bubbled as Peg continued to pat and turn the cod tongues. "The small ones is best. They got to be fried right out until they're golden and a little crisp."

I bet they do, Nora thought, trying to suppress the queasy feeling in her stomach. The smell of cooking had whetted her appetite but the very thought of cod tongues made her shudder. Texture was what was bothering her: soft, slithery, pockets of flesh that need to be "fried right out."

"Just a few for me. I'm not very hungry."

Peg was picking them off the pan and dividing them equally between two plates. "Not everyone likes the tongues, or the cheeks for that matter. But it's nice to have a taste of Newfoundland food now you're here. But no matter, if you don't like them, you can lay them to one side." She then heaped a spoonful of mashed potatoes and a sprinkling of scruncheons on the plates and dinner was ready. "Now sit over to the table." She handed Nora a plate.

Nora contemplated the food. There were six tongues to be eaten. She nibbled on a few scruncheons, swallowed several forkfuls of mashed potatoes, and then told herself that the scruncheons should be saved to help get the tongues down. She had to admit they looked tasty enough and smelled good. If only she didn't know what they were, hadn't seen them. She cut one in half. Something soft and jellylike appeared in the middle. She put a scruncheon on top and swallowed it whole, washing it down with a mouthful of water.

"So now tell me, Nora, you say you work in Montreal?" Peg was busy with her food now.

"I'm a teacher. High school English. I'm hoping to save some money while I'm in Canada and then go back to study for a master's degree in England. There's some interesting work being done there on teaching methods and the different ways people learn."

Peg swallowed and looked at Nora. "Is that right?" It was not a question, just a registering of interest. She turned back to her food. "And do you have a young man, Nora?"

"No."

The clipped nature of the reply was not lost on Peg.

"No, no, I don't," Nora repeated in a softer voice, regretting her abruptness. "Not at the moment."

Peg laid down her knife and fork and was about to say something else when Nora cut her off.

"I was engaged to be married but we broke it off in the spring. Well, he broke it off. He found someone else. I suppose it wasn't to be." She threw a weak smile in Peg's direction.

"I'm sorry to hear that, Nora."

"It's okay now." She touched her ring finger, remembering the beautiful solitaire and how it had sparkled in the candlelight on that magical night when he had asked her to marry him. It had been a big surprise but not near as big as the surprise of finding him with someone else. Startled by the intensity of the memory, she sat upright, quickly hiding her hands below the table top. "That's part of the reason I came to Newfoundland. It was a diversion, something new to focus on over the summer. I suppose it beats having to plan a wedding." A wan smile played briefly at the corners of her mouth. "I work with a woman from St John's and she encouraged me to come here. 'Go on, girl,' she said to me. 'You can stay with Mom and Dad. They'll take you around and show you where to go to find your grandfather, if he's still to be found. My dear, they'd love that. Go on, no sense hangin' about all summer lookin' like you fished all day and caught nothin'.'" Nora laughed as she recounted her friend's enthusiasm. She had been like a mother to her, helping her over the hump. "So here I am."

"Well I'm very glad about that. There'll be others, Nora, you'll see. One of these days I'll be comin' over to Ireland to dance at your wedding." They laughed. "You never know!" she warned. "Now, what about the rest of the family? Tell me about them."

"There are two of us, two girls. I'm the eldest. I had a brother Joe but he drowned when he was ten years old. He was the youngest." She swallowed the other half of the tongue and followed it rapidly with a scoop of scruncheons which she chewed on and savoured hugely. She wondered whether to go into any more detail. It was likely her father Peg wanted to hear about. She paused for a minute, collecting her thoughts, allowing herself to slip into that cool dispassionate place reserved for him. Finally she set down her knife and fork, fiddled about with them for a minute until she had them placed in a perfect V shape on her plate and then took a deep breath.

"We called him 'The Da,' my father, that is. He wasn't a 'Daddy' sort of person somehow, not like other people's fathers, a bit distant, I suppose. He was an intelligent man, intellectual really, but he had no idea how to cope with the practicalities of life. Money meant nothing to him. He'd forget to pay bills, spend lavishly on things we didn't need and then become depressed when everything got out of hand. Yet he worked with money. He was a bank manager." Nora stared at the food on her plate, almost untouched. She picked up her knife and fork and scooped up a small mound of mashed potato. It was halfway to her mouth when she changed her mind, put it back down and pushed the plate away.

"He hated his job," she said. "'Drudgery,' he called it. But he stuck with it because it was permanent and came with a pension. Security, that's what he worked for all his life but in actual fact, what we had was just the opposite." She thought about her father for a moment. "I believe he loved us and truly cared for us but he had no idea of our individual hopes and dreams, no sense of what made us happy or sad, what our ambitions were or what we worried about at night when we lay in bed." She paused before continuing. "I think that he somehow believed that if he could just hold on tightly to the reins and never let go, not for any reason, that everything would be all right and he'd manage to keep it all together."

Nora forced herself to eat some more mashed potato but she had lost all interest in her food. Suddenly she shocked herself by voicing quite coolly the very thought that was foremost in her mind at that moment. "Being abandoned by his father as a little boy must have affected him deeply."

She closed her eyes, imagining his shame, his confusion, his anxiety, hearing the cruel taunts of small boys: "Would ye look at Molloy beyond, his oul' fella's fecked off to America." "Yea, my daddy says he's off with Buffalo Bill chasin' after them injuns, learnin' how to be quick on the draw. Bang, bang. Oooooooooo. Bang, bang. I'd say now, there'll be a couple a scalps in the post from America this Christmas. What do ye say, fellas? Oooooooooo … ooooo." "Nice to have somethin' from Santy Christmas mornin', any oul' thing at all! Eh, Eamon?"

Anger swept over Nora, tangling up her thoughts, snatching at her breath, making it impossible for her to continue. She didn't look at the woman to her left but instead examined the white knuckles of her clenched fists. A voice inside her raged. The selfish, cowardly bastard. How could he do such a thing? How could anyone leave that poor woman and her child in that damp miserable place, in the wilds of bloody nowhere, with nobody to care for them, nobody to protect them, and when the Black and Tan hooligans came and ransacked their little home and burned it to the ground … where was he? Off gallivanting in God knows where, buying bloody fancy hats for strange women. She squeezed her eyes shut, not fully understanding where this sudden fury had come from and at the same time desperate to keep the words that bubbled up inside her from breaking out and finding a voice. But in truth she knew that this would not happen. The words would remain unspoken, contained. The Molloys knew all about staying quiet, knew all about keeping a lid on things. It was a way of life with them.

So Nora and Peg sat together in the gathering dusk, still and quiet, two women in a haze of memory, each seeing a different side of the same man. Finally, when the silence became unbearable, Nora allowed her old voice to emerge from its silent corner.

"His father, my grandfather, to us he was just 'the Da's da,' nothing more, no real name, no face, no identity. Can you believe, Peg, I never in my life set eyes on his wife, my grandmother? I never went to her home and she never set foot in ours, and I don't know why."

For a moment Nora held Peg's eyes but then she looked away, unwilling to confront the other persona of Matt Molloy that hovered close by.

"Everything went wrong for him, girl, everything. It wasn't his fault." Peg's chin came up ever so slightly. She still didn't look at Nora but instead turned to look beyond the horizon where her memories lay, secure and intact. "I'll tell you the truth of what I know, Nora, but first I must make us some tea."

7

Evening was drawing in and already the table by the window was in shadow. Beyond the dark headland the sky was awash with a deep purplish mauve. Tinged with touches of pale peach and backlit by the golden light of sunset, it was surreal in its beauty. A car passed along the road, the headlights sweeping the ceiling and walls. The two women sipped tea and were silent for a moment until the hum of the engine faded away.

"Years ago, Nora, people expected life to go on as usual. On the island, soon as a youngster was old enough, it was expected that he'd go in the boats with his father. I don't know how it was in Ireland then, but according to Matt, it was pretty much that way for him. He had one plan for his life but his mother had another."

"You're cut out for the priests, son, hand-picked by God Almighty." His mother gripped his arm tightly. "What else would you be doing, with all those brains God gave you? Shovelling cow dung below in the byre for the rest of your life? Anyone who flies in the face of God," she whispered urgently, "will have no luck. You mark my words."

"There's other ways to use brains." He wished she'd let go of his arm so he could leave. Instead he said tentatively, "I could be a teacher or maybe work with The Gaelic League."

"Ah, catch on to yerself."

He heard the first note of irritation in her voice.

"The Gaelic League, now there's a bunch of dreamers if there ever was one, just what you need, the poet fella, Yeats, and her ladyship from Sligo. What's her name? Gregory, Lady Gregory. Thinkin' they can solve the problems of the poor people of Ireland by writin' poetry and puttin' on plays above in Dublin. Makin' us the laughin' stock of the world, that's all they're doin'. Yes, Lady Muck herself, grand company for a young fella like you. Don't you go lettin' anyone in the town hear you sayin' the like of that."

"But Doctor Sommerton tells me there's talk now of expanding the university above in Dublin, to make more spaces for Catholic young fellas like me. He says I should apply."

"I might have known." The grip tightened on his arm. "He's the one has been puttin' them daft notions in your head again. Where, in the name of God, does the doctor think the money is comin' from for them grand ideas? The pair of you, dreamin' just like the rest of them oul' eejits up in Dublin! If you listen to the likes of them, you'll be runnin' around with the backside out of yer pants for the rest of yer life and not a penny in your pocket."

"But there are the scholarships."

"But nothin'." She shook his arm, her bright, terrified eyes burrowing right into his brain. "Here's reality, son. I'm here workin' my back off day and night tryin' to keep our end up, to give you a chance, and your father, six feet under, watchin' and waitin' of me to slip up. There was another dreamer. Out day and night with the Fenians, and got himself killed for his trouble: another smart one!"

"We did all right, Mammy." He didn't want her to be angry. Talk about his father always took her down that road.

"Yes, and no thanks to you," she shot back, "with your head stuck in them books all day."

"I thought you wanted me at the books, that you wanted me top of the class. That's why I tried—"

"Look, Mattie." Her tone softened again. "Think of your mammy for a change. Don't I need you up there puttin' in the good word for me with Almighty God, prayin' for me immortal soul? You could have your own parish one day, like Father Walsh. Who knows? Ye might even become a bishop! That would make them all sit up. I'd be able to hold me head high in the town for a change. The bishop's mother, they'd call me. Now, Mattie, I want you to put together all those oul' books of poetry and plays and the like the doctor's been feedin' you and take them back to him this very day, and I want no more talk about scholarships and the Gaelic League. Get along with you now, there's a good lad. And Matt, that oul' book he gave you for getting the exams, put that right on the top so he knows once and for all, we want no more interfering in our business."

A single tea leaf drifted around in Nora's mug. She watched its progress for a while. It was going nowhere; it had reached the end of its useful life. She picked it out with a spoon and set it aside. "His situation wasn't that unusual," she said casually. "In fact, his son, my father, followed a similar route. Many did."

"Yes, girl, I know and it was the same here in Newfoundland. Our smartest young fellas were picked out by the bishop and coaxed away to the priests. Just like where you come from; it was a way to get an education, and for some it worked out grand, but, my dear, there's a lot of them young men should never have darkened the door of a seminary."

She waited to see if Nora would respond, realized it was not coming but decided to continue anyway.

"Your grandfather was one of them. That place got right in his head, it did, and he couldn't get clear of it. Finally one night, the torment just flowed out of him like a lanced boil."

Matthew shifted uncomfortably in his chair, not able to find the words to say what was in his mind. Finally he spoke, his voice barely audible. "It was a sad, empty place, Peg, like a prison in some ways." He leaned forward in his chair, staring into the heart of the fire, the memories coming in bits and pieces. "Long corridors lined with doors that led to bare cells. There was a wall with massive iron gates all around the grounds but the strange thing was that the wall was low enough to be climbed and the gates and doors to the outside never locked, not even at night. Even so the word was, 'It's very easy to get in but very difficult to get out.' The penalty for leaving was shame, abject shame, not only for the man who left, but even worse, shame for his family. It was like a trap, a mind trap that bound us to the place with invisible ties. Nobody wanted to be labelled 'Spoiled Priest.'"

The fire collapsed in a spray of bright sparks. He reached for a log and poked it into the firebox and watched until it caught fire and flamed.

"Frank Roche was from a place called Ballina in County Mayo. He was a grand man. Every night around eleven o'clock or so, when he thought we were all asleep, I'd hear Frank's door across the hall open and close quietly, and he'd disappear down the corridor into the dark with his blanket rolled tightly under his arm. One night, I followed him. He went over the wall with his bundle and disappeared into the night. He's a priest now in Boston. I met him a couple of times, but to this day I don't know where he went every night, or if he knew that I knew."

Peg paused at her knitting. She observed the change that had come over his face: his teeth biting down hard on a tense, rigid jawline, eyes bulging against the rim of their sockets. She wanted so badly to lay down her knitting, to reach out and take his hand into the warmth of her own.

"Tom Murphy was another fellow," he continued, as if to himself. "He was from Mallow in County Cork. He had the room next to me. Every night was the same. After lights out, I'd listen to him turn and twist in the iron bed and every night he'd cry himself to sleep … like a child. One night I went to him, creeping along the corridor like a thief, speaking his name softly as I entered the room. I sat on the side of his bed in the freezing cold, staring at the putty walls, drenched with condensation. Someone had written with a finger on the wet surface in large uneven capitals A M E N. Heavy drops of water ran down from each crooked letter, making a shiny path all the way to the floor. I shook him then. 'Tom,' I said, 'you have to go. For God's sake, go now, before it's too late!' I was whispering in his ear, shaking his shoulder gently. Under the grey blanket the tight ball uncurled slightly and a dark terrified eye appeared above the rim. 'I can't,' he said, the words hanging in a fog of breath. 'I could never go home.' He curled up again into a tight bundle."

The fire shifted and spat a chip of burning wood onto the floor at his feet. He crushed it with the toe of his boot. "Six o'clock every morning, in single file, carrying a jug, we'd walk to the well at the end of the garden to collect water for washing. One frosty morning a few days later, we found Tom, in the well, face down."

He began to rub one palm against the other, back and forth, back and forth. "The church forbids Christian burial to those who take their own life. The official word was that Tom had accidentally fallen down the well and drowned." He became very still. "I was tormented by Tom's memory. I cried for him. I cried because I hadn't done enough to help him and I cried over the whole rotten mess."

Peg set aside her knitting, aware suddenly that the kitchen was unusually quiet. Anxious, she looked towards the window. The wind had dropped, and the snow, just a flurry earlier on, was coming down in thick, heavy flakes and had packed in along the narrow window ledges and against the door frame, cutting out the drafts and quieting the rattle of loose boards and hinges. She turned back to where Matt still sat, transfixed. Tentatively she reached out and touched his arm, but he remained perfectly still, the muscles rigid under her fingers. "Matt," she began, hoping to say the right thing. "Maybe–"

"Others began to notice the change in me," he said, ignoring her and at the same time picking up where he'd left off. "Secretly they'd whisper, 'You're not thinking of waxing now, are you, Molloy?' 'No, no,' I'd say. 'If I leave this place, I'll first tell them what I think of them and then I'll walk out the door, in broad daylight, my own man.'" He crossed his legs, locking his fingers tightly about his knee. "'That's the spirit,' they'd say, 'no slippin' away in the middle of the night. Face up to it.' Those nights, there were times I never undressed for bed."

He turned to face her, as if suddenly realizing she was there. "I'd take off my shoes and get in under the blanket still fully clothed in the black cassock and try to pass the time until daylight. In some strange way, I missed the sounds of Tom crying from the next room. The silence seemed to haunt me more than the sobbing." He paused, took a deep breath and turned again to stare into the flames. "One night I woke with a start. I could make out the outline of the small wardrobe in the corner, the wooden table by the window. I thought for sure someone had called my name. I got out of bed, groped about in the dark and finally moved towards the window. He was there, Tom, right outside the window, dripping wet, his face so white. 'Go, go now,' he was saying, 'before it's too late.' I wanted to tell him I was sorry … but he was gone. I flung open the window. All that was there was the night. I remember thinking, I'm going mad, but then the realization came to me. Tom had come back to warn me with my own words. Right there and then, I made the decision to go. I undid the buttons of my cassock and let it fall to the ground. One step and I was out. I picked up the garment, did up the buttons and laid it out on the bed with the arms neatly crossed in front. I went to the wardrobe, removed the plain black suit, my only temporal clothing, and when I was ready I sat down to wait for morning."

Peg waited, expectant. Finally she said, "You did speak up, Matt, in the morning, before you left?"

"No, I was gone before daybreak."

8

It was after nine o'clock when they finally rose from the table. "You'll stay the night, Nora, no point heading out now." Peg looked at Nora earnestly. "There's other people you should talk to who knew Matt, and besides, there's the garden party tomorrow. Gerry Quinlan may well be there. Now there's one to talk to, and God knows who else will be about. You may as well bide awhile, girl, now you're here. You're in no great hurry, are you?"

"No, not really."

"Then you may as well stay." Peg leaned into the table. "We'll see this one out, once and for all, you and me."

Nora nodded. "I'll get my bag from the car before it gets too dark."

Outside, the community was silent, the evening air still and breathless. When she listened carefully, Nora could hear the ocean tumble onto the beach and the faint rumble of pebbles being sucked away by the ebbing tide. Above her, the sky still reflected the softness of evening. To the southwest a single star, brazen and solitary, winked in the gathering dusk; thousands more peeped out intermittently, awaiting the cover of darkness. She thought about Leitrim and the blackness of the countryside at nighttime, how the sky, frequently laden with heavy rain clouds, would hang overhead like a sodden blanket hiding the brilliance of the stars. She turned away and reached into the car for her bag, making a mental note to have a look at the sky later on when the night was black. With a final glance upwards she headed back into the house.

Peg was not in the kitchen when she returned. She looked about, recalling her arrival that morning as she set her bag down on the floor by her feet. The house was now familiar, the people in the framed photographs no longer strangers. She went to the wall, peering closely at the image of Matt Molloy, trying to find something, anything, to latch onto. He was good-looking, for sure, but his eyes still looked lifeless. Was this how eyes looked in photos? She turned to the other pictures and found a sweet smile, a shy timid look, a strong challenge, a devilish twinkle from the man in uniform. She looked back at Matt Molloy and noticed again the ghost of a smile that barely touched the corners of his mouth. The face somehow seemed more engaging. "Hey, that's better, a smile for your granddaughter." It was hard to look at that cheerless face and still feel angry. The toilet flushed and she moved away from the wall, feeling a tad foolish.

Peg came in from the hallway. "We'll have a little drink now," she said. "I have one nights, before I go to bed. A small drop of whiskey helps me sleep. Will you have one?"

"That would be perfect."

Peg reached into the cupboard below the sink and produced a half-full bottle of whiskey. "Bring a couple of glasses," she called as she made her way to the table.

This woman was full of surprises. Nora, smiling to herself, reached for the glasses. "Big ones or small ones?"

"Well, not too small, girl, but we have to be respectable, in case we have callers. There's some can smell a drop of liquor a mile away and they'd be here in a minute if they thought there was a drink to be had and maybe a bit of gossip to go along with it."

She made herself comfortable at the table and poured two good measures of whiskey. They each added water and took a sip.

"Matt never took a drink, all the time I knew him," she said, wiping a finger carefully along her lower lip as if anxious not to lose a drop. "Years ago, there was no liquor about except maybe Christmas time or the like. The men might have a bit of home brew then or maybe some partridgeberry wine. But even that he never touched. He told me that at one time it was a problem for him, but he always said that the finest drink was good whiskey and a little water. So when it come time I could afford to have a drink and could buy it to the store, I chose whiskey, like he said."

"And you like it?"

"Indeed I do." She lifted the glass to her nose and sniffed. "When I'm alone it takes me out of myself, lifts my mind. It's company."

"I suppose it's lonely, being on your own?"

"Only nighttimes, and mostly in the winter. I know everyone in the community but they have their own families and they're busy with their children and all that. People don't drop by no more, like they used to in the old days." She looked fondly at the child's bouquet on the table. "Times I don't see them too much. But that's the way. I try to keep busy and mostly I manage."

"So he had a problem with drink at one time?"

"Like I said, never while I knew him, but it seems that after he left the priests, he took to the drink pretty heavy. It's funny the way things happen."

She sipped her drink, taking her time, picking at a little spot on the glass with her fingernail. "Walking out the gates of the seminary in the middle of the night was one thing, but what to do then was another. He had no money, nothin' much but the clothes on his back and, as he said, all he could do was head for home. He had the idea that he'd bring his mother around to lettin' him put in again for the King's Scholarship he'd won before he went away. He thought maybe they'd consider him again. That way he could get to the college and become a teacher. Well, I suppose it was an all right plan. Anyways he struck out for home, got a ride in the back of a train part of the way and then began to walk."

It was close to midday when he stepped off the train and into the sunshine. He set a good pace as he struck out along the road for home.

"Can I give ye a lift?" The call came from behind.

Matt Molloy stopped in his tracks. A long low wagon stacked with barrels of stout and drawn by a fine team of dray horses, their brasses gleaming bright in the sunlight, pulled up beside him. He read the gold-edged lettering on the side of the wagon: J. Arthur Guinness. A bead of sweat ran from under the brim of his black felt hat and settled on the end of his chin. He wiped it away hurriedly. Another followed. "Thank you," he said, and without a second thought, he threw his almost empty suitcase onto the wagon and pulled himself up onto the seat beside the driver. The team of drays shifted restlessly.

"Whoa there!" The command was low and guttural. Huge fists, the fingers bristling with coarse black hairs, tightened on the leather reins. "Are ye right so?"

"Yes, yes, I am. Thanks."

There was a sharp snap as the reins hit the horses' rumps and the team pulled away. "Come from Dublin?"

"Yes."

"And where would you be off to?"

"Cullen," Matt said, looking away.

"I can take you as far as Strokestown and drop you by Rulky Bridge. It's just a walk from there."

"Thanks."

The horse brasses jingled, the clip-clop of iron-clad hooves punctuated the silence of the countryside. Horse and driver had found a steady rhythm. Beneath the black cloth of his jacket, Matt Molloy's shoulders relaxed slightly.

The driver gave him a sideways glance. "If you'll take my advice, you'll ditch that black rig-out. Here, give us that oul' hat too. You'll not be needin' that where you're goin'. Ye're out, right? Jumped ship. The hat gives the game away." He held out his hand.

Slowly Matt removed his black felt hat and handed it to his companion. Their eyes met for an instant, and then with a quick flick, the hat went sailing over the hedge and disappeared. The reins snapped. "Now while you're at it, why don't ye ditch that oul' jacket too?"

Without a word, Matt began to remove the jacket, looking about as he did so for a place to lay it down.

"You can leave that there." The driver patted the seat beside him. "By the way, the name's Mattie Duggan. How about yerself?"

"Molloy, Matthew also."

"Ah, go on! I don't know about you but the Mammy called me after Matt Talbot, ye know, the holy fella who looks after the drunkards." He laughed. "She thought he'd look after me too, in that department, keep me outta har'ums way. Piss poor job he's done, I'd say, and me drivin' a wagon for J. Arthur Guinness for a livin'! Sure, isn't that pullin' the devil be the tail? How about yerself?"

"No, nothing like that, just a name."

"Fair enough. So I suppose it's off home now to face the music."

"The music …" He reached for his jacket but a restraining hand touched his arm.

"Hold the head now and take it 'aisy. I'm not takin' a run at ye but tis plain as the hole in a monkey's arse, you've left the priests, right?"

There was no reply.

"What else is a young seminarian doin' walkin' the roads of Ireland, of a Wednesday mornin', in the middle 'eh nowhere, lookin' like he's got the worries of the world on his shoulders." He leaned over then, lowering his voice. "That's why I'm after gettin' ye to ditch the rig-out. There's no need goin' advertisin' the fact, now, is there? Look at ye now, roll up them sleeves over the elbows and ye could be me assistant and no one 'id twig the differ."

Matt Molloy began to roll up his white shirt sleeves, exposing his pale arms with their fine dark hair. "I've let her down again," he blurted out without thinking. "I tried to make a go of it—"

"Now look here, son, I'm tellin' ye now, the mothers of this world are the best and the worst of it," he said with the conviction of a preacher. "Problem is, some of them just don't know when the feckin' job's done. It's simple as that." He paused to take a deep breath and once more unleashed the leather reins onto the horses' rumps. "Time comes when they have to be told where to get off." The horses had picked up the pace and he now had to shout above the clatter. "I remember at school, when I was a young fella, one of the Brothers used to roar at us when we'd be slackin' off: 'Excelsior, gentlemen, onward and upward, and for the love of God, quit blamin' the world for yer misfortune. Get off yer arse and do somethin' about it.' That used to spur us on for a while anyways. That's what I'm sayin' to you now. Don't go lettin' her rule the roost; otherwise you'll never get to crow when it comes your turn. And wouldn't that be a sorry state of affairs?"

There was no reply.

"What you need is a drop of the pure to straighten you out," he said with a new air of joviality. "I always says, Never go into battle without powder in your musket. I tell ye now what we'll do. We'll stop for a quick one before I drop ye off at the bridge and that'll get ye fired up and ready to take herself on. What do ye say?"

"I have no money." His head began to flip back and forth as if seeking a way out.

"I'll buy you a pint, son."

It had been a long day and he was thirsty. The situation at home had also begun to play on his mind. "All right so."

"Now, that's the spirit, son."

"Nora, my dear, that was the beginning of it. Himself and Mattie Duggan got drunk that day and that's how he was when he arrived home. Of course he liked how he felt, liked his newfound courage. He spoke his mind and liked having the guts to do so but once it wore off, he was back to being himself, but by and by, things got out of hand."

"What about the scholarship?" Nora asked.

"That didn't work out or he never tried; I'm not too sure which, but anyways he settled for whatever work was about, just so as he'd have money enough to get out of the house and go to the bar of an evenin'. There were rackets all the time. His only joy back then was his few books." She took a deep breath. "By and by, the mother took things in hand and hooked him up with Sadie Dolan, the one he married: that's your grandmother. The mother and the young one's brother, Mickey Dolan, set it all up."

Nora drew in a quick breath. She could barely fathom what she was hearing. So this Sadie Dolan was her grandmother. She'd never heard the name spoken before. She said it again, under her breath. It didn't rest easy with her. "Mickey Dolan." She said that name. Already she hated it. She hated the very sound of it.

Peg forged ahead, speaking rapidly, her voice strong, tinged with a hint of bitterness. "Indeed she wasn't that much of a young one, seven years older than Matt, she was. She'd been passed over in the marriage department, it would seem, and Matt, not knowin' too much what he was about, was easily led. God love him, he was only a youngster at the time, twenty-one years old."

She poured another drink, held the bottle out to Nora, saw the quick nod and poured.

"One night a few months after they'd met, the Dolan woman tells him she's in the family way and there's nothin' for it but that he do the right thing by her and get married. Yes, my dear, he was on the hook and hauled over the side before he knew it. Just like that!"

"Stupid fool!" Nora could no longer contain her irritation.

"And if he were standing here in the room this minute, you know something? He'd say exactly the same thing. He told me one time, 'Peg,' he said, 'I'm a clever man by all accounts, but I'm a fool.' I was shocked he'd say such a thing but I soon come to know what he was talking about. It had to do with plain old common sense. Ordinary things, little problems you'd have from day to day. Oftentimes he just couldn't decide what was the best thing to do, so in the end he'd head off and do something right foolish. Same when it come to the big things! My dear, he'd look at the facts, up and down and round about, again and again, enough to drive you right cracked, but still he wouldn't know what to be at."

"Reminds me of my father," Nora said bitterly.

Peg picked up her glass and studied the contents for a moment. "I'm sorry to have to be sayin' all this to you, Nora. It can't be too nice to be hearin' all this old stuff, but still and all, it has to be said." She took another sip of her whiskey and hurried on. "Whatever the reasons, he managed to get himself hooked up to a wife in a hurry."

"And a child!" Nora was thinking of her father, the stalwart

Catholic family man, conceived out of wedlock, without love. She stared into her glass.

Darkness had slipped quietly into the room, closing tightly around the two women. In stark contrast against the sky and the sea, the black headland appeared large and brooding. A trickle of silvery light dodged playfully on the water.

"It wasn't even that simple."

Nora's head came around with a start. "What do you mean?"

"There was no child, not then anyways. The child didn't arrive for twelve months or more after they married."

"What?"

"The way it was, Matt didn't even realize that the time had passed for the child to be born. Until one night in the bar, didn't he hear talk from behind a wooden partition. Two women were hard at it, talkin'about him. 'Tis high time she dropped that youngster,' one was saying. 'Sure, wasn't she up the pole way before they ever went near the altar?' 'Aye, indeed. I'd say she'd want to be puttin' a bit of a spurt on or that babby'll be arrivin' with whiskers on!' When Matt heard that, it was only then it came to him that he'd been fooled and that everyone knew but himself."

"God in heaven, don't tell me his own mother was part of that deception? Surely not, who could do the like of that?"

"Who's to know?" Peg's index finger came up in a cautionary gesture. "Remember, that was a long time ago. Back then there were few questions asked and there were even fewer answers given."

"What did he say, Peg? What did he do?" Nora leaned forward, insisting on the truth. "Did he think that his mother knew all along?" She waited, exasperated. "Don't tell me he never asked, never confronted her or that Mickey Dolan or the wife?"

"He did what Matt usually did in those days. He got himself drunk and headed for home."

"*A double blessing, is a double grace*," he announced with Shakespearean flourish as he flung open the kitchen door and tried to focus on the image of his mother and his wife both busy by the hearth. The words were barely out of his mouth when a down draft from the open chimney sent a thick belch of black smoke back into the room.

The mother was by the door in an instant and with a quick shove pushed him out of the way and shut the door. He lost his balance and toppled over.

"A fine state you're in and you with enough drink in ye to flatten a sailor. Get up outa that. Yer a disgrace to yer country."

"Ah," he muttered, attempting to get to his feet, "*enterprise … great pitch and moment … lose the name of action.* Hamlet, Prince of Denmark, now there's the bucco had the right idea when it came to dealing with the women."

"For the love of God, Matt, would ye quit yer cod actin' and get to yer feet. Get up outa that. Whatever it is yer blatherin' about, makes no sense to me. Get up, will ye." A strong young arm caught hold of him and urged him to his feet.

"*Ah wife! The fair Ophelia.*"

"Mother of God, you're gone cracked in the head with all that oul' rubbish you've been readin'. Here, catch a hold of me."

"*Is it my wife has come to help her husband in his hour of need?* Thank you, madam." His hand touched the tight curve of her swollen belly and he let it linger there for a moment.

She tensed, tightened her grip on his arm and then continued to pull him upwards. "Look, over there, Matt, by the fire. My brother Mickey, he's been here tonight with a little cradle was mine once. It could do with a cleanin' but it'll be grand for the child."

He steadied himself, turning slowly in the direction she was pointing. A rough wooden cradle sat on the floor by the hob.

"Now isn't Mickey Dolan the great fella? Knew exactly when to turn up trumps!" He moved unsteadily across the room, stopping for a moment to size up this new treasure and then bending over, he peered into the empty cradle.

"Now there's a fine looking youngster if I ever saw one, and would you look at the size of it!" He moved closer, making little clucking noises. "Now, tell me, wife," he continued. "How is it that our little babby has whiskers?"

There was a hollow silence in the kitchen. The two women glanced quickly at each other.

He straightened up and turned to smile, a strange baleful smile, first at his mother then at his wife. "How is it," he repeated, taking on a menacing tone, "that this babby has whiskers?"

"It was a bit of a miscalculation," his wife rushed to explain, "a wee biteen of a mistake, with the time, is all."

He moved in closer, peering into her eyes, his whiskey breath in her face. "*Confess yourself to heaven / Repent what's past, avoid what is to come, / And do not spread the compost on the weeds, / To make them ranker.*"

"Jesus in the garden! Do we have to stand around here all night listenin' to this oul' gibberish? Your wife told ye, she made a mistake. Don't ye understand or do ye want it straight from the Holy Ghost himself … in several languages?"

He whipped around to face his mother, eyeball to eyeball. "*Beware of entrance to a quarrel; mother dear / But being in, / Bear't that the opposed may beware of thee.*"

His mother stared back, cutting straight through the glazed eyes. She held the stare for a moment then turned away and reached for the Tilley lamp. Holding the light high, she leaned forward, bringing her face close to his. "Yer an eejit, Matt Molloy, of the first order."

The fire spat in the grate.

"I'm goin' to bed. There's some of us have a day's work to do come mornin'. Go on to bed, Sadie, ye need yer rest, and leave our very own Shakespeare here to himself."

His eyes followed his wife as she moved away and disappeared behind the curtain into the shadow of their bedroom.

Peg looked into Nora's startled eyes. "Your father was born not long after that. Not a happy situation, I'll allow. But that's how it was, how your grandfather told it to me."

9

A mixture of anger, pity, and disbelief tugged at every muscle and fibre of Nora's body, leaving her feeling confused and miserable. She pushed away from the table and, turning her back on Peg, gripped her forehead, feeling around her temples the beginnings of a headache.

So often she had thought of her grandfather as a kind of comic figure, a lone Irishman footloose and fancy-free in America; here today, gone tomorrow! That was Maureen's fault, she thought angrily, with her constant playacting, her tendency to make light of everything, always poking fun at the "Returned Yanks" who came back to Ireland on holidays with their gaudy clothes and flaunting their wealth. What would she think now? Would she still find it funny?

"Nora." Peg's voice interrupted her thoughts. She had no idea how long she had been sitting with her back to the woman, lost in her own world.

"I'm sorry, I'm afraid I was miles away." She turned around and pulled her chair in closer to the table.

"Nora." Peg was hesitant. "I know I don't know you well enough to be speakin' so plainly but I'm gettin' on now and want someone to understand how it was between Matt and me. In the past I've tried talkin' to others, my sister when she was alive, a friend or two, but they just thought I was soft in the head. In the end I gave up, because I knew there was no sense talkin' or trying to explain what they didn't want to know or could never understand. But you want to know. Don't you?"

"Yes, yes I do. It's just not what I expected to hear."

"I know." She chuckled weakly and looked directly at Nora. "My father was right, I suppose; I had a liking for wanderers and drifters. But I'm tellin' you now," her voice became serious, "I have no regrets. No, my dear, not the one. I've been lonely in my time and I've cried my fill, but I've never been bitter or felt hard done by. Though there's many a one will tell you different. But I knows the truth of it and I didn't care then and I don't care now what anyone has to say or what they thinks!"

Nora threw a worried glance in Peg's direction just in time to catch a fierce flash of defiance in her eyes, and then it passed and her usual calm returned.

"I don't know, girl, if you can understand what it was really like back then. Times was so hard, always the same, day in, day out, hard work, sickness, poverty, death. They came and went like the tide and there wasn't a whole lot of anything else. I wanted to get away from it all, to be free. I'd have gone to St. John's, gone in service, anything, but it was a dream, nothin' more. There was no way out for the most of us."

She shifted in her chair. "When Johnny went off at the beginning of the war, I envied him. I wanted to go with him. I knew from the talk of people coming back and forth to the island that women were going to France too. War girls. VADs they called them. Voluntary Aids, something like that. They helped with the war, even at the front! I thought I could do that too; I could look after Johnny and the other young Newfoundlanders, and more besides. I was young and strong, able for anything, better able than Johnny maybe. But, I'd promised my mother before she passed away that I'd take care of my father, no matter what, so what was I to do? I told Johnny to go on, thinkin' how he'd come back with all the stories and excitement about England and France and the war. That's how innocent I was. Well, it didn't work out that way, now, did it? The young fellas was killed by the thousands and the ones that come back, the stories they had to tell was enough to give you nightmares. Leavin' the island didn't seem like such a great idea after that."

She finished her drink and poured another. Nora passed her glass.

"Back in those days I used to believe that Johnny knew, when he met Matt, that he wouldn't be comin' back no more, so he sent him to me, special like. By and by, I come to think it was just fate, that all along this is what God had planned for me. Matt's ways were strange sometimes, but he brought me what I wanted most of all, the outside world. He knew about everything it seemed. He was full of information, full of stories, real and not so real. I said to him one time after he told me a few of them Arabian Nights yarns, 'Matt,' I said, 'sure, you're for all the world like that missus Scheherazade, yarn after yarn and no end to it!' He laughed then, or I should say he made a kind of noise like a laugh. He never laughed, not really. Then he just said, 'You'll not chop my head off, if I run out of tales, I hope.' 'I might an' all, so you best look sharp,' I said." She laughed again.

"Not indeed that there was much time those days for tellin' stories. But evenings when the work was done and my father was to bed and I'd have a bit of knittin' on the go, it's then he'd tell the stories or read. Best part of the day it was, that hour before bed. My dear, could he tell a story. Oh, you wouldn't believe! Mind now, there was many on the island those days could tell a good story, especially the old people. We did that all the time at the house parties, especially in the winter. But now Matt, he was different. The voice on him! I don't know where it came from. He wasn't a big fella but, my dear, it rumbled about inside of him like a great swell and when it come rollin' out, well, the power of it! He could command an army with that voice, he could, or be soft enough to put a child to sleep. It was wonderful to hear. And a memory! He never needed a book for the words; it was all in his head, every word. Now times he'd use a book. Said he liked the feel of a book in his hands. I used to watch his long fingers, so elegant, turning pages thin as a butterfly's wing; they'd make a little crinkling sound as he touched them. I liked that sound. Oftentimes when he wasn't around, I'd pick up one of them books with the thin pages, open it up and do the same thing just to see if I could get the same feel."

"And could you?" Nora was amused but touched by the simplicity of the disclosure.

"Yes, girl, but, well, I just wanted to watch him." Peg looked away. "It sounds foolish, I know."

"I don't think it's foolish," Nora reassured her.

In a flash Peg's head came up, their eyes met and her index finger began to tap a determined rhythm on the table top. "It's true just the same; it's how it was." She averted her eyes but not before Nora had seen the glint of unwelcome tears.

"It's important, Peg. It's part of your life," Nora urged. "I want to know."

"Yes, girl, I know but it's ..." She struggled for a moment, trying desperately to hold on to her composure, then she sat forward in her chair, straightened her back slightly and said, "Never mind, let me get on with it."

Nora was thinking that maybe a break might be a good idea when Peg found her voice again. It was strong and purposeful. "You know by now he loved books. It's what he lived for. You saw below in the room." She pointed vaguely in the direction of the spare bedroom. "Beautiful books."

"They are beautiful, and valuable." Nora looked at Peg, wondering if she understood that.

"What you saw is only a part of it," Peg said. "He never stopped collecting them. Some of them have names of famous people written in them, like they gave them to him for a present. It was a job to pack them up and take them with me but I had to do it; it's what he would have wanted."

She nodded her head several times and sipped her whiskey. "After he left home and ran away off, he did what he should have done in the first place, went to Dublin. It was there he really got into the plays an' all that. He used to talk a lot about the Gaelic League and the Abbey Theatre and all of the goings on in Dublin. I remember him talkin' about a pair of actresses called the Allgood sisters. At the time, they were big stars by all accounts. Like them Beatles today! They'd arrive at the theatre every night, a flower pinned to their coats, given them by the flower sellers in the streets. I used to love to hear all that old stuff, all about the fancy clothes and the like. The very idea of sellin' flowers in the streets amused me." She laughed heartily. "They were just ordinary girls, he told me, but they had great talent and worked hard and the people loved them. One girl, Molly, I believe, married the famous man who wrote all the plays, John Synge. But you'd know all about that, Nora, comin' from there."

"No I don't, Peg. Most of it is news to me." Nora was enthralled, her attention now spinning between the collection of books in the spare room, the story of the Abbey Theatre, and to thoughts of her sister and what she might think now of her crazy old grandfather and the fabulous collection of rare books, some of them signed, all stacked in the room down the hall.

"Well, girl, I heard it all that many times I thought I knew them too. He was right in with that crowd, it seems. He had a little job evenings at the theatre just helpin' out with things. He didn't get paid or nothin'. He just liked to be around and I suppose he understood a bit of what was goin' on too. He was there the night they had the big racket in the audience." She threw a glance in Nora's direction to see if she was still interested. "It was the second night after the opening of the play called *The Playboy of the Western World*, you know, the one Matt and I used read together, with Pegeen in it, the one you saw below in the room."

Nora nodded eagerly.

"Here, when it was only halfways through, up she went! Seems the crowd started shoutin' and bawlin' and makin' the biggest kind of a racket … didn't like the way the ordinary people of Ireland was bein' talked about in the play. It got so bad you couldn't hear a word was being said. In the end the police was brought in to clear the decks. That was how it was every night until they shut her down altogether!"

He had been there, Nora thought, this hobo grandfather of hers, there in Dublin, right at the heart of that great revival of Irish literature and culture. She tried to picture him, to put him in the middle of all this excitement. A thought occurred to her. "Did he ever say if he'd met any of the writers, Synge or Yeats or O'Casey? Did he ever talk to them?" She leaned forward, willing a positive response.

"I don't know, girl, but just the same, he said he saw the fella Synge or so he told me."

"He did?"

"Yes, well sort of. There was one night he was in back of the stage helpin' with the curtain. You know, haulin' it back and forth at the right time. Well, standin' in the shadows, right across from him on the other side of the stage, he sees this dark figure of a man. He just stood there watching what was goin' on and then he disappeared. Now the man Synge was dead and gone at the time, but Matt said he knew it was Synge, by the look of him."

"You mean he saw a ghost?"

"Yes, girl. That's what he said."

"And did he tell anyone what he'd seen?"

"That I don't know, but he said there was others talked about seeing a strange figure around the stage after that and they all thought it was the same man."

Peg saw the look on Nora's face. "My dear, he was full of them stories."

"And you remember so well, names, places, everything. I never knew any of this."

"Oh, I don't suppose I remember it all, but it was so interesting, see, and he could tell it so well and make it real. He showed me the old program from that night, all the names and the fine picture of Cuchulainn and his hound on the cover. How could I forget? They're all below in the room, in the drawers, I believe."

The hush in the little kitchen was soothing, dark and cool like the night, but inside, Nora was beginning to be aware of a deep sense of loss.

"I wish I'd known him, Peg. I wish he hadn't run away."

"I know, girl. I know what you mean."

"Did you love him very much?"

The woman beside her tensed slightly. When she spoke, the words came slowly and guardedly. "Yes, I loved him." There was a brief pause and then she added, "In my own way." She was picking her way carefully along a difficult path. "To this day, Nora, I'm not sure that I know rightly what love is. What me and Matt had wasn't like what I had with Johnny, or again, not like what my mother and father had." She stopped to consider the latter. "The way they were, you knew there was something special, something about the way they looked out for each other and for me. But Matt ..." She stopped to consider for a moment. "He was all the world to me. That's all I can tell you and nothing can ever change that."

KATE EVANS

91

Peg had found the little groove in the table again and was rubbing gently, staring at her busy finger with unseeing eyes.

Love. Nora followed the movement. How often in the past few months had she pondered this same question, looking for a simple answer when in fact there was none.

"To begin with, being around him was enough. I just wanted him to stay, but after the racket with Father when he said I should look at marrying the Murray fella, I knew I had to do something. Matt and me were spending a nice bit of time together in and around the house but never outside. Whenever there was a dance or a time to someone's house, I'd always go on my own; he had no interest in that kind of thing. I was content just the same. But with Father's talk about 'getting clear of Buddy' that was enough to get me thinkin'. I decided I had to try and talk to Matt and see what he had to say. So I made a plan. It was simple enough, but the best I could think of at the time."

She sipped her drink, replacing the glass carefully and precisely on the table. "It was getting towards the end of summer, berry-pickin' time. Matt liked to roam the hills so I suggested maybe we'd go together Sunday evenin' and get a few berries to set down for winter."

"We'll go this way." She didn't look back to see if he'd heard but took the path to the left that led to a rocky outcrop and a grove of alders. Her pace was quick and resolute as she led the way up over the grassy slope at the back of the house.

It was warm and close amongst the tall bushes. The sunlight, filtering through the leafy branches, made dappled shadows on the path. Peg knew this spot very well, this little corridor of peace and tranquility with its tiny windows on the sky. To be able to hear the soft crunch of their footsteps on the dry grass thrilled her. Farther along the trail to the left, a robin had nested. She had watched for hours one day in late spring as the little creature busied herself with mud and straw and twigs, crafting the age-old, cup-shaped design of her nest. She had raised two broods during the summer and now it lay deserted. She turned and touched Matt's shoulder lightly, pointing to the nest hidden deep amongst the greenery. He crouched slightly, his face drawing close to hers, his head dodging this way and that as he searched. There was a light rustle of leaves, the robin arrived and perched tense and alert on a nearby branch. She heard Matt's quick intake of breath. Her finger came to her lips in a silent shhh! They stood together, motionless, watching, waiting. Her hair brushed his cheek and he tensed, abruptly pulling back. The robin's head swivelled, beady eyes watchful, her feathery throat thrust forward as she called out. In a frenzied flutter she took off and disappeared. The moment was gone.

They walked on through the alders and emerged into the fading sunlight. "This way." She pointed to the right. "The path will take us to the top of the hill and down over the other side to the partridgeberries."

The climb was steep and rough, pocked with grooves and gullies. They grabbed at roots and scrubby undergrowth, pulling themselves upward. Halfway up they stopped to rest against a huge boulder.

"It's the finest kind of place here when we get a bit of good weather." She looked at him sideways.

"Yes," he said and began to move on.

He took the lead as the climb grew steeper. Close to the top, the trail had been washed away altogether, leaving only a rough, steep area with very little growth. He worked his way slowly to the left, searching for footholds, guiding her along step by step. Her foot slipped on the gravel and she slid backwards. "Here," he said, reaching down to help her over the last hurdle. She reached out, clasping his outstretched hand, and was taken aback by the softness of his skin. In that instant she realized she had never before touched him. "Come on," he urged, and with a little pull she was beside him. He released her hand immediately. Pausing to catch her breath, she took a furtive look at her own hands, rubbing the palms self-consciously, dragging them roughly against the cloth of her skirt. When she looked up he was watching her.

She pretended to brush away a spot of dirt and then pushed past him, lengthening her stride and not stopping until she reached the top of the hill. "The berry patch is that way." She pointed and hurried off down the other side.

She came to a halt by an area of low scrub and with growing anticipation dropped to her knees and reached into the woody undergrowth. Gently she lifted the clusters of tiny glossy leaves, exposing the deep red berries. "Here." With her fingertips and thumb, she gently began to rake a little pile into the palm of her hand. She knew it was best to wait until after the first frost before picking these particular berries but she wasn't about to tell him that. The berries were not important today. She held out her hand for him to taste.

"Tart." She laughed as he made a face. "But good for jam."

They worked together in quiet companionship, moving apart, drawing close, ferreting out the good patches, pausing from time to time to stretch their aching backs. The berries were plentiful this year and the brin bags filled rapidly.

"The light is fading, Matt, I think we should be getting back."

They walked up over the hill a little way to where she knew there was a sheltered hollow that looked out across the water to the far headland, to the place they called Larry's Hill. On a night like this you could watch the moon as it climbed along the brow of the hill right to the top, and then like magic it would lift off and float up into the night sky.

"Let's sit here a minute. Shortly you'll see the moon climb up over the hill."

She set down the bag of berries, propping it carefully between two stones and suggested he do the same. Then she sat down on the grass, easing her aching back against a rise in the ground. "Nature's own daybed," she laughed, "just like home." Her hands settled behind her head and she stared up at the darkening bowl of the sky. There was a slight breeze off the water but the night was still warm. Night came in a hurry at this time of year. She looked around; he was nowhere to be seen. She closed her eyes, anxious, willing herself to relax.

"I've found some blueberries."

She looked up. He was standing directly above her on the rise, his face white against the dark sky. She thought he looked beautiful, like an apparition. He came and sat next to her, holding out a small mound of berries.

"These taste better," he said, "less tart."

"They're a bit puny looking, just about done for this year." She sat up and picked one off the top, taking care not to touch his bare hand, but then she laughed, threw caution to the wind and scooped up a little pile, threw back her head and tossed the lot into her mouth.

A fleeting smile crossed his lips as he tipped back the remainder of the berries. She watched his jaw move up and down and his throat contract as he swallowed. He suddenly appeared clownish, with his lips and tongue stained with the purple berry juice.

"Look," he said.

Her eyes followed his across the water. A white disc edged over the base of Larry's Hill.

They watched, spellbound, as the moon slowly rode the dark edge of the hill, rising gradually and finally lifting off, full and unfettered, into the darkening sky.

"It's beautiful," she said dreamily.

The pale light cast a flickering streak across the water.

She looked sideways at him. He was far away. "Matt." She brought her body around to face him. "Matt," she tried again. "I'm happy when I'm with you. I believe you're happy too. I can feel it right here." She tapped her chest lightly with her fist. "But see, when we're together, half the time I think it's just like we're in another world. We're livin' a fairy-tale life, the two of us; no real plans, not even for the comin' winter. I worry about that, Matt, and Father is anxious too."

"We'll be all right, Peg, don't you worry. The garden this year is fairly good. I'm getting to know the ground here now and what to expect from the season. Later on I'll take a few birds so there'll be plenty of meat, and Pat Tobin asked me the other day if I'd be interested in going caribou hunting on the mainland. So we'll be all right."

"I'm not talkin' meat and potatoes, Matt. I'm talkin' about us."

Alarm swept across his face. His eyebrows shot upwards, making deep runnels across his forehead. Then, just as quickly, they disappeared and he became pensive.

She reached for his hand. It felt limp. With her index finger she began to trace the outline of each fingertip. She felt no strangeness now, only the warmth of his skin against hers. She turned his hand over and laid it against her own, palm to palm, as if for a handshake. Hers were good hands, she decided, strong and well shaped, but his were beautiful and she loved that. On an impulse she brought his fingers to her lips and touched them lightly. "I love you, Matt," she said simply.

The whole world, she was sure, was listening, for at that moment she could hear no sound: not the surf below, not the breeze in the tall grass all around, not their breathing. She looked at him then, feeling happy and confident that at last she had spoken her mind. She waited, expectant.

"Thank you," he said.

At first she wasn't sure that she had heard correctly except that the words kept repeating in her head over and over again … thank you … thank you … like she'd handed him some foolish gift.

She stared at the top of his head, her eyes penetrating, demanding that he look at her. When finally he did look up she saw what she dreaded most of all: that lost sad look that put fear and dread in her heart. It was a look she could not penetrate. At times like this she felt as if he had drawn an imaginary circle on the ground all around him; it meant: keep out. She could not approach him now. Whatever was going on inside had to be settled first before she could try again.

She got to her feet then and walked away, leaving him sitting alone on the grass.

"I can't," he said, his voice just loud enough to reach her and stop her in her tracks. "I can't. I'm a married man."

It was as if someone had just punched her between the shoulder blades and knocked the wind right out of her. She felt unable to move, unable to respond. She heard his step behind her.

"We'd better be getting back. It's late," he said.

He looked ridiculous, his mouth smeared with all that purple juice, and in a flash she realized that she must look the same; the two of them, just a pair of stupid fools. She turned away. "You go on, I'll be down later." She could hardly speak, her tongue felt that dry and thick in her mouth.

"It's getting dark. You might need help around the rough spots." He had begun to move away.

"I'll manage," she whispered. "I'll manage on my own."

She watched the bobbing figure as he made his way down over the hill. Every so often he turned side on to find a better footing. Then she could see his pale profile beneath the black head of curls. Soon he disappeared from sight. She continued to stare down over the hillside, knowing the exact spot where he'd come back into view. He was moving quickly now, almost running on the lower slope. She thought he had stopped once to look back, just before disappearing into the grove of alders, but in the moonlight it was hard to be sure.

She looked around, feeling utterly desolate. The bags stood propped against the rock. He had forgotten the berries.

She walked back to the spot where they had been sitting; the grass lay crushed and flat to the ground. She dropped to her knees and reached out a hand to touch the place. It was still warm, and then she was raking the spot, coaxing the grass to stand up again to be whole and straight. She shuffled and fluffed at it, her hands working frantically, until it stood in crooked ragged spikes. Sitting back on her hunkers she looked at the mess. "Damn, damn," she cried out, her fists pounding the earth. "Stunned, I am. Pure stunned," she yelled. The tears rose painfully from deep within her chest, filling her head, stinging her eyes until finally she let go. They ran freely down over her hot cheeks and fell into the ragged grass at her knees. Why hadn't she guessed? She should have seen the signs. In a rage she stumbled to where the two bags of berries lay propped against the rocks. She grabbed both bags and with all her might flung them one after the other as far as she could. The berries flew from the bags in a shower of shining red droplets and disappeared into the long grass.

"God in heaven," she sobbed, "how innocent am I at all?"

"He wasn't there when I got home." She turned to look at Nora. "I waited up for the longest while and in the end I gave up and went to bed. He came back to the house sometime in the night but I never heard him. By morning he was gone, without a word."

10

The house had settled into a quiet slumber but sleep would not come to Nora. The room was hot and stuffy and the pressures of the day had sapped her energy, leaving her restless and depleted. She wondered about Peg. Was she by some miracle feeling the opposite, unburdened and content, fast asleep in her bed?

Nora's earlier attempt at opening the window had failed, but this time, driven by heat and frustration, she threw back the covers and hit the floor at a trot. The small slider window was set a little too high on the wall for easy access, so she had to struggle hard, pushing against the glass with her palms, finally managing to inch it open just enough to get her fingers around the edge and pull. The night air rushed in. She closed her eyes and pushed back the tangle of her hair, relieved to feel the cool breeze on her face and neck. She was about to climb back into bed when she remembered the night sky. She moved back to the window. It was a golden night, thick with stars, bright with moonlight. Suddenly she wanted to be outside, to stand again on the little rise at the back of the house where she had stood earlier in the day. She whipped the coloured blanket off the bed, threw it around her shoulders and quietly crept to the bedroom door and eased it open. The whiskey bottle, ominously lit by a streak of moonlight, stood on the kitchen table, solitary, like an actor at centre stage, his moment done. She tiptoed to the back door, her bare feet making no sound. The cat! She looked around, but remembered then that she had seen it follow Peg into her bedroom. The back door was unlocked. She opened it cautiously and stepped outside onto the cool grass. Except for the gentle heaving of the ocean below, the night was eerily quiet. It felt strangely romantic, standing there in the moonlight, a lone figure on the mound, her nightdress flapping around her bare legs. What if anyone should see her? She looked about but there was not a soul to be seen. On the far headland a single light pierced the darkness. In the community of Shoal Cove several houses were still awake. She pictured the people inside, clustered around the TV or drinking mugs of hot tea at the kitchen table, possibly discussing the young woman from away, who, that morning, had shown up on Peg Barry's doorstep looking for some relative or other. The night, clear, sweet and uncluttered, brushed aside such thoughts.

She searched the sky, picking out the Plough and the North Star and the Great Bear, but that was the limit of her ability. If her grandfather were alive today, she mused, he might have walked her to the edge of the bluff and stood there beside her, guiding her through the maze of the constellations. He would surely have known about things like that. Her mind drifted to a sheltered hollow long ago, the moon climbing up over Larry's Hill and a figure fleeing down the side of the hill. Was he shy, or scared? Unable, or unwilling, to give it any more thought, she pulled the blanket tightly about her shoulders and walked back to the house, closing the door softly behind her.

Back in the little bedroom she sat on the edge of the bed and picked up the first book on the pile by the bed. It was a collection of poetry. She made herself comfortable against the soft pillows and began to read. Gradually she drifted into a kind of easy contentment and when she finally turned out the light, sleep came easily.

She was awaken by shuffling noises in the room. Instantly alert, she lay rigid in the bed, her face to the wall. For a moment she was confused, unable to recall where she was. Her heart thumped painfully, loud and insistent. The window … immediately she remembered where she was. She had left the window open. There was someone in the room. She could hear little crooning noises now, more shuffling. She raised her head slowly, terrified. Across the room she could see the outline of a white figure by the bookshelf. In an instant she realized it was Peg, her pale wisps of hair loose and hanging down the back of her nightdress. A thin hand, feverish and agitated, searched the shelves of books and finally eased one from its place. Nora watched the white figure, now quiet and content, turn the pages. After a little while Peg closed the book quietly and put it back in its place. Then slowly she turned and began to make her way across the room to where Nora lay petrified. Peg paused for a moment and then leaned forward, her eyes hovering just above Nora's. The faint smell of stale whiskey was on her breath. Nora pulled back against the pillow but the eyes, glittering like two polished marbles, came closer, pinning Nora to the spot. Suddenly, as if sensing she was unwelcome, the white figure turned and left the room, closing the door quietly behind her.

Nora, rigid with fright, listened for the sound of Peg's bedroom door closing. The house fell silent again.

Nora awoke feeling sluggish, her eyes still heavy with sleep. She rolled over, dragging the bedclothes over her head. Something was not right in this befuddled world of bedclothes. She sniffed, sniffed again, pushed back the bedclothes and slowly raised herself on one elbow. Only her eyes moved as she scanned the room: the stack of boxes, the books neatly arranged on the wooden dresser, the open window. She sat bolt upright as it began to dawn on her. Someone had been in her room during the night, over by the window. She remembered the little whimpering noises, the pale shadowy figure coming towards her, the staring eyes. A loud clatter coming from beyond the bedroom door made her jump. She could smell baking. Peg, of course, she had been in her room last night, rummaging about in the dark. In an instant Nora was out of bed, across the floor and standing in the kitchen.

Peg was by the stove, her back to Nora.

"You're all right?" The words rushed out and immediately seemed misplaced.

"Oh, good morning, my dear," Peg called over her shoulder. "Yes, of course I'm all right. Once the sun's up, I'm up. Did you sleep well? It was hot last night, too hot for my liking."

"I was fine. I left the window open all night."

Peg turned and smiled at her young guest. "That's fine. I never lock the house." Her hand brushed against her apron, sending a poof of white particles into the air.

"Good." Nora could think of nothing else to say. A night had passed and things had shifted, but she was relieved to see the same Peg looking back at her. She realized suddenly that she felt very protective of this woman.

"I'll just have a quick wash and get dressed then and I'll be with you in a minute."

"No hurry, my dear. You just take your time."

In the bathroom Nora splashed her face with cold water. When she raised her head and looked in the mirror, she saw uncertainty. What in the world had been going on last night? Peg obviously had no recollection of her wanderings but she must have had a very troubled sleep. Nora told herself to be careful, to pay more attention to how things were progressing. The whole thing had to be emotionally very trying. With that resolve she went to dress.

There were freshly baked blueberry muffins and mugs of hot tea on the table when she returned to the kitchen.

"You've been busy."

"I promised a plate tart for the garden party today, so I had to get that on the go. It was no trouble to do up a few muffins at the same time. Eat up now. I'm nearly done here." Unsteady hands lifted a tart from the oven and set it on top of the stove. Nora watched as Peg lightly touched the golden crust with her fingertips.

How could everything seem so normal? Nora began to doubt her memory. Had she been dreaming? But the thought of the luminous, vacant eyes coming towards her in the darkness sent a shiver right through her and made her realize that it had been no dream.

She heard Peg give a little grunt as she reached over and turned off the oven. Systematically, Peg did a quick check, touching knobs. Finally, nodding her head, she made her way to the table.

"Did you sleep well, Peg?" Nora put the question casually.

"Oh, best kind, but I was some tired. It was a bit late when we shut her down." There was no sign of unease or embarrassment, no indication that anything was other than normal.

"I've been thinking, Nora, maybe you'd like to take a run down to visit Bird Rock today." Peg poured more tea, using both hands to steady the pot. "It's a wonderful sight to see this time of year with the thousands of birds feedin' and busy with their young and it's not too far from here. I used to go there with my father the odd time, when I was a girl, but I haven't been there in the longest while. I wouldn't mind seeing the place again and it would be nice for you too."

"I'd love that. It's not too far, you say?"

"No, just a few miles down the road, a nice little run in the car. Years ago, the fishermen used to row down there and then across as far as Golden Bay to the fishing grounds. Those days it took nine and a half hours of solid rowing just to get to Golden Bay. They'd set out on a Monday, fish all the week and come back again Saturday." She reached for a muffin. "My father had an engine on his boat so it was an easier run for him, but on the way back, if I were with him, he'd pull in for a spell near the rock to watch the birds. It was just a bit of fun."

"We'll do that then."

Peg's face lit up. "Right, soon as we get clear of the dishes, we'll be off."

11

They drove south, through Great Barasway, Ship Cove, past Gooseberry Cove and Angel Cove, the narrow road cleaving tightly to the edge of the ocean. To the left, brown rocky barrens pocked with massive boulders and great clumps of low stunted bushes stretched back to where a great big sky met the horizon. Nora was glad to be out and about. It was part of her reason for coming here. She hadn't placed a whole lot of hope in finding a link to her grandfather but she was interested in seeing this remote place, reputed to be the closest thing to Ireland on the North American continent. On the way back she'd hoped to stop and explore some of the little communities along the way. The road began to climb into an area of low hills covered with thick lanky spruce. The dark earthy smell of the woods filled the warm air.

"You know, Nora, he came down here one time," Peg began tentatively, "with a student of his; he wanted to see the birds. Of course he wouldn't hear tell of going in the boat, so they walked all the way. They went in across the path from St. Bride's, but here on the way home, all of a sudden, didn't the fog come in as they were crossin' the barrens. In no time they were lost, but the young fella with him, smart enough, knew what to do. Got in under the tuckamores, them's the low bushes you see out there, and settled down 'til morning when the fog lifted. They got home none the worse for the wear, but God knows what might have happened had he been by hisself. He wouldn't have had the sense to lie low and wait."

"You said he had a student with him?"

"Yes. He taught school on the island for a spell. It was after he come back home one time. The young teacher to the school up and left suddenly, to get married: I believe there was a love child on the way. Anyway, the parish priest, Father O'Reilly, was to the door the next day lookin' for Matt to take on the job. Matt wanted none of it but there was no sayin' no to Father O'Reilly. He would have him."

"So when was that?"

"October 1928," she said without hesitation. "He'd been back a year or so by then."

"So, he'd been gone for a long time, seven or eight years?" She looked for confirmation but there was none. "Did he just show up after all that time, just like that, right out of the blue?" She couldn't keep the disbelief from her voice. "In all that time, did he write, send a postcard, anything?" She threw a worried glance in Peg's direction but Peg quickly turned away. A wire hairpin dangled from the knot of hair at the top of her head. It danced about as she moved but hung on tenaciously.

"No. There were no letters."

Nora had to resist an urge to reach out, take the hairpin and tuck it back into place.

"I was some pleased to see him when he come back."

Nora turned again to take a quick look at Peg.

"Havin' him around again was like seeing the ice break up in the spring of the year; winter was gone and the good weather was on the way." Her mouth worked slightly in an effort to find the right words. "My father had been dead several years by then and I was alone. I had my chances, mind, while he was gone, just like father said I would, but there was none could match him, not to my mind anyways, even with all his faults. He had been in New York all that time. Things were booming there, plenty of work to be had and good money to be made, so he said. The old crowd from Dublin had shown up also, doin' a tour with their plays and he met up with them all again. The two sisters he thought so much of, they were there as well. He talked a lot about them. They were makin' piles of money on the stage in New York and had all the finery to go with it: silks, velvets, furs. I was a bit jealous, tell truth, but just the same time I wanted to hear all about them." She laughed at her own foolishness and suddenly startled, pointed her finger to a turn off in the road. "My dear, I've been talkin' too much. Here's where we turn off."

A narrow dirt road pointed straight to the horizon. "You're sure we can drive in?"

"Yes, girl, this is the way the locals come now."

The narrow path stretched away in a straight line as far as the eye could see. Edging the car carefully along, Nora sat forward, straining to avoid the potholes, praying not to get a flat tire, and trying not to think of what might happen should they become stuck. She brushed aside a fleeting image of herself and Peg huddled under a bush for warmth.

"Can you change a flat tire, Peg?"

"No, girl, but I've been in tighter spots than this and managed." She chuckled, knowing exactly what was in Nora's mind as she picked her way along the bumpy road. After what seemed like an endless run, the sea appeared, a flat dark blue streak above the craggy cliffs. She parked on a grassy spot and rolled down the window all the way. The scream of the birds rushed in on a stiff breeze.

"What a racket! There must be thousands of them!" Nora had to raise her voice to be heard.

"That's nothing. Bird Rock is across the barrens a little ways, towards the cliff. That's where you want to be." She pointed off to the left.

"You're not coming?"

"No, my dear, I'd forgotten how wild it is here. I'll just sit in the car. Off you go and take your time. I'll be happy here just listening to the birds."

"You'll be all right on your own?"

"Yes, off you go and take your time."

Nora hurried across the wild exposed terrain, battling with every step the fierce wind off the Atlantic. She stopped to catch her breath. To the right a lighthouse and keeper's home sat comfortably on the point, but otherwise, there was no other sign of human habitation. A small bird, unafraid, alighted by her feet and pecked away at the earth, quite unconcerned. Tiny purple harebells, dwarfed by the wind, struggled to show their sweetness through the grassy terrain. She turned into the wind again and continued on.

Up ahead, the sky was alive with a great jumble of flapping feathers, birds circling, diving, screeching and squawking. The great dome of the rock appeared above the cliff. As Nora came closer to the edge she saw that the dome extended and widened, the massive walls reaching down hundreds of feet in a great cone, to the ocean far below. Every nook and cranny of this vast roost was occupied, every square inch staked out by a dense mass of birds clinging perilously to the rock face. All around, the cliffs were similarly inhabited. It was magnificent.

Cautiously she stepped down over the edge of the cliff onto a little sheltered plateau where there was a large flat stone that over the years had obviously been used as a seat. It was smooth and glossy and, strangely enough, unlike the surrounds, totally clear of bird droppings: Visitors are welcome and encouraged to stay! She took her seat, laughing with delight at the sheer miracle of it all.

A gannet with a soft golden head and dark velvety wing tips swooped right by. Nora followed its flight. Gliding and soaring, it flew in a perfect figure-eight pattern and then disappeared from view. Another gannet flew in close, this one trailing a strip of tattered cloth. It reminded Nora of those cards that show a plump dove trailing a ribbon that says *PEACE ON EARTH* or *HAPPY ANNIVERSARY*. She watched the bird swoop and dip, showing off its treasure before heading for home.

He had sent ribbons one time. Well, someone had sent ribbons all the way across the Atlantic. Years later Maureen and she, for want of a better solution, had decided it was the Da's da who had sent them, but at the time it was a mystery, at least to the children. The American Parcel. That's what they had called the big brown package with the strange stamps and the hard red globs of sealing wax that had arrived unexpectedly from America, just before St. Patrick's Day. Her mother had told them that it was from Daddy's cousin who lived in Boston. There was never any talk before of American cousins, but in the excitement of the moment nobody cared.

She had been the one who had answered the door and taken the big package from the postman. In a funny way she felt it gave her ownership or certainly a special claim to the treasure within. Her mother whipped the package from her hands, turned it over several times, and headed for her bedroom, closing the door behind her. Believing there was strength in numbers, Nora went immediately to break the news to her brother and sister, and they gathered outside the closed door, ears cocked, until finally they found the courage to edge their way into the room to a vantage point by the bedside. All eyes were fixed earnestly on this wonder from America.

"Who's it for, Mammy?"

"It says: The Molloy Family."

"That's us."

"Yes, that's true, so maybe we should wait 'til Daddy gets home."

"He'll make us put it away 'til Lent is over."

"Sure, by then we might forget all about it. Mightn't we?"

"Go on, Mammy, open it up."

"Well, maybe that would be all right." Their mother began to unwrap the big package.

It was a wonder: a book for her father. She couldn't recall the title but it was brown and shiny and she had never seen it again after that day. There were comics, ten or more, bright and colourful: the Lone Ranger, Roy Rogers, Buster Brown, three copies, crisp and new, *Buster Brown Goes to Mars, Inter Planetary Police vs. The Space Siren, Time Masters.* Nora remembered clearly the smiling face of Roy Rogers looking out from the front page of the comic book. He had on a soft white cowboy hat and a red shirt with long fringes dangling from the sleeves. He was leaning casually against the top rail of a white wooden fence, his hand resting on a striped blanket. She thought he was gorgeous.

There was a slim black dress for her mother, very simple except for a wide band of blue and green beadwork that ran all around the neckline and formed a shimmering heart at one shoulder. Mrs. Molloy held the dress against her body. "Well, take me to Garbo," she murmured to herself, admiring her reflection in the long mirror on the back of the wardrobe door.

"You look beautiful, Mammy."

Mrs. Molloy touched her hair, turning slightly to one side as she draped the dress across her slim body. Gently she ran her hand over the soft fabric, smoothing it over her flat stomach and nipping it in at the waist. Her head came back as she drew her knee slightly upward, the toe of her shoe brushing the floor. "Look at me now and the day you got me. Hit me now and the child in me arms!" She laughed outright with delight.

Maureen, catching the drama of the scene, began to mimic her mother's actions.

"Don't be bold, Maureen, and stop that cod actin'. Your daddy will be home in a minute and he'll settle you." She folded the dress, set it aside, and picked a roll of green satin ribbon from amongst the treasures. "Look here, girls, bows for your hair, three inches wide!" She ran the ribbon off the roll, measuring from hand to hand pale lengths of apple-green satin. "Three quarters of a yard makes a perfect bow so there's plenty here for two each. You'll be great style altogether for Patrick's Day."

"Wait till Da sees this. Won't he be surprised?" Nora jumped about, clapping her hands in delight.

"You'll not breathe a word, not to a soul. You hear me now, not a word, not to your father or anyone outside of this room. She looked from one to the other. I'll talk to your father in due course."

"Can we have a couple of the comics now, just a couple?" Maureen begged. "I'll hide them under the bed where he won't see them."

"All right then, just a couple, but remember, not a word to a soul."

But Maureen had told. She had blabbed it all a couple of days later. Sitting in a pew at the back of the church following choir practice, she could keep her secret no longer. She had leaned over and whispered the news in Helen Duffy's ear, and had made her promise not to tell a soul. Soon the whole town knew and there was hell to pay.

Nora smiled now at the memory. Years later it came to her that maybe the parcel had indeed come from her grandfather or that he'd had a hand in it somehow. She liked the idea that he had thought of them but she also knew that her father had felt quite differently when he found out. The parcel was never mentioned again, her mother never wore the dress, and the ribbons disappeared. Every so often the couple of comics under the mattress made an appearance. They had been read and reread and then had been returned to their hiding place.

This and the letters were her only real connection to her grandfather, and even the parcel was pure speculation but the letters were real enough; she had them here in her handbag. She reached for the bag and removed the discoloured envelopes. She chose the one addressed to her father and put the other away safely. She could now picture the man who had written this letter and the woman who stood close by, urging him on. Carefully she drew out the single folded sheet. *My dear Eamon.* She began to read again the now familiar words. Where do feelings come from when one writes such a letter? A heart nourished by fantasy and fragmented memories? Did he retain a visual image of his abandoned child? Could he recall how his hair felt beneath his hand, the look in his eyes or the sound of his voice? She continued to read the words again and again, trying to connect with the man who had written this letter. *I have found a degree of happiness and contentment in my life for which I am grateful.* She read this last sentence again. The words seemed to fly right off the page: *a degree of happiness.* Was this the sum total of his feelings for Peg and the life they had shared? Was that it: *a degree of happiness*? Nora slipped the letter back in the envelope and returned it to her bag. Maybe a cold rejection from his son was all he deserved.

12

Nora shivered as she hopped into the car, her cheeks pinched, her hair whipped into an unruly mass by the wind. "It's turned chilly all of a sudden." She was breathless, having sprinted the last hundred yards to the car. "One minute it's a beautiful sunny day and the next it's freezing."

"Look!" Peg pointed towards the lighthouse where a thick bank of grey fog had appeared on the horizon and was slowly creeping towards the land. "That's the way with the weather around here. It can turn quick as an eel in a barrel."

Nora shivered again. "That's a truly wonderful place out there. It's nature at its very best. I can't believe I had it all to myself, just me and the birds. The isolation is part of the magic." A light mist had begun to settle on the windshield. She smiled and turned to Peg. "I'd never have ventured out here without you. I'm so glad we came. Now, where is Golden Bay where you used to go with your father? Can we drive there?"

"No dear, you have to walk across the barrens or take a boat."

"How far to walk?"

"Oh, two or three hours, I suppose. You don't want to be at that now. It's a shame you'll not be around a while. Pat would be glad to take you on the boat, but maybe you'll come see us another time. I'd like that."

"So would I."

Nora put the key in the ignition but as she was about to turn it, she stopped. "When I was sitting out there all alone I thought about him, my grandfather. Tell me, Peg, was he a generous man? Would he have been the type who'd take the trouble to send gifts to people he didn't really know?" She sat back, leaving the key dangling. "We had a parcel one time from America. We didn't really know who sent it. The story was that it came from cousins, and to tell the truth I didn't care one way or the other, but later on I wondered if he had anything to do with it. Would he bother with the like of that?"

"Yes, he would. He never came home empty-handed. There was always something, no matter how small."

"But to strangers? Did he ever mention anything to you about sending a parcel to us?"

"No, I never heard tell of it. He wasn't the kind to talk about the like of that. He'd just do it. Was there nothing to say where it came from?"

"I don't know. My parents never said."

A long wail sounded from the lighthouse as the fog slowly crept inland. The tip of Bird Rock disappeared into the mist.

"We should be getting back." Nora was beginning to feel apprehensive, even a little frightened by this sudden change in the weather. They were terribly isolated and not a soul knew where they were.

"He wasn't a selfish man." Peg was oblivious to Nora's concern. "He was good-hearted, you have to understand that. It was more of a thoughtless way he had." She sounded slightly exasperated. "Most times he just didn't know what was needed of him. He didn't know what to do." She dragged out the last word for emphasis. "Life and living comes easy to some. It just follows along one day after the next, but for others, it's just an endless struggle." She was looking downwards, rubbing her swollen knuckles.

"You must think I haven't been listening to you, that I haven't tried to understand what you are saying, but I have," Nora said, feeling a little hurt. "You see, until now I've always seen him in a poor light, as someone who didn't care about anyone or anything, so it's not easy to suddenly turn around and think of him kindly. You had a different experience, you saw his good side." She glanced nervously in the direction of the advancing fog.

"I saw all sides," Peg insisted.

Light rain covered the windshield like a fine gauze. "We'd better go." Nora turned the key in the ignition.

"I had a child to care for when Matt returned that second time.

The keys clanged against the shaft of the steering wheel.

"Not my own child," she added quickly. "My sister's child. She died having little Sheila. Her husband had two others to care for and couldn't manage everything on his own, so I took the new baby to raise. She was a dear little baby, but Matt would have nothin' to do with her. I could understand that. After all, she was nothin' to him, but just the same it's hard for most to resist a little motherless child."

Not for him, Nora thought. He resisted his own, no problem. But she kept quiet. The engine hummed patiently. She needed to move, to at least get back again on the main road, but she couldn't brush aside this startling revelation, not even temporarily, and besides, Peg obviously had no intention of quitting and she needed to give driving her full attention.

"By and by, Nora, I noticed him watching me when I'd be talkin' to the little one, you know, goin' on with old nonsense to make her smile. He was takin' it all in but I pretended I was paying no heed." She gave a long sigh. "One day I came on him. He was leaning over the side of the cradle, his hand stretched out above the child's face. I couldn't think what he was doin'. He stayed like that and not a budge out of him for the longest while. My God, I thought, what's he at, at all? He'd take his hand away and then bring it right back to the same spot." She made the motion with her hand. "By and by he put his hand to the child's head and began stroking her little cap of hair. The baby never stirred. He touched her cheek and ran his finger along to the point of her little chin. I could tell it was all a wonder to him. He was just trying his hand at something new."

She looked straight at Nora, making sure that what she said was being understood. Satisfied, she decided to continue.

"I remember at the time thinking about my father, how when he'd get home after days on the water, he'd pick me up in his arms and hold me to him. There'd be the smell of the day's work on him, sweat and fish, and I'd bury my face in it all, breathin' it in, 'til I'd have to break away burstin' for a breath of air. It was a wonderful comforting feeling. We all need the comfort of another human being sometimes."

Inside the car it was very quiet, all fears and apprehensions set aside for now.

"This may sound foolish to you, Nora, but I decided one night that it might be a good idea for him to try his hand at holding the child."

"Isn't she a picture," Peg said proudly, holding her out for him to see. He had watched furtively as she bathed the infant at the kitchen table and got her ready for bed, and now, he came forward tentatively. He reached to touch the little outstretched hand. Right away, the baby latched on to his finger with a firm grip. Taken aback, he looked at Peg, unbelieving, certain that something remarkable had just happened. She nodded encouragement, and indicated that he should take the baby. He fumbled around with the blanket for a moment, and then, awkwardly, took hold of the bundle. Immediately, the baby began to scream, arms and legs thrashing about, furious at being disturbed. Straight away, he thrust her back into Peg's arms and stepped back, convinced that he had done something terribly wrong.

"She's just tired and needs her sleep," Peg assured him, as she expertly tucked the child against her shoulder and took her off to bed. When she returned to the kitchen a few minutes later, he was sitting by the fire with his head in his hands.

"I have no way with children. I don't know what to do with them," he said without preamble.

"It'll come to you, you'll see. All you need is a bit of practice. It's just like anything!"

He wrung his hands pitifully and stared into the fire. "I saw a young child one time, maybe four or five years old, running after his dog down the lane by his house. He fell hard onto the rough ground. His knees and hands were all scratched and bleeding. I was just a few yards from him. I never moved, never went to him, just stood there listening to him cry, watching, fascinated, as a ball of white snot pumped in and out of his left nostril. Funny the things we remember, isn't it? It was the dog that came to the rescue. It came bounding back over the path, fussing and whimpering around the boy, and then settled down beside him and began to lick his bleeding knee. The dog knew better than me what to do." He shook his head, confused. "Why couldn't I help the little lad?"

"Don't go payin' no heed to the like of that." She looked in his direction and decided to take her time before trying again. The following evening, however, he appeared at the kitchen door, all cleaned up and looking like he was ready to go out somewhere.

"You're going out?"

"No."

"Oh!"

"I thought I might have a try with the child again."

"Oh! Right. Well, you've come at a good time, she's just about asleep. Come and sit here in Father's big chair and I'll settle her."

He crossed the room and sat on the edge of the seat.

"Just take it easy now. Sit back in the chair and make a crook with your arm, like this, see. That's it." Firmly, but with great care, she laid the sleeping child in the cradle of his arm.

He stared for a long time in disbelief. Then he looked up into Peg's face. "I can feel her warmth," he said softly.

"I'll never forget the picture of the two of them that night, Nora. He sitting there so still, his long fingers, splayed out so protectively around the tiny body. He had a little poem he used say sometimes to put her asleep. I heard it that night for the first time."

"Do you remember it?"

"I don't know if I can remember all of it but it was something like this: *House, be still, and ye little grey mice, / Lie close tonight in your hidden lairs. / Moths on the window, fold your wings, / Little black chafers, silence your humming. / Things of the mountain that wake in the night-time, / Do not stir tonight until the daylight whitens!*

"I can't remember no more but he could say it so beautiful. Sheila loved that poem best of all. No matter what stories he had to tell, she'd still go on to him, 'Say the one about the mice!' He got to care for that youngster in his own way, and she for him."

"What do you mean, 'in his own way'?" Nora was frowning.

"Oh, you know, looked out for her. Got her little treats."

"So what became of her? Does she live in the cove?"

"No, my dear, she's long gone. Married an American boy with the armed forces she met down to Argentia. There was all kinds stationed here in the forties during the war and many of them married

Newfoundland girls and took them off back to the States when the war was over. They went to California, where he was from. She's still there and has three children of her own."

"And do you ever see her?"

"Oh, yes. From time to time she comes home to see us all, and I've been to California to see them too. Yes, my dear, I got to see a bit of the world after all."

Nora put the car in gear, turned around, and headed cautiously into the fog.

13

They left the fog and rain behind at the cape but the sky had clouded over, taking the blush off the day. Since leaving the headland, they had driven along in silence. Nora wanted to ask Peg about people's reaction to the living arrangement at her house, but when she glanced across, Peg's head was nodding forward onto her chest. The woman needed her lunch and a rest, not more chatter, so she let her be.

Nora tried to imagine the set-up. They must have made an odd group back in those days: an attractive young widow, a small child deprived of her mother at birth, and a good-looking lodger who turned up from time to time and lived with them. It would certainly have caused a stir where she came from, but in the small island community, having the parish priest firmly on your side no doubt had helped. Without his approval there would have been no refuge for Matt Molloy at Peg Barry's house, certainly not after her father died. The whiff of scandal would have found its way to the door, and only Father O'Reilly's unqualified acceptance of the situation could have stilled the wagging tongues. The priest would have been like God in such communities, and somehow Matt Molloy had gained his trust.

"My dear, I'm nodding off. Where are we?"

"We're almost home, another ten minutes or so and we'll be there. Is Father O'Reilly still alive? It might be interesting to meet him."

"He is indeed, and I was thinkin' you should go and have a chat with him. He lives close by, in the priest's house down to Placentia. He's retired now but he still helps out doin' the odd bit of parish work around here. He's getting on now, mind, but I'm told, his mind is good. Take a spin up there after lunch, why don't you, while I have a little nod of sleep."

"Maybe I'll do that and then I'll come back for you and we'll go down to the garden party together. How would that be?"

"Don't worry about me, girl, you go on. Pat will come by if I needs a run."

"What's he like, Peg?" she asked, conjuring up an image of a crusty old parish priest.

"Oh, best kind. The people always liked him but I haven't heard tell of him this while. He must be up there now. In his late eighties, I'd say."

"But he knew Matt quite well, you say?"

"Oh yes, they were friends."

They rounded the bend above Shoal Cove. Without the sunshine the community looked bare and desolate.

"He won't be shocked then to have a granddaughter of Matt Molloy's show up out of the blue?"

"No, you won't find anyone around here too shocked. Nobody asked and nobody was told, but everyone seemed to know that Matt was bound somehow to another life. For certain they all had their own ideas, and in their own minds they were convinced they knew the truth of the matter.

Nora gave her name to the woman who answered the door and

asked if she might speak with Father O'Reilly. The woman, whom Nora presumed to be the housekeeper, looked her up and down, her searching eyes taking in every aspect of the visitor. Nora smiled her best smile, hoping to make a good impression and thereby gain easy access to the inner sanctum of the presbytery. The woman, like a seasoned guard dog, held her ground, blocking the entrance to the house. In those strained moments of intense scrutiny, Nora returned the woman's gaze, aware of a low wheeze coming from the woman's chest.

"Well, now." The wheeze had become a hoarse bark. "He's a busy man. An appointment would–"

"I can come back later, when it's more convenient." Nora turned as if to leave, knowing full well that she would not be allowed to go without at least saying who she was and where she came from.

"Come in then and I'll see what I can do." It was a grudging invitation but the woman never budged. "What was it you said you wanted?"

"That's fine now, Mary, I'll see to the visitor." The voice came from the dark hallway.

Reluctantly the woman stepped aside and opened the door just enough to allow Nora to step inside. A tall portly man in clerical dress stood in the shadow. As Nora moved into the hall he pushed open a heavy wooden door to his right. A thin shaft of light fell across the polished floor.

"Come in, Miss Molloy. Mary, maybe you could rustle up a pot of tea for us and then you can leave early and go on to the garden party." He then dismissed her with a nod and held the door open for Nora. After a quick glance back into the hall he closed the door behind them.

"I'm Nora–"

"Yes, Miss Molloy, I know who you are. News of a stranger travels fast in a small place, and Mary had it before most." His large hand trembled slightly as he reached out to shake hers but his grip was firm. "Father Charlie O'Reilly," he said, introducing himself. "You are a relative of Matt Molloy. His granddaughter, I believe?"

"That's right."

"Come and sit down." He indicated an ornate upholstered chair to the side of the fireplace. Nora took a moment to look around. It was a solid, sombre room laden down with shelves of dusty books, heavy furniture, and plum-coloured velvet curtains. An assortment of religious icons provided meagre relief. A wooden prie-dieu with a velvet kneeling pad stood in one corner, and above that, a small crucifix. A large bay window looked onto the front garden but sheer, white curtains cut off the outdoors. There was a smell of tobacco in the room.

She turned her attention to the priest as he made his way across the worn carpet to a large armchair across from her. He walked with a heavyset assurance, his large pigeon-toed feet securely laced into stout black brogues. Despite his years he held himself erect. Slowly he lowered himself into the armchair. He had a benevolent look about him, this man of God.

She had expected some small talk about Ireland or the family, but there was none. As if knowing exactly why she was here, he went straight to the point.

"Your grandfather ..." he began. Watery grey, slightly bulbous eyes scrutinized Nora from above heavy horn-rimmed glasses. There was a query there, or was it a challenge? Nothing terribly obvious but one she found to be unsettling. She held his gaze for a moment, waiting for him to continue. Finally he averted his eyes and settled back into his chair, pushing his glasses back onto the bridge of his nose with a pudgy index finger. He began again. "We spent a fair bit of time together, your grandfather and I. I expect you are aware of that. It was part of my pastoral duties to visit Berry Island every couple of weeks to say Mass and administer the sacraments. I travelled by boat of course so the weather often dictated the frequency and length of my stay. There were many occasions when I prayed for bad weather just so I could stay on longer and be in his company. I can confess that now." A smile appeared at the corner of his mouth and his chest heaved as he gave a little "heh," the bare beginnings of a laugh.

There was a pause. "We got along well together, the two of us. We'd talk for hours, maybe play a game of chess. You'd be surprised at all the topics we would discuss. Mind you, I have to admit, there were times I didn't know what he was talking about, but I enjoyed listening to what he had to say. He was full of what he called, 'the new order in the world, the shift in society, new ways, new ideas, new forms.' Music was being rearranged, 'disordered,' I believe, was a word he used. He talked of 'shifting planes' and about 'geometric forms' in art. People were dancing with their toes turned in! Now I didn't see that as strange. I'd been doing that for years." There was a sputter of coughing as he tried to laugh.

He pulled himself up in the chair. "I could see a funny side to it all. From our point of view, here on an island at the edge of the Atlantic, it was all ridiculous nonsense. 'Imagine now, Matt,' I'd say, 'the fine time a fella like Picasso would have rearranging the likes of me.'" He began to cough uncontrollably.

Nora sat there, conjuring up an image of the heavy, pigeon-toed priest rearranged, squared off, Picasso style, a big watery eye plucked from its socket and set halfway down his cheek, stepping out, doing a nimble Charleston right there on the presbytery floor. She looked up and found him peering at her again over his big glasses. His lips had parted into a broad grin showing long tobacco-stained teeth. She laughed.

He began to cough again and while struggling to bring himself more upright in the chair he produced a crumpled white hand-kerchief and buried his face in the folds. There was a loud blow followed by a great intake of breath and he continued, "I said to him one night, 'You know what we should do, Matt, you and me? We should invite them boys to Newfoundland, have them down here to do a job on the whole place. Reorder, remake, rearrange. Think of the time they'd have with that.' He got furious with me then. He thought I wasn't taking him seriously enough."

There was a knock on the door and Mary appeared with a tray. She looked from one to the other. No doubt she had heard the laughter. For a moment Nora thought she might turn on her heel and walk straight back out the door, taking tray and all. But she planted it down with a rattle on the small table beside the priest.

"I'm off then, if you have no further need of me."

"Thank you, Mary. That will be grand." He watched her leave.

"I think she's jealous," he said softly, still in his jovial mood. "Mary has been around for a long time and thinks it her right to know everything that goes on in this house."

Nora didn't quite know what to make of this man. Perhaps she had come with a preconceived idea of how this small-town priest might be and he didn't quite fit.

He pulled himself around in the chair and, having poked his glasses back on his nose, proceeded to pour tea. He passed the cup to Nora, inviting her to have milk and sugar and a tea bun if she wished. He then helped himself to four spoons of sugar and stirred vigorously as he poured a stream of yellow creamy milk into his cup. She had black tea.

"What was interesting about your grandfather," he was looking carefully at the buttered tea bun he held between his fingers, "was how he embraced the concept of change with such enthusiasm. It excited him. He explored new ideas and talked about them with a kind of passion that didn't seem to transfer to his everyday life. The idea was what mattered. Whether in fact it had any practical use was of no importance. I don't honestly know whether he liked Picasso's work or Stravinsky's music or if he liked the innovations in the theatre that he talked about so much, but he loved the shift in creative thought and loved to speculate on where it might lead. He was a fascinating man."

"Did you think of him as a friend?"

He studied her over the rim of his eyeglasses. "I was a bit older than him but that never seemed important. I enjoyed his company. Quite often he did the talking and I listened; I was a kind of sounding board. However ..." He leaned forward, his index finger stabbing repeatedly at the black cloth on his thigh. "When we got into philosophy, that for me was our best time together. I was well able for him then." He settled back in his chair. "I was on home turf. Thomas Aquinas, St. Augustine, they were the two. We'd go at it hammer and tongs well into the night." He was excited now, munching steadily on his bun, taking great gulps of strong tea.

He was avoiding her question. She needed to turn the conversation around and she didn't have all day. She looked across at the old priest and shifted position.

"He didn't exist for me. Can you understand that, Father O'Reilly? He was a non-person, a kind of a legend. The same applied to my grandmother." She waited. "I'm trying to find out why he left. Until I met Peg Barry I knew nothing about him, and she has been generous in sharing her memories. She thought you might have other insights that you would like to share before it's all too late."

He was silent.

"As a friend," she continued, "I thought you might know what happened. I mean, did he ever talk about his past life? Did he ever bring it up?" She pressed. "Did you ever ask?"

He put the last piece of tea bun into his mouth and chewed, looking pensive. His glasses had slipped again and he pushed them back onto the bridge of his nose. "We didn't discuss our personal lives." He was staring beyond her. "He never mentioned his private life and I never asked. It was a mutual understanding, unspoken."

"You didn't know him very well, then?"

The teacup rattled precariously as he returned it to the tray.

"He was a good man." He spoke as he might from the pulpit, a note of authority and finality in his voice.

Good, she wondered, and what does *good* mean? She searched the shabby carpet at her feet. Pious, holy, virtuous, sound, slap on the back, good man yourself, sterling, satisfactory, good to the last drop, *GUINNESS is GOOD for YOU*! She took a deep breath to quiet the rant going on in her head. Across from her he was pensive, his elbows resting on the arms of the chair, hands clasped in front of his face, the fingers solidly intertwined, index fingers straight and pointing heavenward. He tapped his pursed lips silently with the steepled fingers.

Childhood nonsense rang in her head: *Here's the church / There's the steeple / Open the door / There's the people.*

"A good man," he reiterated.

She drew a deep breath. "How would you know that?" Her question, she knew, was blunt, too blunt, but she didn't care. She was beginning to find him irritating.

He shifted, crossing one leg over the other. "When one serves in a community for as long as I did one tends to get to know one's parishioners quite well. That's part of the job."

She could feel the gulf widen between them. It made her more desperate, more insistent. He was preaching at her again and that annoyed her. She felt an overpowering urge to tell him that she wasn't here for a sermon, that she was not a pesky parishioner who could be cowed by a stern formal tone. But good sense or good manners, one or the other, took over and she decided on another approach.

"There must have been talk around that would have been of concern to the parish priest?"

"There is always gossip in small communities." He was looking directly at her over the rim of his glasses.

She held her ground. "Gossip you could ignore?"

"The man came and stayed from time to time. He taught school for several years and he boarded with Peg Barry. There's no crime in that now, is there?" He wasn't asking her. She was being told.

"So, you had no reservations about hiring him to teach the children on the island?" She pressed, her pounding heart threatening to garble her words.

"No, I did not. I made what inquiries as were necessary. I offered him the job and he accepted."

She wondered about the inquiries. How did one inquire about the likes of Matt Molloy?

"Did you know that he had a wife and child back in Ireland?"

He hesitated just a bit too long before answering. "Yes, I did."

She could see the old power there, the well-honed ability to shut down any further inquiries. She decided to change direction again. "I understand he refused the position to begin with."

"We had little to offer in those days. We were very fortunate that eventually he agreed."

"Maybe he was the fortunate one. Perhaps Berry Island was a better alternative to Boston or New York in the Dirty Thirties."

"I'm sorry I can't be of more help to you. Peg is the one who knew him best. She is your best source." It was his parting shot. He got to his feet, abruptly bringing the conversation to an end.

She rose, thanked him, said goodbye and walked to the door.

In the car she went over their conversation bit by bit. Things had started off quite well. She had liked his humorous, straightforward approach but somehow things had turned around. She acknowledged that she had been too strident in her approach, not diplomatic enough but time was her enemy. Tomorrow she would have to leave. She was convinced that he knew more about Matt Molloy than he had let on. She could feel it in her gut. Why couldn't he just come straight out and tell her what he knew? At this stage what was there to lose? She was thinking about turning back and trying again when it occurred to her that maybe the nosey housekeeper might know a thing or two, and she was going to the garden party. Maybe she could corner her there and wheedle a few details from her.

Beyond a grassy meadow she could see a long stony stretch of beach. She pulled to the side of the road, hoping the fresh breeze off the water would clear her head. She hurried across the field, eager to get to the water's edge.

Sitting on a rock she watched the ebb and flow of the tide, the grey waters lapping the shoreline, running silently into every nook and cranny, painting dark shiny crescents on the beach rocks and the rough sand. She picked up a flat stone and threw it far out in the water. It made a loud plop and disappeared, leaving behind ever expanding circles that spread wider and wider and finally disappeared.

14

There was no need to ask for directions to the garden party. The brightly coloured bunting beckoned with a mad kind of excitement as she drove down into the cove. Hoopla was the last thing she needed right now but she had to go for Peg's sake. When she'd stopped by the house to pick her up she found that Peg had already left.

Lively dance music crackled from a loud speaker as she stepped from her car. Two girls in tight bell-bottom jeans, one clutching a huge purple stuffed dog, went by arm in arm, heads close together, giggling and whispering. Across from where Nora stood, a crowd had gathered around a Wheel of Fortune. A couple of lanky boys, hair slicked back, hands jammed deep into their pockets, broke away from the crowd and hurried after the two girls. How in the world was she going to find Peg in this melee? Nora moved closer to the crowd.

"Last five tickets before the spin."

"Twenty-five cents, any takers, any takers?"

"Keep her goin' there, b'y. We need a quarter, just one quarter, to stop the wheel."

"Who's goin' to be the lucky one?"

"Yes, my darling, they're all yours."

"We're ready now, here she goes!"

In one swift motion money and tickets changed hands.

"Take her away, Paddy. Watch your numbers, ladies and gentlemen."

Brrr. The wheel spun round and round, the rubber finger slapping the metal spikes. A hush fell on the crowd.

"Twenty-six," Paddy called out with authority.

"Jumpins, I'm twenty-six!" A white head bobbed up and down and a thin hand slid a blue strip of tickets to the vendor.

"Yes, indeed, Aunt Carrie, my duckie, and I'm Santa Claus. You'll get no argument from me. Give the lady her prize, Paddy, if she says she's twenty-six, then, by God, she's twenty-six!" The crowd cheered and laughed.

He was playing the pack, a seasoned expert holding their attention, making eye contact, coaxing them shamelessly to part with their money. They were having a grand time. A blue flurry of spent tickets fell to the ground as the next spin got under way.

Eager to be part of the fun, Nora moved in closer, pulled out a dollar bill and reached above the straining heads. "A dollar's worth," she called tentatively, not sure if she would be heard above the din.

"Ha, ha. Make way there, ladies and gentlemen, for the last of the big spenders."

Heads turned.

"Step right up, my dear. Four strips for the lady from away."

She reached forward, her green dollar bill dangling between her fingers. He laughed, showing his big white even teeth, his dark eyes full of merriment. She took in at a glance the neat set of his collar and tie, the tanned flush of his skin and the neatly combed head of greying hair. He put her in mind of one of the travelling peddlers of long ago, full of banter and charm but with a certain craftiness. Yet he cut a dashing figure. He took her dollar bill and held out four blue strips of tickets. She grasped them but he held on momentarily as if to say, "Not so fast lady." In that moment he looked her straight in the eyes. It was an honest look but strangely disquieting, devoid of the merriment she had seen there earlier. Then it was gone and he moved on to his next customer, joking, laughing and selling. The crowd pressed closer to watch the next spin. She didn't win but decided to move on.

She had a go at the ring toss but again came up empty-handed. She wished she could locate Peg. A roar of laughter followed by loud clapping came from a group over by the tent. She began to hurry across the open space to the shelter of the crowd, aware that people sometimes stepped aside to let her pass. Was she the only one in a hurry? She wished that she had worn something less conspicuous. Her long maxi summer dress that she had hurriedly put on for her visit to the priest might be fashionable in Montreal, but here it made her even more conspicuous. She edged her way into the crowd and stood on tip-toe looking for Peg. The crowd was thinner over to the side so she went that way. Up front she could see a young man stripped to the waist, sitting precariously on a makeshift ledge a few feet above a huge plastic tub of water. Above the tub hung a large black bull's eye painted on a piece of wood. She strained to get a closer look. The woman to her left turned to leave and suddenly she was at the front of the crowd.

"A clean smack and down he goes. Three balls for a quarter. Here we go, ladies and gentlemen. Try your hand."

"Gimme a couple of them there balls, Foxy, and I'll wipe the grin offa that young whelp's face. Time someone teached him a lesson."

"Go for it, Ronnie b'y, give 'er a smack." The crowd was all fired up, hollering advice at the little man to Nora's left.

"Clear the decks there, b'ys, and give the man a bit of room."

In a flash his jacket was off and pressed into Nora's hands for safekeeping. "Hold on to that, my duckie. I'll be done the minute." Bright eyes darted from the jacket to Nora, a caution to take great care of his bundle. He flexed his skinny muscles, pushed his tweed cap to a warlike angle and stepped up to the line. "Hang on to yer drawers, b'ys," he yelled, as he wound up with an exaggerated motion, "Ronnie is about to blow the arse right out of her. She's goin' down." The ball soared straight above their heads and tumbled back into the crowd.

Abuse came from all sides.

"Look, Ronnie b'y, the target's here, right above me head." The young buck on the ledge pointed to the bull's eye.

"The sauce of that!" He wound up again. A quick flick and the ball once more flew into the air above the crowd.

"Ah, I'm not meself today, lost me touch!" With that, he turned, took his jacket from Nora and thrust the last ball into her hand. "Here, girl, have a go. Give it to him, right in the chops!"

She had no wish to participate. She just wanted to watch, to be a part of the crowd, yet she couldn't help but feel sorry for the little man who was getting such a hard time from the raucous mob. She was his partner after all; she had held his jacket.

He leaned in to her and whispered in her ear, "Go for it, girl. A clean hit an' he's in there, eyes and face. Give it all ye got."

She felt the weight of the ball in her hand, turned it over several times, and with a knowing glance at her partner, stepped up to the line.

Now she wanted to do it. She wanted to bring that smirky face down and it wasn't just for the fun of it. She was shocked momentarily by the intensity of her feelings but she quickly pushed them aside. She eyed the lad on the perch. It didn't matter anymore that people stared, that they pointed and whispered behind her back. She was going to show them. She was going to enjoy this one.

K A T E   E V A N S

She took careful aim, her eye fixed on the black circle above his head. Her arm arced back slowly. A quick flick and the ball flew from her fingers, hard and sure and straight. She heard the thump as it hit home. Another thump immediately followed and then an enormous splash. The crowd whooped and yelled in delight and then she too was laughing, wiping splashes of water from her face and forehead with the back of her hand. Ronnie, beside himself with glee, grabbed her by the waist and danced her round and round on the grass in a fumbling victory waltz.

"Yes, girl, you got 'un good."

As she twirled round and round she caught a glimpse of her victim as he emerged dripping from the tank, hair plastered to his head. He was grinning broadly. She waved to him, mouthing her apologies. He winked approvingly.

"Feels some good, don't it?" Ronnie, delighted with his new buddy, continued with his victory dance.

She realized suddenly that it did feel good. It felt great.

When finally she broke away from the crowd, she was once more trying to decide what to do next when a voice spoke right in her ear.

"He had a good eye, too."

She spun around. It was the ticket man from the Wheel of Fortune.

"You frightened me, creeping up like that."

"Sorry."

"What do you mean by that, 'a good eye'?"

"Mr. Molloy, he had a good eye too. He was a crack shot, right on the target."

"Oh, yes, so I hear. Peg told me." Nora looked at him carefully. He had an amused look in his eye.

"Gerry Quinlan." He held out his hand.

"Oh, Peg mentioned your name. I'm Nora Molloy."

"Did she now? She's looking for you, wonderin' if you got here. She's in the tea tent just over there." Without asking he put his hand on her elbow and ushered her across the grass.

It was good to see Peg looking rested and relaxed amidst the noise and hubbub of the tent. Nora walked over to where she sat with another lady having tea.

"Ah, there you are, child, and Gerry too. Come and sit down, the pair of you."

"Aunt Peg, my dear, you're looking great, yourself too, Treese." He nodded to them in turn.

"Get away with you, Gerry," Peg said, dismissing the compliment, but she was obviously pleased to see him. She turned to Nora. "Are you enjoyin' yourself?"

"I'm having a grand time. I just dumped some poor young lad in the water outside there."

"Oh, that'll be Gerry's boy, I suppose. He's a great sport. Loves a bit of fun."

"Your son?" She turned to Gerry.

"Yes, my dear, you never know who's who in Newfoundland." He was mocking her.

"You might have told me."

"Never got the chance."

"Treese." Peg turned to her companion. "This is Nora Molloy from Ireland. You remember Matt Molloy, taught school on the island years ago? Well, this is his granddaughter. She's here for a visit."

"Hello," Nora said, offering her hand to the woman sitting on the edge of a folding chair. Nora was looking at a face full of scrutiny, one suffused by a deep frown, so much so that her eyes were all but lost to view. Only a glint of light coming from where the sockets were located gave this face any semblance of life. She was regarding Nora intently. For Nora, it was like looking at a mask.

"Something to drink, Nora?" Peg asked.

"Thank you, but no, I had tea with Father O'Reilly."

"How was your visit?" Peg gave Nora a cautionary look and ever so slightly inclined her head in Treese's direction.

Nora caught Peg's warning. "Very good. He's a remarkable man for his age."

There was a lull in the conversation. At her side the ticket man was still, his banter shut down. Mustering a bright smile, Nora decided to change the subject. "It's quite the event out there," she said, looking from one to the other. "It's just like home."

"Is that right?" Peg came to life and moved in closer to Nora, partly blocking her view of Treese.

"Yes, there were always events like this when we were children," she continued, speaking directly to Peg. "There were all kinds of prizes to be won, not toys like here, but practical things mostly. I remember one time coming home from the fair with a set of white dishes with blue flowers painted on the cups. I forget now how I won them." She rushed on. "We also had a game that I loved called Roll Away. I don't see it here. It was a huge round table like a checkerboard caged in all around with heavy mesh. The squares were just big enough to hold one of our big brown pennies." She drew the outline of the old brown penny on the palm of her hand. "All around the cage were little openings, with a wooden chute at each one. You literally rolled your pennies away down the chute. However, if the penny landed right smack in the middle of a square without touching any lines then you won whatever amount of money was marked on the square."

"We had the very same years ago. Didn't we, Treese?"

Nora knew without looking that Treese had not taken her eyes off her from the moment she sat down. Nora glanced in her direction. Still no eyes and no reply!

"I remember that was the most exciting game of all," Peg continued, ignoring the silence. "To win money, that's what we all

WHERE OLD *Ghosts* MEET

wanted. Yes, girl, I can remember fixing the chute right at the big money square and then how it would roll away straight into buddy's pocket."

"That's right." Nora was grateful for Peg's participation. She knew she was talking too much, but still she barrelled on, unable to stop herself, still speaking directly to Peg and ignoring Gerry and Treese. "One day, didn't I win the big money, a pound note! That was a lot of money then."

Peg laughed, a slightly strained, exaggerated laugh. "I suppose it was."

Nora could see the bright pink plate of her false teeth with its even row of cream dentures. Peg was trying to help her out.

Suddenly Treese's voice cut the space between them. "What I'd like to know is this. What drove him out of Ireland?"

The question hit Nora like a sharp slap. A crackling silence followed. Nora now scrutinized the face in front of her. "Did you know him?" The calm assurance in her own voice surprised her.

Treese sat back in her chair, pulled the two sides of her knitted cardigan across her chest and held them in place with folded arms. "No," she said, dragging out the word. "Not exactly, but I knew about him."

Nora examined her fingernails for a moment, taking time to pick her words carefully. She looked up. "Then, I don't imagine you would want to be bothered with all the ins and outs of my grandfather's life. It's a long story," she added, sweetening her tone but leaving no doubt that she didn't intend to continue the conversation.

They regarded each other across the table, both impassive. Two hot spots of indignation burned on Treese's cheeks. The frown had lifted like a fog from the wrinkled face and two rather nice hazel eyes appeared in its place. Nora noticed for the first time her fine head of thick white hair. It was a shame that Treese hadn't discovered the worth of a smile, Nora mused.

Treese made a move and got to her feet. She turned to Peg. "I've got things to be doin', so I'm off. I imagine I'll be seein' you by and by." She nodded in Gerry's direction and left.

The music had stopped playing outside and suddenly it seemed very quiet in the tent.

"I'm sorry," Nora began. "I hope–"

"No, my dear, don't you say a word. Treese was just fishin' around, lookin' for a bit of gossip. She's been sittin' here waitin' all afternoon, knowin' you were bound to show up. That's the way with her. It's none of her business. Now, how did you get along with Father O'Reilly? I didn't want you to say in front of Treese, but the question was out before I realized."

"Oh, he was very welcoming, brought me in, gave me tea, and chatted about Matt, but I think there was more he could have told me but for whatever reason, chose not to. He certainly didn't want to answer any questions. You can only go so far with these things …" She was about to add "without causing offence" but decided to leave it alone.

"Gerry here, he was a star pupil of your grandfather's. Maybe you should have a chat with him."

The music started up again outside.

Gerry came to life and began to beat out the rhythm on his knee as he hummed the tune. "'Up the Pond,' great tune," he said and continued to beat out the rhythm. "I don't know about a star, but a pupil, yes."

"You did well for yourself, Gerry. Better than most."

"Are you ready for home yet, Aunt Peg?" Pat had appeared at the tent opening.

Peg got to her feet. "Yes, Pat, I'm ready. You two can stay on and talk about old times. Gerry here's a grand man to talk when he gets goin'. I'll go on now and see you later."

Gerry stood as she left and planted a kiss on top of her head. "She's some wonderful woman," he said, watching her leave.

"Yes, she is. I've become quite attached to her in the short time I've known her," Nora said.

He sat down again, placing his arms on the table. "It's a pity that you've come now, now he's gone, I mean. I could never understand why a man the like of him was so alone in the world, alone except for Peg, of course."

"You're not surprised to know that he had a family in Ireland?"

"No, we all thought there had to be some kind of a problem, some reason he didn't have Peg. She was willing, for sure. You could tell the two of them were close. In her day, Peg was a fine lookin' woman, with a fine house, and he was presentable too but a bit of an oddball. It was only natural that there was talk around. I used to love to listen in on the old fellas below in the shed, sittin' around talkin' about the pair of them. They were worse than a bunch of old women. One of them would start up the conversation with a comment like, 'Buddy now, the boarder, what's stayin' above to Peggy Barry's place, now, he's somethin' else. Walkin' about the year like a gentleman without his swallowtail. They say he puts in his day sittin' about readin' his books and the like. Now that's a queer way to be goin' on, wouldn't ye say? Don't put no bread on the table, that's for sure.'" Gerry grinned, flashing his set of magnificent white teeth, and inclined his head to one side as if to say, "Now, what do you think of that?"

Nora began to giggle and leaned in closer. "Shh. Keep your voice down or the whole place will hear you." She glanced nervously over her shoulder.

But the devil seemed to have taken hold of Gerry as he continued to mimic the men in the shed. "'No, and it's not bread I'd be after either if I had me feet under Peggy Barry's table. Guaranteed! It's under her skirts I'd be. Yes, by the Jesus; I wouldn't be at no books.'"

"Gerry!" Her eyebrows arched.

In an instant, the grin was gone and a new persona emerged. He looked at her with mock earnestness. He seemed to be enjoying himself, feeding shamelessly on Nora's anxiety as he continued his rant. "'There's no call now to be talkin' like that about the poor woman. It's her business. There'd be no yap the like of that out of you fellas, if the skipper was still above. Buddy'd be out the door on his arse.'" Gerry thumped the table with his fist and paused, feigning mock consideration of the situation. "'Still an' all now, I wish I had his head. I never seen the like of him. I've had occasion to be down to the priest's place doin' a bit of work and I've heard the two of them talkin' about stuff and I can tell ye, b'ys, the words'd be comin' out of him like farts from a goat. Never heared the like in me life.'"

Nora burst out laughing, loving how he straddled the very core of the gossiping men. Covering her mouth, she said, "Gerry, I think we'd better go."

"It's you they're interested in, not me. Pay no heed." He sat back in his chair and stretched out his long legs. "That's how they'd go on, Nora, they'd have a few laughs and usually end up speculating as to what it was had a hold on him. The general consensus was that it had to be either God, the law, or another woman. The latter was the most popular belief. They were a hard crowd when they got goin'. But now, I have to say, the gossip didn't seem to bother Peg. She just went her own way."

The crowd had begun to drift into the tent in search of refreshment. The tension that had gripped Nora since leaving the priest's house had begun to dissipate. She was surprised also to find that she felt quite at ease with Gerry. Perhaps it had to do with Peg's liking for him and his obvious respect for Peg, or maybe it was just his easy, humorous way, but, whatever the reason, when he asked her if she'd care to have a beer with him, she accepted.

"I didn't get your last name, Gerry," she said as though assigning him a final stamp of approval.

"Quinlan. My family came to Newfoundland from Ireland in 1838. I'm glad to meet you, Nora Molloy. It's like meeting a long lost cousin."

15

He drove a big, swanky black car with sleek tail fins and an abundance of chrome. With one arm resting on the edge of the open window and the other gripping the smooth rim of the steering wheel, Gerry Quinlan looked suave and confident.

"There's only one place around here to have a beer. It's a few miles up the shore in Angels Cove." He looked at her sideways, his right eyebrow cocked, waiting for her reaction.

"That's fine, I'm in no hurry."

"It's a bit rough now. Not too many women go there. It's a tavern really." He glanced her way again.

She caught that now familiar look of amusement in his eyes. "I've been in a tavern or two."

But she had never quite seen the like of this place. It was a small dark room with a low ceiling, not much more than a shed, attached by an adjoining door to an equally small and rundown house. The room served also as a kind of shop with a few shelves behind the bar that were strewn with an assortment of boxes, aspirin, matches, nails. There were a few loaves of bread, odd bottles with various liquids, and a number of cheap plastic toys in dusty wrappers. The air was sluggish with the smell of stale beer, tobacco and smoke. Behind the door and set back in a corner was a small wood-burning stove, which, despite the warm weather, was alight and throwing a fair amount of heat into the tiny room. A solitary figure sat slumped over the fire, his head heavy in his hands.

"Paddy." Gerry nodded in the direction of the figure by the stove. There was no reply. He turned and closed the door, shutting out most of the light to the little room. In the gloom, Gerry put his hand under Nora's elbow and guided her to one of the small tables set along the back wall.

"I'll get us a beer."

Nora looked around her. The lights of a shiny juke box appeared like a mirage out of the shadows. It winked silently, inviting her to play. The loud clang of a bell startled her. Gerry was tugging at a dangling rope attached to a thin wire in the ceiling. He gave it another tug. The adjoining door opened and closed and a short stout man stood behind the bar. In the dim light Nora guessed him to be in his seventies.

"Gerry. Marvelous bloody day," he boomed, jolting the room into life. "Too goddamn hot for my likin' but all right just the same, I suppose." He had reached under the counter, produced two bottles of beer, and had them uncapped and set on the counter before Gerry had time to draw breath.

"Grand day." He poked his head around Gerry's bulk and raised a hand in Nora's direction.

She nodded.

"Nora Molloy, from Ireland." Gerry pointed to where Nora sat. "Dave Broderick."

"Bloody fine women over that way, I'll allow." He slapped his hand on the counter, set his head to one side, and smiled admiringly at Nora. Language aside, his round balding head with its fringe of white hair and his plump fresh cheeks put her in mind of Friar Tuck.

"Welcome to Newfoundland, my dear." Raising his voice even more, he roared across the room, "Paddy, don't forget the goddamn fire." With that he turned and disappeared back to where he'd come from, leaving behind a stunned silence.

The man by the stove never moved.

Gerry shrugged, picked up the two bottles of beer, and brought them to the table. "I'm afraid there are no glasses." He sat down. "What do you think?"

"Different, I have to admit. Who's he?" She inclined her head towards the man by the stove.

"Paddy Broderick." He dropped his voice. "A kind of relative. Comes in here every day, first thing in the morning, stays all day. Just tends the stove."

"Does he speak?"

Gerry shrugged his shoulders. "Not to me." He raised the bottle to his mouth and took a long draft. "You handled Treese well this afternoon."

Nora shrugged but made no comment.

"It's been forty-odd years now and she's still sniffin' about like the crackie dog after a bone, unwillin' to let go. She was all set to tear into you this afternoon, couldn't wait. But you kept her right at bay. More power to you. I liked that."

"I thought she was a friend. The way you were dishing out the compliments, I thought maybe you were related."

"Well, you know how it is. In a place like this you want to stay on the good side of all." He winked.

"So why would she want to take a run at me?"

"An old battle from years ago. Her brother wanted the teaching job on the island, the one Mr. Molloy was given. He was local, see, from down Red Island way. He had just grade eleven, whereas your grandfather was more educated and also from away, which made him not only better in some people's eyes, but more important. He was also a friend of Father O'Reilly, and he wanted him in the job so that was the end of it. There was quite the racket brewing at the time and Treese wasn't beyond spreading rumours around. However, another position was found for the brother and all was smoothed over. But Treese never forgot the 'slight' to the family and has held a grudge ever since."

"Maybe she had good reason to be annoyed. I'd say Father O'Reilly was looking out for his own interests."

He looked surprised. "What do you mean?"

"I'd say he wanted him to be a permanent fixture on Berry Island, for the company. He liked having him around, it seems."

"You're a bit of a crackie yourself, I'd say." He laughed. "You weren't impressed with the padre then."

"No," she said reluctantly, "I didn't take to him much. He's not your uncle or anything like that, I suppose."

"No, no." He laughed again and then added, "It's the same today. Someone you know gives you the nod for a job and you're in. It's simple as that."

She looked across at him. He had that infernal look of amusement on his face again. Normally his attitude would have irritated her, but again, she found herself liking his frankness. "I'm surprised he accepted a job when he didn't really want it. From what I hear he just didn't seem like the type."

"That may be true, but back then, not many said no to authority. I was only a youngster at the time but I'd say he didn't really care too much one way or the other, and he likely wasn't aware of the racket that was afoot." His finger traced the rim of the bottleneck, round and round. "Mr. Molloy was a man of few words so it was hard to tell how he felt. When he was pleased he had a habit of saying, 'Well, well.' Anger, on the other hand, made him pace like an animal, small even steps back and forth on the floor, his jacket pushed back to one side with a white-knuckled hand spread wide to hold it in position. Words were not needed then. Soon as the pacing stopped, you could watch out."

The man in the corner moved, his chair scraping the floor.

They both turned to look but nothing seemed to have changed. Gerry threw his head back and tipped the bottle. The muscles in his neck contracted. Finally, with lips pursed he made a small sucking noise and lowered the bottle. He gave a contented sigh and then his face was still. Fine lines at the corners of his eyes lay slack and open, exposing thin white furrows on his tanned skin. He took another swig.

She followed his lead, allowing the cold carbonated bubbles to rest for a moment on her tongue. The liquid was cool and refreshing. She drank again, this time deeply.

He had begun to pick at the label, digging for a starting point with his thumbnail. A loose spot in the corner gave way and crinkled into tiny damp accordion pleats. "He let me down, you know." For a brief moment his cocky self was gone and he looked vulnerable as he picked away at the label. His head came up then and he gave a short careless laugh. "It's all past and gone now. But I sure as hell didn't see it that way at the time. It was like he got me all fired up to take on the whole bloody world, and more besides, and then when I'm ready to go, he tells me not to be so goddamn foolish. Jesus, at the time I was mad as hell. I wanted to smack him one right there and then." His fist jerked upwards and tightened into a hard ball. A devious smile spread across his mouth. He regarded the half empty bottle, trying with his thumb to smooth away the wrinkle. "My dreams were all bound to him. I hung on every word that fell from his lips, every move he made, every shift in his imagination. I stored it all away, like a precious stash, deep inside. I was in awe of him." He paused and drank again.

"Did you have dreams, Nora?" He turned to her, his old jocular mood back.

She shifted but remained silent, feeling a tiny jab of intrusion, like the sudden prick of a needle penetrating a soft fingerpad.

"You're right," he said. "Guard your heart. Keep them to yourself."

But the dream surfaced nonetheless, vivid and uninvited: Alicia Markova, prima ballerina, the breathtaking grace and elegance of the ballet. That was what she dreamed of. She had the physical attributes, the athleticism, the vision, but she had never even owned a pair of pink satin slippers, let alone learned to dance. She had studied pictures of the ballet, committing every detail to memory. She had read every book on ballet in the public library, devouring the words, and today the dream still lived in her imagination, vibrant and lovely as ever, for her eyes only.

"*Thuras amac*. Do you know this expression?"

She was jolted into the present. "Sorry, yes, of course. Yes, did you say *thuras amac*? This is Irish. A *thuras* is a journey and *amac* means out or outward, so I suppose an outward journey would be the direct translation."

"Well, down this way when I was a child, it was often used as an expression meaning a bit of a disturbance. Someone might say, 'Now, that was a right ould *thuras amac* last night.'"

"Really!"

"Yes, but *Thuras Amac* was the name he gave to an imaginary ship. The last half hour every day, all hands boarded the *Thuras Amac*. 'All aboard,' he'd call out. 'Hoist the mainsail, McGrath to look out!' That was the signal to cover up the windows in the schoolroom with coats." Gerry laughed a deep throaty laugh that filled the tiny room. "We were pirates then, heading for the high seas, at least that's how we youngsters saw things. We loved it." He looked across to the old stove in the corner. "There was a stove just like that. When we were shipshape and all seated around the fire he'd throw open the doors of the stove and the red glow of heat and light would spill into the darkened room. We were there with him, every man jack one of us, ready and willing to be transported to wherever he chose."

He began to mimic the boys' excited voices: "'I knows where we're to, sir. It's called Tahiti, sir. This is an island, sir, in the Pacific Ocean, but it's not even a small bit like Berry Island because the sun is always shining here and it's lovely. The people are all the colour of the kelp below on the beach and they go around wearin' half nothin'. There's millions of big bright flowers grow all over the place and the trees is full of yellow oranges and the water in the sea is warm as the rock pools on a hot day below to the beach, and so the cod fish couldn't live in that water at all. Too warm, see.'"

Gerry set his beer on the table and assumed an air of authority. "'Very good, Pat,' he'd say. 'Now one day in the year 1769, as the hot sun disappeared below the crust of the earth, a great ship with white sails reaching high into the heavens sailed over the horizon and anchored off the shore of this island. The ship was called the *Endeavour*. The captain on board ...' That's how he'd go on, Nora, encouraging us to be colourful and imaginative in our speech and writing, but at the back of it all was learning, learning about the world beyond our island. 'Knowledge is power,' he used to say. Times like that, if he told us we were off to the moon in a dory we'd have believed him. It was something we all looked forward to at the end of the day and nobody wanted to miss the trip. It even became a game that we played in our spare time, down by the water, but then it was all about pirates fightin' and robbin' and killin' each other. I believe that half hour every day kept many youngsters in school. Nobody wanted to miss the *Thuras Amac*. School wasn't compulsory then, so normally any excuse and the children were gone."

Nora tried hard to picture this quiet distant man who was her grandfather surrounded by serious little faces, all still and attentive, burning bright with the fire of imagination: a pirate ship, scarlet blossoms, big ripe golden oranges, outstretched hands, a grey stone building, iron fencing, a lonely little boy standing on his own in a schoolyard. Images slipped in and out, forming a curious montage of past and present, light and dark.

"Was it a nice school?" Her voice was distant.

"Well, it was pretty basic, a wooden frame building, clapboard walls, peaked roof. That was all. It was painted red." His eyes brightened. "A poor excuse for red, the weather saw to that, but red nonetheless." He chuckled. "Inside was fresh and clean and white and cold. I used to wish they had done the paint job the other way round, red inside, white outside! It would have made more sense to me anyways."

Nora kept very still, half afraid that he might tire of reminiscing. "Go on," she said with just a hint of urging.

"We travelled the world on that ship," he said. "Up the Yellow River into the interior of China, climbed the Great Wall, beating off hoards of fierce tribesmen." Gerry was a little boy again laughing heartily. "It was grand," he said with a certain longing. "We sailed across the Arabian Sea and into the stifling heat and colour of Bombay." He looked right into her eyes. "He had an uncanny knack of making everything seem very real."

He got up, went behind the counter and helped himself to two more bottles of beer and continued the conversation, barely breaking stride. "My favourite journey, the one I remember best of all was our trek through the tropical jungles. We had read several of Kipling's stories. Now, can you imagine being a child living on our little island having *The Jungle Book* read to you and knowing that at three o'clock we were all headed there on our very own ship? It was pure bloody magic no matter how old you were. Jesus, I could hear and smell the jungle." His eyes were shining. "We all thought we'd been there! I still do," he added, laughing. He passed her a bottle of beer.

"Another day," he pushed on, "we went to Paris, to the great cathedral of Notre Dame. 'The walls rose from the ground like the cliffs out of the ocean.'" The hand that held his beer bottle rose into the air to demonstrate. "'The glass in the windows blazed with crimson and gold and blue, all the colours of a fierce sky at the close of day.' We had no concept of a cathedral, so that's how he described it to us. That day he balled up a bundle of old rags and stuck them under his jacket. Up and down the schoolroom floor he went, dragging his foot, his great hump half hiding his face, his hair askew, clanging the school bell. Quasimodo, high in his cliff tower, addressed the upturned faces in our little schoolroom."

He shifted around and spoke to the bottle held in his hand. "I came to understand the extraordinary power of the imagination. I saw how easy it was to get people to believe and accept almost anything, provided the mind was open and it was presented in the right way."

A damp patch of perspiration had begun to collect around his temples, but he seemed oblivious to the heat and discomfort. "At times like that he was a different man, full of strength and energy and conviction. There was fire in his belly then, real passion. It seemed to me that he was at his best when he was being someone else." He turned to face her. "I was fascinated by that."

It was a while before either one spoke and then she said, "He must have been an extraordinary teacher."

"Well ..." The word left a trail of uncertainty in its wake. "If you were smart then he was the best kind but he had a hard time dealing with the 'dunderheads,' as he called them. He had no patience at all with slackers and even less with those who were just plain stunned. He didn't seem to take into account that many of the youngsters had never even seen a book until they came to school and that their parents oftentimes could barely read or write or couldn't read at all. But he couldn't see that. He put it all down to laziness and that was the end of it."

He drew the back of his hand across his forehead and sighed. The dark hair on the back of his wrist was flattened by sweat into an oily slick. "There was a fella by the name of Joey Coady. He was a bit of a hard case, like a jack rabbit, off in all directions. Maybe I shouldn't be saying this but …"

He rubbed at the damp patch on his wrist until it disappeared and the dark hair stood up on end. For a moment he looked uncertain but then decided to continue. "There was one day he had Joey to the board. I remember it all so clearly, big white numbers on a blackboard: 26 X 17, that's what he wanted him to do. Multiply the two numbers. Joey hadn't the clue. Mr. Molloy started pacing the floor, back and forth, hand on hip. We all knew what was coming. Joey still hadn't learned the tables or didn't know how to do what was asked of him, but that day he laid the cane on that youngster and left big purple welts on his arms and legs that lasted for weeks. He went right off the head, lost it completely." He rubbed his hand back and forth on his forearm. "It was terrible to watch. Somewhere inside that man there was a mean cruel streak that reared up in him every so often, and there was no telling where it came from. It always seemed to be directed at the most unfortunate … like Joey, poor youngsters who had no one to pick up for them and couldn't pick up for themselves either."

Her hand came to her throat, her voice thin. "Did that happen often?"

"Often enough. Not as bad as that day, but every time it happened I felt sick to my stomach, but back then I could never bring myself to blame him."

She reached for her drink. The beer had become warm and sickly, but still she drank deeply as if somehow she could wash away what she had just heard. She felt claustrophobic and was thinking about making a move when suddenly Gerry stood up and went across to the juke box. Rummaging in his pocket, he scanned the flashing dials, dropped a few coins into the slot, punched the buttons and returned to the table. "Another one?" He pointed to her half-full bottle but she declined. He helped himself at the bar again and came and sat down just as the slow whine of a female country singer hit the air: *I go on walkin' after midnight / Out in the moonlight just a hopin' / You may be somewhere / Out walkin' after midnight / Searchin' for me.*

Nora hated country music and wished she could get away, but her driver had settled down with another beer and showed no inclination to leave.

"Patsy Cline," he said with a jaunty air. "I love Patsy Cline. How about you?"

Nora cleared her throat. "She's got a great voice," she replied, mustering up a smile. Until a short time ago she had been delighted, even fascinated, with this strange little tavern in the wilds of Newfoundland, with its blustering landlord who handed his customers their first beer and then conveniently disappeared, leaving them to fend for themselves. Her companion, too, was lively and talkative and seemed happy to take the time to tell her what he knew about her missing grandfather, which was why she was here after all. So what did she have to complain about?

"Ever been to Nashville, Nora?"

"No."

"You should. It's a great spot. I've been there twice."

She watched his body take on the rhythm of the song. She wouldn't have put him down as a Nashville type. It just didn't seem to fit. He had an easy grace and charm about him, she had to admit that, and an assurance and sophistication that she liked, yet, from time to time she sensed a shrewd side to this man and fancied that in different circumstances he might surprise her. She had wanted several times to ask what he did for a living but shied away from the intrusion.

Instead she asked, "How did he let you down, Gerry?"

He waved his hand as if to brush the thought away. "Ah, you don't want to know about that. It was just a lot of old foolishness, the mad dreams of a youngster."

Yet it was important enough to mention earlier on. She looked at him steadily. "I'd like to hear if you wouldn't mind telling me."

He sat back in his chair and regarded her over the rim of the bottle. "I was his protégé. I suppose that's how people would see it today. He worked with me for a nice few years to bring me along, all the time making me believe that if I worked hard at the books, I could be whatever I wanted to be. I believed him absolutely."

He crossed one leg over the other, shifting most of his weight onto his left buttock and twisting his body around so that he no longer faced her. "I was the only one on the island at that time going for grade eleven. I worked a lot on my own and he taught me after school, at the weekends or whenever we could get a few spare hours. I was even allowed to go to Peg's house, if I was sore in need of help with my work. I loved to go over there. It was warm and cozy, always neat and clean and peaceful; merciful God, it was so peaceful. A haven of contentment, or so it seemed to me. You could tell there was steady money coming in there. Those days every other house in the community was full of half-starved youngsters, but there was only Sheila there, all bright and smiling and well cared for. They had it all, everything I wanted, or so I thought. But you know, the fact that they were not a real family didn't occur to me in those days."

He glanced at her sideways and continued on. "When he left I couldn't believe he had walked away from that perfect, sheltered life. In fact I was ragin'." There was a long pause. "I also couldn't believe that he had walked away from me, leavin' me twistin' about in the wind not knowin' where to go or what to do. I thought I was important to him."

"I'm sorry," Nora said, not quite knowing or understanding what she was sorry for. Was she feeling guilty about this strange long-lost man, this relative of hers, this …? She didn't want to use the word grandfather. *Blood is thicker than water*, a voice inside suggested. She wanted to be rid of that voice. She wanted it gone. Out! Peg, now she was the loyal one, the kind one, the one who knew him best. She was his … Again she was stuck for a label, a naming word, a bonding word. Immediately she felt ashamed of her rush to push her guilty feelings onto Peg, but at the same time she wondered whether Peg had ever taken on these same guilty feelings.

"So he ran out on everyone a second time. I didn't know that. What happened? Can you recall or do you know?"

"Oh yes, I know. It was my fault but I was only a youngster, and as I said, it was all a bit foolish. You want to hear that, too?"

She nodded.

"It was Christmas time and us youngsters decided to put on a concert. We wrote the skits, did up the songs and decided on the stories. I put it all together, taking into account all he'd shown us about setting things up and creating atmosphere, making believe. We held it down to our place on Old Christmas Day. Being Christmas and all, my mother got right into the spirit of things and made a big boiler of soup with doughboys enough for the crowd. Everyone was there, all packed into the kitchen. For a while we thought he wasn't going to show up, but just as we got under way he arrived and stood down back by the door beside my father, even though there was a seat specially set aside for him up front by Father O'Reilly. We had a fine time, everyone doing their bit. Young Joey Coady, I told you about, did the best kind of take-off of Father O'Reilly giving his sermon on Sunday. Up on top of a chair he was, decked out finest kind in an altar boy's outfit, lookin' like butter wouldn't melt in his mouth, wagging his finger at the congregation and givin' it to her good as Father O'Reilly any day. It was a grand bit of fun and the crowd loved it and I was glad for Joey."

"And the priest?"

"Oh, he was the best kind."

"And did you perform?"

"Yes, I took my turn." He drew in a deep breath. "I was expected to play the accordion and maybe give a song. That's probably what I should have done. But I was seventeen years old, getting ready to write grade eleven exams in the summer of that year and I had a plan. This was my chance to show him what I had learned. We had been studying Shakespeare's *Henry V* together and had talked at length about the dignity and manliness that the king had shown in his great speech to his men before the battle of Agincourt, and how those qualities had inspired his army to rise above the boastful frivolity of the French and eventually win the day against all odds."

She nodded and, smiling, quoted in a low voice, *"And he which hath no stomach to this fight, / Let him depart."*

"You know it." He beamed. "I loved that speech. It was burned into my imagination and I lived every word of it that evening. *"This day is called the feast of Crispian: / He that outlives this day, and comes safe home, / Will stand a tip-toe when this day is named, / And rouse him to the name of Crispian."*

He laughed as she added a new line. *"This story shall the good man teach his son."*

They touched bottles with a soft clink, confirming their togetherness at that moment.

"We few," he began and she joined in, *"we happy few, we band of*

brothers; *For he today that sheds his blood with me, shall be my brother.*"

Then, all of a sudden it hit her. Her heart began to thump. He need go no further. She knew, she just knew, with absolute certainty what was coming next: the curt dismissal, the bitter blow that in a matter of seconds would shatter a cherished dream, and then the aftermath, the misery of feeling silly and stupid and sorry, so bitterly sorry for having tried to reach for something that was out of the ordinary, something exciting, ridiculous. Her father, his own son, could do the same in an instant, without a second thought or a hint of remorse. She knew from experience, and the memory hurt her more than she could have believed.

"I was good, you know!" His laugh pierced the quietness in the room.

She felt a surge of relief that seemed to calm the frenzy in her chest.

"Next day there were high expectations of praise amongst the youngsters and he did manage to dole out a few well-chosen words but that was it. So after school, when the others had all gone home, I approached him."

"Sir?"

"Yes, Gerry."

"I have a plan, sir, for when I finishes grade eleven."

"When you finish, Gerry. You must get it right."

"Yes, sir."

"And what is your plan, Gerry?" He continued to read and make corrections to the exercise on the desk in front of him.

"I want to be an actor, sir." His voice was steady. He waited, aware that he had drawn no comment. He waited a moment longer then continued to plough on, staring straight ahead at a dirty smudge on the white wall behind the desk. "If I could just get to New York, sir, and if you could help me a bit, maybe I'd have a chance to get started. I'd work hard and do whatever was necessary to get—"

With a clunk, the heavy black fountain pen with the gold band hit the wooden desk.

The young man's eyes went from the pen to the face behind the desk and saw a look of utter disbelief.

"Don't be talking such bloody nonsense." The voice behind the desk was cold, quiet as death and with a hint of fear. "We are aiming at getting you to the university college in St. John's. That," he spat the word out, "is what we are working towards."

Unexpectedly, the man who never laughed, laughed. It was a quiet dismissive laugh that lingered with mocking candour on the chilly air. The heat rose in the young man's body, and like a flash fire, a crimson flush spread across the back of his neck and swept over his cheeks and forehead, rising into the very roots of his hair.

"I didn't know we had decided on that, sir." He was staring at the dark spot on the wall again. "I don't remember ever discussing that." His eyes hurt.

The teacher's fist came up suddenly and landed in a crashing thud on the desk. "Well, we're discussing it right now, young man!"

"We!" The pent-up anger spurted out like bright blood from a new flesh wound. "Who is this 'we' you're talking about all of a sudden? In case you didn't know, it's my bloody life that we're discussing and just because you've made an arse of yours doesn't mean to say I've got to do the same with mine. Now, if I wants to be a bloody actor, I'll be a bloody actor, whether it's all bloody nonsense or not, and I'll do it with or without you." He stood his ground, hot with fury, his breath visible in the frigid air.

For a moment there was a stony silence in the room, both realizing that a line had been crossed.

"For now, if you take my advice," the voice was cool and controlled again, "you would do better to concentrate on learning the correct use of the English language." He picked up his pen then and resumed marking the exercise in front of him.

Patsy Cline was done on the juke box and the place felt empty. "Of course, later on I regretted everything," Gerry said with a smile. "I was glad I'd picked up for myself but it was like losing a friend, more than a friend. I knew things would never be the same again. I was no longer the boy he'd brought along. If he hadn't laughed, maybe things wouldn't have been so bad. Anyway, shortly after that he left and I never went back to school again."

"So what did you do?"

"I wrote my exams and went to St. John's to the university college ... eventually. So he had his way. But, it was my choice and not his."

Suddenly she could stand the heat no longer. She had to get out of the place. "Maybe we should be off." She made a move to leave.

He finished his beer in one swallow, went to the bar, counted out several bills and threw them on the counter.

Nora made her way to the door. The lone figure by the stove had raised his head and was looking at her with the blank stare of a cow looking over a fence. He blinked once, and for a second she thought he might speak but then he lowered his head and returned to his crouched position. She opened the door and stepped out into the late afternoon sunshine.

"Sorry if I upset you," he said when he caught up with her. "But you did ask, and I gave it to you, warts and all."

They had reached the car and she smiled across the black dome of the roof. "I'm glad of the truth. Thank you." She got in and closed the door.

16

"*You* wouldn't know but it was the Queen herself was come to visit us. Father O'Reilly has been on the phone twice lookin' for you, and Pat came by wantin' to know if you'd fancy a run over to the island tomorrow. He'll be goin' by there to check his traps and he can drop you off on the way. If you like, that is. There's not too much there now, just the old houses but it's nice just the same, nice to spend a couple of hours on a good day."

On the stove, a white enamel lid danced an urgent rat-a-tat-tat, the steam bursting in furious puffs into the kitchen.

"I'd love to go." The very thought of actually setting foot on the island, seeing the house, the garden, of walking the path up over the hill through the alder bushes to the berry patch was all very exciting. "How long would the trip take?" Second thoughts had made her cautious. "I've got a flight to catch on Tuesday morning so I need to be back in St. John's tomorrow night."

"Oh, it's only a couple of hours run, maybe less."

"Then I'll go. I'd love to." Nora paused a moment. "I don't

suppose you would come too?"

"No, girl, I'm done with the island now. It makes me sad to think of the old house all neglected. Too many memories," Peg said, raising her voice as she reached over to lower the heat beneath the bubbling pot.

"Then I'll bring back a memento of some kind, something special you can keep."

"Yes, do that, girl. I'll let Pat know then." She was already heading for the phone.

"Thank him for me. It's very thoughtful of him," Nora called out. She went to the table and sat down on the corner of Peg's chair. The child's bouquet, although still bright and colourful, had begun to droop slightly, but it still held its place of prominence in the middle of the table. The faint smell of honey from the lupin brought her back momentarily to her mother's garden. She could see exactly the spot where the purple and lavender spikes stood tall and majestic in the perennial border, making a glorious splash of colour in early summer. She reached over and touched the velvety bloom. Everything in this tiny house was treasured: every scrap of clutter, every ornament and souvenir, every picture, every letter and card all had a connection to life. Her eyes fell on the big chair by the fireplace where the cat lay curled up asleep. Even the dust from the island had been saved. It was all important to Peg, keeping her together body and soul in an urgent drive to keep going. Nora could hear her now, busy making plans. There was a click as the phone was returned to its cradle.

"That's all set then. He'll come by for you tomorrow about eleven o'clock. I'm glad you're going to see the island. It was Matt's home. It was where he belonged and where he is laid to rest."

"I wondered where he was buried. Will I be able to find his grave?"

"Yes, my dear, that's easy. It's well marked, I saw to that."

Things were moving along very quickly and her time was getting short. She hadn't quite known what to expect when she decided to come to Newfoundland. Her plan had been to take her time, to contact her friend's family in St. John's, to get a feel for the place, look for information on Berry Island, maybe seek out Peg Barry's whereabouts and find out if Matt Molloy was still living. She wanted, if necessary, to be able to put things on hold for a while and maybe, when the time was right, make personal contact with a letter or a phone call. But encouraged by how simple it had been to track down Peg and buoyed by the great weather and a wonderful few days in St. John's with her friend's family, she had no trouble deciding to rent a car and head out into the unknown.

However, it was only when she was outside of St. John's and well on her way that she began to think that maybe she should have made a phone call first. What if Peg Barry was a crotchety old woman who was bitter and truculent and difficult to deal with? She might even cut her off right there and then, and that would be the end of it. She resolved to go carefully and to leave room for a quiet exit if necessary, but of course, on coming face to face with a real living Peg Barry, she had immediately thrown caution to the wind, forgotten all her resolutions and jumped right in.

"You've been very kind to me, Peg," Nora said on impulse. "Thank you."

"It's not easy what you're doin', girl," she said. "News of you is on everyone's lips now, but you don't want to worry about that. Your grandfather gave more to this place than he ever took away and he never hurt no one. Now, you go sit down and I'll take up your supper."

"What do you think Father O'Reilly wants with me?" She reached for the plate held out to her.

"Maybe he's thought more about it all and has something he wants to tell you. When you've kept your distance all your life from the ordinary people, it's hard to change. That was part of the clergy's power years ago. People were afraid to come near them, never mind come straight out and ask a question."

Nora remembered that feeling of being in awe of the men in black. But that was then, now she felt differently. She'd make a quick phone call after supper and see if he wanted to be more forthcoming. She turned her attention to the piece of crispy pan-fried cod on her plate and began to eat.

"This is delicious." She realized that she hadn't eaten all day.

"Did Gerry have much to say about Matt?"

"Gerry had plenty to say about Matt but he seems to think he let him down. I suppose you knew all about that?"

"Yes, I knew about all that. Who didn't? Things were bad enough during the thirties but the teacher leavin' was the last straw. There was some racket about that, people layin' blame with this one and that one. The school was doin' good. The youngsters were there every day, and not only that, they wanted to go and that was something in itself. Gerry and a few more were making great strides. We were some proud of our school then." She looked out the window, browsing the landscape of her memory. After a little while she laid her fork down and stared at her plate, holding the rim lightly with both hands.

"You're disappointed, I know, to hear Matt took off like that again. It's hard to understand but I believe he was afraid for Gerry. He thought he'd done wrong by him."

"What do you mean?"

"He blamed himself for filling Gerry's head with all that actin' stuff. He never meant to do that. Gerry was smart but more important, he had no fear in him. He had the guts for anything. He's still the same, goes for the big haul. When he gets something in his mind, there's no holdin' him back. He'd have done as he pleased no matter what. That's what Matt didn't understand."

Peg touched each side of her mouth with her index finger in her usual way, checking for stray scraps of food. "Gerry was in some state that night. He came by the house about eight o'clock. It was January month, bitter cold with a gale of wind comin' in off the water. He stood back from the door a ways, his two feet planted on the ground like he was anchored right to the spot."

"Come in, Gerry." Peg opened the door wider. "Come in, for the love of God, before the wind makes away with you."

"Is it true?" he bawled out. "Is he gone?"

"Yes, Gerry, it's true," she said. "He's gone."

"And what about me and my exams? I don't suppose he happened to mention before he left, what I was supposed to do."

"No, Gerry, he didn't. You're on your own now." Peg had to shout to make herself heard above the wind. "You got to look out for yourself and keep on with what you're doing. Any time you wants a quiet place to study, you're welcome here. You've just got to go do it yourself."

"To give him his due, Nora, Gerry did just that. I believe myself, it was the makin' of Gerry Quinlan. He had a new determination about him, like he was cut free. He was the first youngster on the island to get his CHE exams and he passed with wonderful marks. That was some achievement in those days, coming from a one-room school. He came to the door with the letter to say he'd passed. 'Aunt Peg,' he said, 'I've done it.' Then if he didn't pick me right up off the floor and swing me round and round. Pure delighted, he was."

Her smile broadened and the straight line of perfect teeth pressed down onto her lower lip as if holding back an unbearable delight. "I was some proud of him that day. It was like he was my own." She picked up her fork and continued with her dinner. "It was another year or so before he managed to get away to the college in St. John's, but by then it was the politics was drivin' him. There was no more talk about acting."

Nora's eyes widened but Peg continued on, "He finished his education and was apprenticed to a lawyer in St. John's when he first met up with Joey. His timing was perfect. All he wanted then was the politics. Funny how things turn out, isn't it?" She gathered the last remnants of her dinner together on the plate and piled it onto her fork.

"I didn't know he was into politics."

"He didn't tell you?"

"No."

"My dear, Gerry's been tucked in there, right next to Mr. Smallwood on the top floor of the Confederation Building since the beginning. He's all set now to run for the Liberals in this district come election time. He's a born politician, can work the crowd like no one else I know. He's smart, see, and understands the game." She looked out at the fading sunset. "He'll go far, will Gerry. He knows how to get the crowd on his side." Her finger tapped at the table top. "He'll go to Ottawa one day, right to the House of Parliament." Her hand came down firmly on the table.

"Who is Mr. Smallwood?"

"My dear, the premier of the province, Joe Smallwood. Brought us into Canada."

There was a new vigour about Peg and Nora had spotted it. "You like politics, Peg?"

"Yes, girl, I just wish I was younger. I'd run myself! But imagine now, he didn't tell you all that?"

"Well, we talked mostly about Matt, but I did wonder what he did for a living."

"Well, girl, you're lucky you got to meet him. The garden party brought him this way today. It's a good way to see and be seen."

"So that's what he was at today, canvassing." She smiled. "His boyhood dream wasn't too far off the mark. I wonder what Matt would think of his star pupil now?"

Peg leaned forward, her chin tucked into her shoulder. "He knew what Gerry was doing but he didn't have much time for politicians," she whispered, her eyes sparkling with mischief. "That crowd, he'd call them." She giggled girlishly.

"Did Matt know that you liked politics?"

Peg drew herself upright. "And that he did, but that was my business. Politics is part of life here. I've always been into it, picked it up from my father." She began to clear off the table. "You haven't phoned Father O'Reilly yet, it's getting late."

"I'll do that." Nora got up from the table and went to make the phone call.

A few minutes later, she hung up the phone. "He'd like me to come by tomorrow morning sometime," Nora said. "There are, he says, a few details about Matt's life he's aware of that I might be interested in. Now, can you believe that? I said I'd drop by in the morning, before we head out to the island. I wish he'd said what he had to say when I was there this morning."

"Maybe he forgot, girl, the memory isn't so sharp when you get older." Her eyes were soft. "It's not easy, you know." She passed Nora a mug of hot tea and poured one for herself. "I wish you could stay on for a while, girl. I love the company and it's grand to talk and not worry about gossip and the like." She brought the mug to her mouth, her lips hovering nervously as she tested the temperature. She decided to wait a while and set the mug back down. "It changes a person, you know, having to be cautious around others, always careful with what you say and do. I was always one for company

K A T E   E V A N S

165

and a bit of fun. I liked to talk and have people about but …" She hesitated. "It just changes you, that's all. You learn to live with it."

"Did you resent that?"

"From time to time, yes, I suppose I did. Especially when he wasn't about. People weren't so quick to come forward then. I suppose they didn't know where they stood or what to be sayin', and neither did I, tell truth."

"Was he fond of Sheila?" Nora asked, thinking of the little girl caught in this strange triangle. She wasn't sure if fond was the right word but that was what had come out.

"I believe he was. Well, I know he was, maybe not in the same way as you or I might be fond of a youngster." She pondered the situation, searching for words to explain. "When she was little and he'd come through the door of an evening after school, she'd go right to him, slip her little hand in his and guide him in. He never did get past his awkward way with her. But now just the same, if she wasn't there, the first thing from his mouth would be, 'Where's Sheila?' He bought her a doll one time. Ordered it from the catalogue, the best there was. There wasn't another on the island the like of it. She loved that doll. There was nothing could take the place of it." Peg drew in a deep breath. "Once she started school and he was the teacher, there was a distance come between them that wasn't there before. It just grew more noticeable as the years went by. But she thought a lot of him just the same. When he died, she came all the way from California to bury him. That was good now, wasn't it?"

17

The cat had found a spot in the sunshine, and with impassive eyes watched as Nora washed the supper dishes. It was a relief to have something practical to do. On the shiny surface of a plate she caught a passing glimpse of her reflection. She shut her eyes and abruptly dunked the plate back into the suds. She suddenly realized that she wanted to get away from the Molloys, to talk about something else, anything other than the Molloys.

She hit on an idea. "Tell me about Sheila, Peg. What did she do with herself? Did she finish school?" Nora spoke over her shoulder as she lifted the plate out of the water and set it on the dish rack.

"Indeed she did. Sheila's a nurse. It was all she ever wanted growin' up, to go to one of them big hospitals in St. John's to be trained."

"Really! You must have been delighted. Was Matt pleased?" Too late she realized her mistake.

"Pleased? Of course he was pleased." A sharp note like the ping from a tuning fork sounded above the clatter of dish washing. Nora stopped what she was doing and looked over her shoulder. Peg was sitting in the same spot, her hands clenched tightly in front of her mouth. She refused to look across at Nora.

"It's always the same," she said finally, sounding peeved. "People always quick to think the worst of him, always seein' him as 'the selfish ole bugger who only looks out for hisself.'"

There was a loud clatter as a dish was placed randomly on the rack.

"I heard those very words spoken," Peg said indignantly. "But I knew better. I knew it wasn't hisself he was thinkin' of then. He was thinkin' of me. He wanted what was best for me."

Nora moved quickly. Wiping her hands against the cloth of her dress, she hurried across the floor and eased herself onto the chair alongside of Peg. She rubbed her damp hand once more along her thigh and then gently placed it on Peg's rigid arm. She felt a long quiver, like the fluttering of a frightened bird. It was followed by another. Nora stroked the wrinkled arm, momentarily surprised by the warmth and life that still ran in the slack aging flesh.

"It was a comfort to think that someone was lookin' out for me." The cat silently got to its feet and in an effortless leap was on Peg's lap. Peg began to stroke its soft fur lovingly. "I was frightened, that's all, afraid for the first time in my life of being alone."

Nora was at a loss; her glib comment had obviously touched a nerve, but there was something else going on and she had no idea what it was. She was about to say she was sorry once again but changed her mind at the last moment and instead asked, "Why were you frightened?"

The hand stroking the cat became still for a moment and Peg's mouth began to work furiously in that funny little way she had when having difficulty voicing her thoughts. She began to pet the cat again. "Matt wasn't hisself when he come back that last time. He'd been gone quite the while and had gone away to nothin'. He wasn't altogether right in the head either. Tell truth, I don't know how he found his way back to the island and he never did say, but he was dyin', inside and out, by the time he got to my door. I took him in of course and cared for him. By and by, he come around and things were like they'd been before but it was a struggle just the same." She took another deep breath. "By then, Sheila had finished school and was makin' ready to go off to St. John's. Everything was the finest kind, until I was taken sick with consumption. TB they call it now." The stroking stopped again momentarily.

"I was only fifty-five years old the first time the TB boat came to the island. Those days it used to come in the bays and coves all around the coast, to test the people." She turned to stare out of the window. "It was a grand sight first time she come around the headland, the bull horn blastin' away, the coloured banners snappin' in the breeze. Once she was tied up to the wharf the music started up and 'Mocking Bird Hill' came singin' out over the microphone. It was like a garden party. I remember everyone runnin' down to the water to see what all the excitement was about. We were all invited on board to be tested. Nothin' to it, we were told, just a little scratch on your arm and that was it. 'The scratches,' we used call it after that. All true, but here ten days later, I gets a slip saying the test on me was positive and that the boat would be by again in two weeks to do a chest x-ray.

"I wasn't so happy next time the boat came about. Turned out the rotten part was lodged there in my right lung this while and I was to go to the hospital in St. John's for treatment. I told the doctor I felt just fine but he said that was the way sometimes. If I didn't get treated, in a few months' time, I'd be in hard shape. Worse still, I could pass it on to Sheila and others. Well that was it." She pushed back a wisp of hair from her forehead. "One day I was best kind, next I was sick and lookin' at going to the hospital for a spell. What was I to do? Up until then, I don't believe Matt had ever interfered in my life, but what he had in mind for me and Sheila that time got me right upset."

Furious with what Sheila had told her, Peg came barrelling down over the stairs calling out Matt's name. Sheila passed her in the hallway in tears as she ran out the door. She found him at the table reading the newspaper.

"I hear you've been tellin' Sheila what she must do and what she mustn't do."

"Yes, that's right. I pointed out to her that she'll need to be around to take care of you when you get back from the hospital. It's her duty. She can't be going off and leaving you now. You don't know what that disease can do to you. You–"

"I don't know, don't I? I suppose you think I just rolled up on the beach with the last lot of caplin. Well, I'll have you know something, Matt Molloy. I've been livin' about these parts all my life and I've seen life come and go, watched strong men hackin' and coughin' their way to the grave, seen little children come to nothin' but skin and bones, their faces blue from tryin' to catch a mouthful of air, and you tell me I don't know. Oh yes, I knows all right. I knows lots of things, Matt Molloy, things you'll never know nothin' about. And there's something else I knows for certain. Sheila will have her chance to do as she pleases with her life and there's nothin' or nobody's goin' gettin' in her way. You may think that child owes me somethin' for raisin' her up, but that's not how I sees it. What I did back then was out of love for her mother, my own sister, and now it's for love of Sheila herself, but then again I don't expect you to understand the like of that. So don't you go tellin' me what I must do? I knows what to do."

He had begun to move away from her fury, folding the newspaper and carefully placing it under his arm. "You'll learn," he said from the doorway before climbing the stairs to his room.

"My dear, after that spat, I was that upset I didn't know what I was doin' or sayin' no more, but one thing I was certain of, Sheila would have her chance in life. I was goin' to see to that, no matter what. On that day, Nora, at that moment, I valued my independence more than I'd ever done in my whole life."

A shadow fell across the kitchen and made them both look up. The sun had slipped behind a cloud. Dark murky fingers reached silently across the grey expanse of water, while on the far headland, dramatic tonal patterns merged on the sculptured blackness of the trees. A momentary stillness hung on the air and then abruptly, as if giving a signal to continue, the sun reappeared from behind the clouds and the evening continued its silent progress.

Peg cleared her throat as she tried to reclaim her story. "Anyway, when the dust settled I was glad I spoke up. It lifted my spirits, made me feel stronger and in control again. It had cleared the air, and after that I knew in my heart that somehow everything would work out."

"Sheila was happy to go along with your decision?"

"It took a bit of time. She had come to believe Matt was right and that she should stay home, but I told her it would be a comfort to me to have her close by when I was to the hospital in St. John's, and being a nurse in trainin', she'd be able to deal with the doctors and all. Anyways she finally agreed. Little did I know that before I ever saw the island again, Sheila would have her trainin' done and have met her young man and be gone for good."

"You were gone for a long time then?"

"Yes, girl, several years. I never expected that. Anyway, me insistin' Sheila go away for her trainin' put Matt in a difficult spot. After our words he kept to hisself a bit more. I could see he was doin' a lot of thinkin'. It was comin' up time for us to leave and I was busy with preparations."

The folded laundry lay in neat piles on the table. Matt came in from the yard, hung his hat on the nail behind the door, and stood for a moment to take in the scene.

"Sheila and me, you know, Matt, we're off in a couple of days. What are you plannin' on doin' with yourself?"

"I don't know but I'll see you safely to St. John's to begin with. If you wish, that is."

She looked up from what she was doing, surprised and delighted. "That's kind of you, Matt, to think of that, being as neither one of us has ever been off the island. That would be a wonderful help."

He sat to the table, resting his arms between the piles of laundry, his hands tightly clasped, and began twirling his thumbs round and round in maddening circles. From the corner of her eye Peg watched the action, recalling how, on his first night in the house, she had watched, fascinated, as his long thin fingers had worked the same crazy rhythm. Time and again since then, she had observed the same action, circling, circling, forwards, backwards, going nowhere. Sometimes it would drive her crazy and other times it would bring out a certain fondness, a desire to soothe and comfort. Now she wanted him to stop. She decided to try again.

"Matt, there's something I've been meanin' to say to you." She wanted him to look at her. "Matt," she began again, edging forward in her chair. She could hear the faint rush of his breath between his teeth. A pulse throbbed at his temple. "I'd like for you to bide in the house while I'm gone."

"That won't be necessary." The reply was there, ready on the tip of his tongue. "I'll be on my way as soon as I get you settled in St John's." He made a move to get up.

She placed a hand on his arm. "Matt, sit down a minute and listen to what I have to say. I'm asking you to help me." Her words set up a barrier blocking his way. "When I'm lyin' in that hospital bed in St. John's," she persisted, "I want to be able to think of this house as being warm and lived in, with the smell of food cookin' on the stove and a light in the window. I want to come back to a home, not a house. It would be a great comfort if you could stay on and do that for me."

"I don't know anything about things like that, Peg. I–"

"Maybe it's time you learned about things like that," she said with a firm but gentle air of finality.

"There's always Pat," he began.

"I'm asking you, Matt." With that she rose from the chair and left him to make his decision.

"It was the end of the line for me, Nora. I had to look out for myself and if he wasn't prepared to help me, then that was it. He could take off if he wanted. I didn't care no more."

A loud knock on the door made them both jump. A voice called out, "Anybody home?" Gerry Quinlan stood in the doorway of the kitchen. It was then Nora realized that the sun had disappeared altogether and that they were sitting in the semi-darkness, oblivious to the world outside.

"Not a stir in the house," he said, "and the two of you sittin' in the dark." He took the chair at the other end of the table. "Is this Irish woman leading you astray by any chance?"

"More like me leadin' her astray. My Lord, what time is it at all? It's almost dark."

He glanced at his watch. "Going for nine o'clock."

"Imagine, the day slipped away and we never noticed. Sit down, Gerry. Fetch yourself a glass and we'll have a drink."

"I thought you'd both be above to the supper and dance tonight."

"My blessed Lord, I forgot all about it and I'm supposed to take a plate tart for the supper. You go on, Nora girl, you'll enjoy the dance. Gerry will take you along. Won't you, Gerry?"

"Not without you. We don't want tongues waggin' now, do we?" He winked at Nora.

"Go on with you now, you knows I'm too old for that racket." She scratched her head aggressively as if to shake it clear of such nonsense.

"Maybe you are, but now Aunt Josie Nash from St. Brides is above and is askin' about you, and Treese is about too."

Peg thought for a moment. "Well, all right. Maybe I'll stir myself. This time next year I might be pushin' up clover to the churchyard and then I'll be right poisoned with myself."

18

The doors to the church hall were wide open and held in place by a couple of chairs wedged tightly beneath the handles. Outside, the night air was cool and inviting, but inside, it was suffocating with the smell of overheated bodies and leftover food. Everyone seemed to be on the move, the women hurrying to and fro, carrying stacks of dishes, laughing and calling out to each other as they went. The men, their stomachs full, were heading outdoors, some lighting up as they went.

To Nora, it looked like total chaos but nobody seemed bothered. The crowd was in high spirits, all dolled up and ready for a good time. There were a few familiar faces around, people she vaguely recognized from earlier on in the day, but no one spoke to her nor could she see anyone she knew by name, but the odd nod from a friendly face made her feel better. A young girl standing off to one side looked her over carefully but a smile from Nora sent her fleeing for the door. Nora looked around for Gerry. The last she had seen of him, he was making his way across the hall with Peg by the arm to where Treese sat by an open window with another woman. Along the far wall there were long tables spread with white paper cloths and strewn with the messy scraps from a meal. Chairs had been pushed aside or tipped over. A vigorous clean-up was underway. She decided to move closer to the small stage at the front of the hall where an elderly fiddler sat knee to knee with a young woman who had just slipped the straps of an accordion over her shoulders. Oblivious to the racket all around them, they began to play softly, dipping and swaying into the music, coaxing their instruments to find the tunes that would see them through the night.

"You had your supper, m'love?" A large woman with a frizz of mousey hair and kindly eyes stopped as she went by with a stack of plates. "There's all kinds out back."

"Thank you, I've eaten."

"Okay, m'love." A nod and she was gone.

Over the tops of heads Nora could see Peg settled in her spot. She was in deep conversation with the women. There was no sign of Gerry. A long loud drone from the accordion gave the signal they were ready and sent an immediate buzz of excitement through the crowd. Dancers elbowed their way forward, their necks straining, eyes peeled for possible partners.

"Hello, missus." The voice came from behind her. She turned, not sure if she was the "missus." A slight man stood by her elbow. He was about her height, no more; she was looking him straight in the eye. "I hears you're one of the Molloys from Ireland," he said without preamble.

"Yes, that's right." She smiled, pleased with the distraction.

"Well, missus, I'm pleased t'meet ya," he said, extending his hand. Small fidgety eyes regarded her intently. A quiff of dark hair rose in a stiff wave above his forehead and fell off into a tail over his left eye. He wore a brightly coloured shirt patterned all over with red and blue and yellow circles, gaudy by any standard. He put her in mind of an exotic bird that had been in a racket of some kind and had emerged looking slightly battered. All the while he spoke he shook her hand.

"I come to speak with ya, missus, seein' how Mr. Molloy done me a great service. I wants to acknowledge that now. I'm Joe Coady, missus. I'll call ya missus now, if ya don't mind, that is." His grip, bony and urgent, tightened as he continued to shake her hand.

In the background, the accordion player swung into a waltz and the crowd pressed forward. Still gripping her hand he pulled her to one side. "Watch out there, missus."

"Sorry, what did you say your name was?"

"Joe Coady, missus."

The name and then the image came to her in a flash: a small boy, white numbers on a blackboard. Nora felt her throat contract and heat begin to rise at the back of her neck. She tried to avoid his gaze but his eyes followed hers until she was compelled to face him again.

"He teached me to read and write, missus, is what I'm sayin'."

She waited for the harsh words that must come, looked for the twist of bitterness about his mouth. There was none, just a funny little cockatoo of a man who shifted from foot to foot in a restless dance. He still gripped her hand, giving it the odd shake from time to time as if to ensure her attention.

"By the Jesus, he had some hard time gettin' that stuff in me head, but he done it." His head twitched a couple of times, dislodging the quiff and causing it to fall forward onto his forehead. She stared, unable to utter a single word, unable to accept the fact that this was the poor little scrap that her grandfather had walloped with a cane because he couldn't do his sums.

As if reading her mind, he laughed, his whole face gathering into tiny weathered wrinkles, his mouth opening slightly to show gaps in a row of narrow yellow teeth. "Ya know somethin', missus, when the Yanks come durin' the war and was buildin' the base down to

Argentia, Joe Coady was ready. Yes, b'y. I was good with me hands and I could read them Yankee blueprints best kind, and I could make anything they wanted with a bit a wood and a few nails, I could so, anything they wanted, and they sure wanted plenty. Made some good money, I did, enough to build me own house handy to the base." He was in full flight now, shifting from one foot to the other as he pumped out his story. "Yes, by the Jesus, the women was after me then. I had the pick of the bunch. Mad for me they was."

He laughed again, batting at the quiff of hair with the back of his hand. "Before that, Joe Coady was nothin'. Pussy Boils, they used to call me. Yes, indeed. But once I had the few Yankee dollars in me pocket and a good job to the base, the women was plentiful as tomcods. And he done it, Mr. Molloy did. Nobody paid me no attention 'til then, thought I was stunned. But we showed them, him and me. Mind now, missus, he beat the livin' shit out of me doin' it. Those days I didn't want to know nothin' about school but not now. No, b'y. My youngsters, they all been to the university." He leaned forward. "Education is the key, missus," he whispered philosophically, his eyes shining like polished marbles.

Nora was transfixed. She opened her mouth to speak, but the words dried up on her tongue. Around her the music and the dancers swirled fast and wild. For an uneasy minute it crossed her mind that he was having a bit of fun with her but his eyes were so utterly serious, she quickly dismissed the idea. He waited, expectant, and when she still didn't speak, his jaw dropped, the exuberance wiped clean from his face but he continued to look at her intently like a sad clown, willing her to say something. She swallowed hard, ran her tongue over her lips and said the only thing she could think of saying, "You're a bit of an actor too, I hear."

"No, girl, nothin' like that, but I tells the odd yarn time to time."

"I heard you did a fine imitation of Father O'Reilly one time." She was beginning to find her voice.

"Ah, that oul' would-be politician you been hangin' round with been goin' off at the mouth again. Likes to hear hisself, he does, all wind and business he is, mostly wind."

A cheer went up from the crowd, followed by clapping.

"The men is dancin' up," he said, straining to see what was goin' on. He urged her forward. "Give the missus a bit of room there now. Clear the decks, b'ys."

In a small clearing, an elderly man danced alone, his legs jiggling about in a complicated shuffle, punctuated every so often with a loud stamp on the floor before taking off again. When he finally showed signs of tiring, another dancer took over, trying in turn to outdo the previous performer with fancy footwork. Up on the stage the accordion player leaned into her instrument, while by her side the fiddler whipped his bow back and forth, his foot tapping out the rhythm. The crowd whooped with delight. When Joey Coady took the floor the yelps grew wilder, and the more they yelped the better he liked it. His bony legs, as if rubber below the knees, waggled hither and thither, his feet stamping the boards, rocking side to side on the outer edges of his shoes, kicking out randomly to the point where Nora was certain he'd end up in a heap on the floor. But Joey was surefooted and now his arms were into the action, swinging back and forth in front of his body. All the while he looked at his feet. The quiff, having bobbed along with him for quite a while, had now come undone and hung in a sweaty mass across his forehead. The fiddler continued the frantic pace, the accordion player waltzed her instrument back and forth to keep up, and Joey danced, his steps becoming more exaggerated by the minute until just as suddenly as it all had begun, the music stopped.

He dragged his sleeve across his forehead and saluted the crowd. Some reached out to thump him heartily on the back. He caught Nora's eye, gave her a nod, and disappeared into the crowd. She looked around again, hoping to spot Gerry. He was nowhere to be seen. She spotted Joey heading outdoors. She followed and found him on the steps, his legs spread wide, elbows resting on his knees, a bottle of Pepsi in his hand. A dark sweat stain spread between his shoulder blades, dulling the brightness of his shirt. A car spun away out of the parking lot, leaving behind a cloud of dust.

"It's nice and cool out here," she said.

"Yes, girl." He turned to look up at her.

"Do you mind if I sit with you? It's hot in there."

"Yes, girl, I mean, no, girl, you sit down."

"You're a great man to dance," she said, taking a seat on the steps.

He set down his bottle, reached into his shirt pocket and pulled out a packet of Craven A cigarettes and a silver Zippo lighter. He tapped the packet against his index finger and picked out a cigarette, pushed it between his lips and held out the packet to her. She shook her head. The lighter lid flipped back with a clunk. It flamed, a tall arrow of white light, and for a brief moment the deep pockmarks on his face and neck were clearly visible. He inhaled deeply and with his right hand pushed back the hair from his damp forehead.

"I'm glad you think of him kindly," she said after a while.

Smoke came from his nose in little puffs and then from his mouth as he spoke. "Don't you go feelin' bad," he said as if reading her mind. "Him and me, we was the best kind." He hesitated a moment. "Buddies, we was."

"You were friends?" Her surprise was a shade too obvious.

"Well now, missus, far as I'm concerned, he was my friend. I'd 'ave done anything for that man." He tapped the white shaft of his cigarette, rolled it about in his fingers and tapped again. He inhaled. The red tip glowed hot. "Isn't that what a friend is?" He looked across at her through the curtain of smoke.

She nodded, then nodded again.

"When he come back that last time, he was in hard shape. I mean to say, not right in the top story, ye know." He touched the side of his head with his cigarette hand and waited a moment before taking a deep draw. "I seen him one day, walkin' out across the headland toward the Big Gulch. It was the spring of the year, freezin' rain comin' down and the ground hard and slick. He had nothin' on his back but that suit of clothes he always wore. It come to me that was a strange thing to be doin' on a day like that."

He kicked at a stray pebble and it landed on the gravel below. "I made out across the path after him, keepin' an eye on the black flaps of his jacket as they batted about in the wind. He was goin' at some rate and when I caught up with him right by the gulch, I calls out. 'Mornin', Mr. Molloy sir, tis good to see you come back. It's Joe Coady,' I says, but he just kept lookin' in the distance like he'd not heard a word I said. Enough to scare the livin' shit outa ya, it was. So I just kept talkin'. 'I've got work down to The Base in Argentia now, with the Yanks,' I says, 'steady work. I'm back to see me mother. I've done good, and I'm gettin' married the fall. Tis all thanks to you, Mr. Molloy … me bein' able to read and all. You done some fine job, you did, more power to ye.'"

He stopped to take another drag on his cigarette. "Jesus, girl, I didn't know what to be sayin'. All I knowed was that I'd best keep talkin'. So I took a step closer and coughed a bit, the way he'd know I was still there. After a spell he says, 'Thank you, Joe.' Just the same, he never budged, just kept on starin' ahead. So I starts up again. 'The seals is whelpin' down to Rook Cove. Maybe we could take a walk over.' He said nothin' for the longest while but by and by didn't he turn away from the edge. 'I'll be going on home now,' says he. It was all I could do, missus, not to reach out and catch hold to him for fear he'd slip and be gone over the side. He started to walk away and then he turns back and says, 'I'm sorry, Joe, very sorry.' He made like he wanted to say more but gave up and then took off back across the barrens, the wind tearin' into him."

A long white ash had formed on the tip of his cigarette. It hung there precariously and then fell to the ground, making a little white mound between his feet. He stared at it for a moment and then scattered it with the toe of his shoe and, taking a last draw, flicked the cigarette butt onto the parking lot. It made a little arc of smoke and sparks and landed a few feet away in the gravel, still glowing. He picked up his drink. The muffled sounds of the music came from behind. The dancing was still in full swing.

"Next time I come on him was months later. Aunt Peg was after takin' care of him and he was shapin' up finest kind. Always spoke to me on the road after that, asked after me mother and the like, but we never said nothin' about that day ever again and I never told no one 'til now." He finished his Pepsi and set the bottle down by his feet. "He liked to keep hisself to hisself."

The community of Shoal Cove stretched out below them. On that lovely summer night it looked idyllic and peaceful, tucked in close to the water, tight to the land, protected by the headland.

"I'm glad that we met, Mr. Coady. I'm glad he had a friend like you," Nora said. The cigarette still smouldered on the ground, glowed like a tiny beacon in the black gravel. "He was my grandfather but I never knew him, knew nothing about him until I came here." She looked across at him.

"I knows, missus. I knows what ye mean."

Nora wondered if he did know, if he could understand what it was like always to wonder where you had come from and what might have been.

His voice broke in on her thoughts. "We spent a bit of time together, him and me. If ye wants I can tell ye how that come about." He turned to look at her and she nodded.

"After Aunt Peg took sick and went to St. John's, I used to come back to the island the scattered time. One weekend me mother says to me, 'Here, take a loaf of bread and one of them chickens in the yard to that poor man above to Peg Barry's. He's got no one now to do for him.' So I picks out a nice hen, ties up the legs, shoves her in a brin bag and heads up to the house. By and by, he comes to the door and opens it just the smallest bit."

"I've got a bit of new bread and a chicken here, from me mother," Joe said, and tipped the squawking chicken onto the doorstep.

"I can't accept that. Thank you." Matt Molloy began to close the door.

"I hears you're a good hand with a gun," Joe persisted. "Maybe ye could show me sometime. I'd like to bring in a few birds for me mother for the winter. If ya don't mind, that is. I could come along sometime when you're goin' by yerself."

Matt didn't answer for a while then he said, "We'll see."

"You think on it, sir. No rush." He set the loaf of bread on the doorstep and before her could utter another word, he left.

"See ya now," he called back over his shoulder.

"After that, when I'd be home, we'd often go in the woods. He'd set up a target, a bit of sod or the like on the branch of a tree and show me how to load and take aim. One day we was in the woods practicing. I was to one side watchin' while he was showin' me what to do and didn't the sod fall to the ground before he got the shot away. Like the foolish gommel I am, I runs up to set her back in place and BANG! The gun goes off. I falls to the ground. He's by me side in a minute, holdin' me head. 'Oh, Mother of God,' he's sayin'. 'What have I done to this decent, lovely man?' He brings his head down to me mouth to hear if I'm still breathing and I whispers in his ear, 'Ah, b'y, yer not such a great shot after all.'"

His thin shoulders heaved slightly as he recalled the incident. "But I tell ya somethin', missus. I was the one got the shock. When I popped me eyes open I'm lookin' right in his face, and here the two eyes in his head is filled right up with tears. I never told that to no one neither. It was between him and me."

Nora didn't know whether to laugh or cry. "Was that the end of the shooting lessons?"

"No, missus. I learned to keep me head down, and by and by, I got me own gun. I wasn't good like he was but he always shared his bag with me, said it was for me mother. She'd take him up the few bottles of turrs in return and do him up a bit of bread. He was the finest kind with her, gave her the run of the garden. She could have all the cabbage, potatoes, turnip she wanted. That's how we became buddies, him and me."

Behind, in the hall, the accordion played a slow waltz and she could hear the crowd singing along.

"Will we try a waltz?" he said suddenly. "I likes the waltzes, I does."

19

Nora removed her jacket and laid it on the arm of the big overstuffed chair. There was a faint smell of fish in the kitchen, the memory of a meal shared. It had been a long and tiring day and she was glad to be back in the cozy clutter of Peg's home. She couldn't live with it, she decided as she looked around, but when Peg had caught her eye at the dance and indicated that she wanted to go home, the thought of the little kitchen with the inevitable cup of tea was very inviting.

"It was terrible hot in that hall. I don't know how people could dance. I was wishin' we'd paid no attention to Gerry and stayed home where we were comfortable. We barely caught sight of him the whole night. Off politicking, I'll allow. But I saw Joey Coady bendin' your ear there a while. What old foolishness was he on about this time?" Peg was busy with the kettle.

"Oh, telling me what he knew of Matt."

"I suppose, but now you wouldn't want to pay too much attention to Joe. He grew up hard, Joe did. Himself and his mother lived in a small tilt below Little Brook. He was a love child. Some shareman or other came around one summer helpin' with the fishery, put her in the family way and then took off. When Joe was born, his mother wouldn't hear tell of parting with him so it was hard for them always. Still an' all, he done well for himself and so did his youngsters. I'll say this for him, he never forgot his mother."

The kettle began to sing on the stove.

So, Joey Coady understood very well about "not knowing." Understood better than most. "I liked him." Nora looked across at Peg, but she was busy with the tea and didn't seem to hear her. "I liked him a lot," she murmured to herself.

"You fetch some cups and milk and I'll make the tea and we'll finish off that drop of whiskey."

"I enjoyed the dance," Nora said reassuringly. "It was just like a country dance at home. Did you always go to the dances, Peg?" She was about to add, "even when he was around," but stopped herself just in time.

"Yes, my dear, I always loved to dance." Peg set the tea on the table. "It was mostly in people's kitchens those days. We'd just get together and have a 'time,' that's how we call it, a kitchen party, you know." She sat down heavily. "Nora, if you slip into my bedroom you'll find an old-fashioned oil lamp on the dresser. Bring it here to the table and I'll light it. We'll have it nice and low. That way we won't have Gerry or the like droppin' in on the way home from the dance. If they see the big light on, they'll be to the door and I've had enough of that for one night."

Nora found the lamp as Peg had said. As she left the room, she noticed a little metal plaque hanging on the wall by the door. It had a pie-crust edge and was decorated all around with painted red roses. It said: *Lord grant me all things / That I may enjoy life. / The Lord gave me life / So I might enjoy all things.*

She closed the door behind her and brought the lamp to the

table. Peg carefully removed the glass chimney and turned up the wick. She struck a match and held it to the wick. A blue-gold flame leaped upwards, pushing a tail of black smoke into the air. Nora was startled and pulled back.

"You've never seen a lamp lit before, have you?"

"No, I haven't." The pungent smell of kerosene made her catch her breath.

Peg's crooked fingers, unsteady but practiced, turned the knob and carefully lowered the flame. Nora watched, fascinated, as she replaced the glass globe and adjusted the flame still more. "Close them blinds onto the road like a good girl, Nora, and turn off that big light and then we're all set."

A warm amber glow filled the room. Their reflection, soft and muted, peered back from the window.

"There's more I want to tell you that's important and as you'll be off early tomorrow, it's got to be now." Peg stared into her mug, stirring slowly, memories swirling.

"I suppose the Lord had no room for me back then." She scratched her head. "By rights, I should have died. But I made it through, hung on, and when I come home, not only was Matt still there but I was now a Canadian. While I was to the hospital the great debate had taken place and the vote taken. Newfoundland was no longer a country in its own right, but a province of Canada. We were dragged into this country of Canada barkin' and complainin' like harp seals on a whelpin' pan, but Canadians we were and that was the end of it." She laughed. "I wish I'd been about them days, they were exciting times. That vote was some close."

"How close?"

"Fifty-one point nine percent."

"Very close."

"Yes, there were some rackets about that, I can tell you." She settled in close to the table. "It didn't seem so important to me then. I had other things to be concerned with. The house was in a state when I got back: after three years you can imagine, but, my dear, Matt was best kind, with the ground all turned and ready for planting, and not only that, the garden was twice the size it used to be, with a proper fence all around. Joey Coady, if you please, put the fence in place for him. The extra ground was to be for special seed potatoes he'd got from St. John's called Forty Folds. They had come from Ireland, brought to Newfoundland by a man from Kilkenny, I believe. Well, I watched from my chair by the kitchen window as he worked the soil, getting ready for planting these special potatoes. It was like his life depended on it, and I'll tell you, girl, there was something real wonderful about those young shoots when they first come up, strong and healthy out of the dirt. Later, when the flowers came, they were beau..ti..ful." Her lips pursed as she spoke each syllable and her fingers bunched to make big imaginary clusters.

"I never seen the like." She paused. "Evenings he'd take me for a walk around to show off those plants. I was happy for him but nights I'd lie to bed thinkin', Who in the name of God was going to gather in this field of potatoes and lay them down for winter? It was wonderful and terrible at the same time; put me in mind of the year of the big tide, 1929. The vegetables were still in the ground and ready to harvest, and here in the middle of the night the sea come roarin' in right up to the house and tore the ground right up. People farther along the shore to Burin lost everything that night: houses, boats, even their chil'ren. It was some bad. The mornin' after, I was outside goin' mad tryin' to save what was still on the ground for fear the sea would rise again, take it all away, leavin' us with nothin' for the winter. He just ignored it all. He said it was all spoiled anyways, nothing there to save. Times like that he tried my patience sore. There was no talkin' to him.

"When I sees the beds of potatoes enough to feed the whole shore, all I could do was pray that come the fall of the year, I'd find the strength to bring them in. But at the time I could barely walk the length of myself, I was that weak, so I used to pray to God to send what help was needed."

The low buzz of a housefly sounded somewhere in the kitchen. It stopped momentarily, started up again, whizzing about in the darkness behind them.

"It was comin' up to the end of September, when one afternoon he come through the back door with a rake of potatoes stacked along his arm. They were just like a load of junks for the stove. My dear, they were this big!" She held her hands about eight inches apart. "I never seen the like."

"'Them's some potatoes, Matt,' I said. He held one out to me, the black dirt still stuck to it but, my dear, it was perfect, neither scab nor blemish." She paused. "I was some happy for him, Nora, happy he was proud of his work. We set about cooking them up that evenin' for supper, watchin' them boil up until they split right out of their jackets. 'Laughing at us,' was how he put it."

Nora watched Peg's face. The soft lamplight had smoothed away some of the ravages of time and sickness, leaving a faint trace of the younger woman, open, vulnerable, eager.

"I need not have worried. He brought them in that year hisself, workin' from early mornin' to evenin', layin' them down in perfect rows against the back wall of the root cellar, and what we didn't need, he gave away."

Nora was listening attentively and following every word Peg spoke, but there were other things on her mind and time was running out, so when a lull came in the conversation she asked the one question that had been floating about in her head like a leaf in a murky puddle. "Peg, in all those years did he ever express regret for what he had done to his wife and his child?"

Peg stroked the back of her hand, pausing for a moment, only to continue more vigorously with the same motion. "Not too much, except for the day he had that letter back from your father sayin' he didn't want to hear tell of him no more. It all come up that day just like he was sick to his stomach. The bits and pieces of his life come rushin' out."

20

There was comfort in the drink that Peg had passed to her and she was glad of it, but inside she longed for the luxury of a hot whiskey heavy with the pungent smell of cloves and the tang of lemon. Most of all she needed the comfort of a warm bed and sleep. Nora leaned her elbows on the table, giving support to her weary body. Peg too looked tired, but Nora could tell she had settled in with her drink and still had a way to go before heading to bed. "Do you have the letter my father wrote in reply?" she asked.

"No, girl, I don't." Peg took a deep breath. "Matt was some upset by that letter. I don't know if it was because of the way it was written or because he just felt cast aside or both, but after that it was like he didn't care no more. He just balled that letter up and pitched it in the fire. He watched until it was nothin' but ash and then walked out the door. This time I knew he'd be back, but I didn't want him off roamin' about by hisself in that state. I called out to him that if he was about to go for a walk, I wouldn't mind a bit of air myself. Before he had a chance to reply, I had my coat on and was to the door. I could see there was a bit of weather on the way so I grabbed his coat off the nail too."

He was well ahead of her, setting a fierce pace, not bothering to look left or right. Neighbours, busy with cutting wood and mending nets in preparation for winter, paid no attention as Matt Molloy scurried by, but when Peg appeared shortly thereafter, carrying his coat and in just as big a hurry, they turned from their work and followed her progress until she disappeared over the hill.

She held her tongue until she was out of earshot of the neighbours and then she shouted out to him. "Blessed God, Matt, will you hold on? I was lookin' for a walk, not a gallop. I'm havin' a hard time catchin' up."

He slowed down then, and waited for her.

"That's a lazy wind, Matt. Here, put your coat on or it'll go right through you." She held out his coat and helped him with the sleeves. Low dark clouds overhead promised rain. She pulled the collar snugly around his neck and began to do up the buttons. "I'll have to see to that before winter sets in," she said, noticing the top button was missing. She held the lapels for a moment in an effort to get him to face her, but he was focused on a different horizon and completely unaware of her gentle maneuvering. She tucked one lapel inside the other to make up for the lost button.

He hasn't changed much over the years, she thought, looking him over. He still wore the same kind of dark suit with a shirt and tie and wool pullover. Over time, the pullover had changed in colour but not style. In the old days it was grey, now it was brown. Cautiously, she looked over the thin, clean-shaven man in front of her. He still had a full head of hair, but the spring was gone from the curls and they were now a lovely silvery grey. He was still handsome, she thought, but today, he looked pitiful.

"Sadie Dolan," he said suddenly. There was an acute bitterness in his voice. "I should never have had anything to do with her."

Peg stepped back. "What's that you said?"

"Mistake after mistake. The curse of my life," he muttered. Then, stepping to the side, he went around her and set off again over the path.

Peg hurried after him, half running to keep up.

"She came into Dowd's one day. I served her." He halted abruptly on the path, causing Peg to bump into him and stumble. He reached out, steadied her. "I was a shop assistant there at the time, men's drapery." A fleeting look of wonder crossed his face and his voice momentarily lost its edge. "I can remember seeing strands of red-gold in the dark of her hair. They were glinting in the light as she turned her head. On the spur of the moment I asked her if she'd like to go for a walk, after the shop closed."

He set off again, picking up the pace, taking long angry strides. "There was no baby there when we got married. I'd been fooled and everyone knew but me." Then he began blathering to himself in a kind of singsong whine. "Spoiled priest, foolish daddy, hangin' round waitin' for the babby. Sniggering little snot-nosed brats," he muttered angrily under his breath.

"Matt." Peg had to shout again to be heard. "I don't know what you're goin' on about, but I'm beat out."

He turned and came back to where she was standing, tapping at her chest with a closed fist.

"It's no good, Matt. I can't keep up." Out of sheer necessity she stepped in closer and took his arm. Feeling the closeness of his body, she realized with a start what she had done but to her surprise, she felt no resistance in him. Glad of the support, she drew closer into the comfort and warmth of his big coat. "You had every right to be angry," she said reassuringly. He made no reply but she thought she felt his arm tighten momentarily around hers but she couldn't be sure.

"It seems, Nora, that after that he turned right against his wife: couldn't even bear to look at her and her swollen belly. When, eventually, the child was born, she, in turn, shut him out. Never let him near his son. That was his punishment. He went and reclaimed his books from the doctor who had kept them safe for him. The books were his refuge. For the next few years there was nothin' but bad feelings and bitter words between them. Now, when his mother died and they had the place to themselves, things eased up a bit. But, you know how it is. In time, we must reap what we sow.

"Matt." She began to play with the thin gold ring on her finger. "I want you to listen to what I have to say, just this once, listen, and don't walk away." His wife took the seat across from him and placed her hands lightly, one on top of the other, on her lap.

He shifted, sensing danger.

She sat very still, waiting for him to acknowledge her but he keep his eyes glued to the book in his hand as if he hadn't heard her. She drew in a deep breath. "All my life," she began, "I ... I've been pushed around doin' everyone's biddin'." She looked around as if by some miracle help would come from the walls or the ceiling or seep out of the cracks in the floor. "In my father's house I owned nothin'." She threw her hands in the air in despair. "Nothin'," she repeated, her voice rising. "Nothin', but the few clothes on my back. Sadie had no needs or wants. What could I be in need of? Where would I be goin'? I was just there to tend to the needs of a crooked, complainin' old man and his miserable son, my brother. I was just a skivvy, twenty-eight years old and not a single offer. I knew I was no great catch and they never let me forget it."

She leaned over and poked her husband in the arm. "You know somethin', Matt Molloy? It was my brother sent me to the shop that day to get him a new shirt. He had his eye on a girl in the next town and

WHERE OLD *Ghosts* MEET

194

wanted 'to put his best foot forward,' so he said. I heard talk that you were home and that you were workin' at Dowd's shop." She opened and closed her hands as they lay in her lap, as if they were the gateway to someplace deep inside of her.

She lifted her head and looked at the man across from her. "I caught your eye over the counter and in that minute I thought I saw something there. Maybe twas only pity, but it came to me that maybe, just maybe, you might understand what it's like to be cast aside to be lonely and … well, maybe, maybe, you'd know what I mean when I'd say that, sometimes, in the quiet of evening, I can hear the grass whisper to me below in the meadow or that sometimes in the early mornin' when—"

The book snapped shut and made her jump.

"My God, Matt! You frightened me, you did."

"Did she know? Tell me now, did my mother know?"

"Know what? Blessed God, can't we forget about her, Matt? She's dead and gone!"

"Tell me." He still hadn't raised his head.

"Can't we just make a life for ourselves and Eamon, and not have her, like a crazed old magpie, forever between us? Forget her."

"Tell me now."

"Gentle Redeemer." Hands flew from her lap. "Wasn't she abroad lookin' for a wife for you, soon as you set foot back in the town? Sadie Dolan wasn't exactly what she had in mind to help her save face, not good enough for Matt Molloy, no, but just the same she had to get you out of the bars and settled down where she could keep an eye on you now, didn't she? So when she heard I'd been walkin' out with you and, Lord preserve us, in the family way, that was it." She paused to take her breath.

He looked at her then, attentive to every word.

"My brother it was, told her," she announced with a degree of satisfaction. "He wanted me gone so he could make way for a new woman in the house. He had no use for me anymore."

"But you weren't, damn it!"

She sighed. "To begin with, I thought I was." Her voice had dropped so that it was barely audible. "I wanted to tell you straight out. You see, I'd missed twice." She stole a glance at him but he had turned away. "I was terrified." Her voice collapsed in a deep sob. "Can't you understand that? Terrified of my own father and brother. My brother knew I'd missed. I don't know how he knew, but he knew. Goddamn him, he knew everything about me, even that. When I discovered it was a false alarm, twas he urged me not to breathe a word. He wanted me gone, kept tellin' me that there was no place for me here and that this was my only chance."

Pitiful eyes turned to the man at her side. He hadn't moved.

"Jesus, Matt, is it myself I'm talkin' to?"

"You still haven't answered me. Did she know?"

"Of course she bloody knew. They fixed it all, didn't they?" Her cries hit a peak and then collapsed again into a low rattling sob.

"And you agreed."

She made no reply, just stared into the dying embers of the fire, making no effort to stop the flow of tears that ran down her face and formed a dark patch on the front of her dress.

He opened his book and returned to his reading.

In a flash, her hand came back, and with a single swipe, the book went flying from his hands onto the hot embers of the fire.

A howl, tormented and pitiful, came from deep within him and in a single movement he sprang, ripping apart the very space between them. He was on his knees, his bare fingers poking at the glowing coals. The pile of dying embers collapsed, the book sinking farther into the hot ash. His hand touched a red hot coal and he pulled back, bringing his scorched fingers to the cool wetness of his mouth. Then he was back in again, determined. He got hold of the soft leather cover and pulled his beloved Shakespeare from the fire. It was smouldering and coated with hot, white ash. Desperate, he dabbed at the charred pages, spitting on his fingers, touching the glowing edges, brushing the ash, ignoring the agony of his hand.

She watched transfixed as he battled fiercely with the hot coals to save his precious book. "I was wrong," she said calmly. "You're no different from them."

"Mammy?" The child stood in the doorway that led to the back room, his eyes wide with fright. "Mammy," he said again, louder this time, his petrified gaze fixed on his father's face. He began to gnaw on his tiny clenched fist.

They looked at each other, father and son, a long, lost look. He could find nothing to say to the boy. There was nothing to say, nothing to do, so he got up and, taking the charred remains of his book, walked past the child and out the door.

Peg took a deep breath. "When I heard that, the chill inside of me was worse than the chill of that October day on the hill. I never did have a child of my own but …"

Even in the gentle light of the lamp Peg looked pale and dazed. "I don't know if …" Her voice faltered. "It's too difficult." She reached for her drink and finished it in one gulp. "How can we know what goes on in someone else's head?" It was a question that didn't invite an answer, so she turned away to speak to the night. "He told me that he wrote from New York one time, asking them to come to America. He said he had money saved for their passage. But he never heard back from them, not the word, and he never tried again."

"That's true!" Nora was suddenly alert. "That is absolutely true. I have the letter here in my handbag." She reached down for the bag by her feet. Where was it? The chair by her coat. She got up. "It was amongst my father's papers," she said, rummaging in the clutter of her bag. The light was poor and her hands awkward. Finally she produced the two letters. "This one," she said, holding on to one and dropping the other back in her bag. "It came from New York; it's from him." She slipped the folded single sheet from the envelope and passed it to Peg.

Peg looked at Nora and then at the paper in her hand, her eyes wide and incredulous. Here it was, in his neat handwriting, his effort to make amends. She took her time to read, savouring every word. How typical it was of him, short and to the point: his way of protecting himself. You had to know that, to understand.

"I don't think Sadie ever received that letter. Somehow her brother Mickey Dolan intercepted that letter and kept it from her. Look at this." Nora handed Peg the envelope.

The familiar handwriting looked back at her. She touched the letters. Mrs. Sadie Molloy, Ballyslish, Cullen, County Roscommon, Ireland. Her hand flew to her chest, pressing bony fingers against the cloth of her dress in an effort to control the pounding inside.

"Read the back," Nora urged

Peg turned over the envelope. Different handwriting. Nora heard the breathy mumble as she read. "This letter was found amongst the effects of Mickey Dolan. It was unopened at the time." Peg looked from the envelope to Nora.

"Who wrote that?"

"My father."

"Your father! You're sure about that, Nora?"

"Yes, I'm absolutely sure. I don't know how he got hold of it but it was with his papers when he died, that and the other one from Matt, both together."

"The brother never even opened it then. Is that what you're saying? Never even bothered to see what he was keeping from her? Why would anyone do the like of that?"

"Maybe he wanted to hold on to her as his housekeeper. Remember, they were living with him then. I know he never married, never got the woman he was after. An old man in Cullen told me he was a bachelor."

"My God, you'd have to be some evil to do the like of that." Peg studied the envelope again. "Evil." She read the letter once more then slipped the single page back into the envelope. They fitted together perfectly. She looked at it once more and then passed it to Nora. "I knew it was the truth," she said. "Knew it right in my gut but I'm glad to see it wrote down."

"Well, my father knew, but obviously it didn't carry much weight with him. He still decided to shut him out. My mother told me that fear was the reason. She whispered that to me one day shortly before she died, when I tentatively approached the subject of our missing grandfather. 'Your father was afraid he might turn out to be a drunken old blackguard, like the tinkers. He knew he had a problem with the drink,' she whispered just before she drifted off to sleep. The subject was never mentioned again."

There was no reaction from Peg. She had withdrawn into her own world.

"Maybe he was right," Nora mused to herself. She knew about the tinkers. She had seen them many times and they frightened her. On the Fair Day in the town, they parked their caravans under the street light at the end of the road. It was a noisy busy encampment during the day, with cooking and washing, repairing pots and pans, ragged children chasing each other around the area, but when the pubs closed at night, the fighting and brawling could be heard all over the town. One night, she had watched from her bedroom window as a man took a horse whip to a woman as she cowered on the ground, screaming. The children, huddled together, watched from the half-door of the caravan.

Nora shuddered. "Maybe he was right," she said to herself.

21

"*Joinin'* up with Canada in '49 was a mixed blessing. Everything was changin', and changin' very fast. It was hard to keep up sometimes with all the changes. There was talk about movin' people off the islands. Services like schools and health care to all those isolated spots was costin' the government too much money. They couldn't pay for it no more, so we were told. The plan was to move us to what they called 'growth centres,' where there were jobs for all and a decent livin' to be made. We could 'burn our boats,' so they said. Imagine! Well the rackets! Some couldn't wait to be gone. Others, well, there was no way they were being told what to do. Families that had been there for generations weren't about to tear up their homes and gardens, and families, all they ever knew.

"In the late '50s it all came to a head for us on Berry Island. There was an allowance to be had from government to help with the move: $300 to $600 depending on the number of children in the family. The catch was that all hands had to leave. Anyone stayed behind, then the deal was off. They were on their own. Well, my dear, up she went!"

Peg rose to fill the kettle again. "I remember one night there was a meeting called to the school. I went to that meeting. I'd been to many over the years but this was to be the final one. I had my mind made up. I was gettin' on and I could see a time comin' when I'd need a few services handy to me and besides, there was nothin' much on the island for the youngsters no more. Things were closin' down all over the place. The priest was gone, the school had only a few youngsters and the store was shapin' up the same way." She laid a plate with thick slices of homemade bread on the table, with a dish of margarine and a pot of dark red berry jam. The pot of tea arrived and Peg poured, the hot steam rising over the table. It smelled good.

"As I saw things then, it seemed like every day brought something new. We were part of a big country now and we had best get aboard or be left behind." She began to spread margarine on the bread and pile jam on top.

Nora followed her lead. "And Matt?"

Peg swallowed a piece of bread and jam and licked the tips of her fingers. "Matt," she said hesitantly, "he was a bit tormented over the whole idea of movin' but I thought he'd come around. Tell truth, I was kind of surprised he was of that mind, havin' moved about so much in his life. I wouldn't have thought it would bother him too much. But when I come to think on it afterwards I suppose it was understandable for him to be concerned. He was content where he was to, best he'd ever been. By then he'd been livin' on the island on and off for a good many years, and here by all accounts he was to be forced to pull up and leave. 'There's nothin' decided yet,' I told him, 'but if you want to be a part of what's goin' on you'd best come and hear what others have to say.' So the night of the vote I persuaded him to come down to the school."

There was standing room only in the schoolhouse that night. The women had come early and sat in rows, jammed into the wooden desks, their heads swivelling back and forth, watchful and expectant. The men stood shoulders to the walls, unshaven, the look of a long hard day set in their faces. A few young people hung about by the doorway in a loose group, detached, awaiting a decision. Matt Molloy sat on the wood box, partly concealed by the belly of the stove. He had not been in this room since the day he'd had the confrontation with Gerry Quinlan twenty or more years before.

Now the tide had turned. Gerry was back for tonight's vote. He stood up front behind the teacher's desk, suitably attired in a dark suit, shirt and tie, a lawyer representing the Government, adviser and confidant of the merchant who now stood alongside of him as Justice of the Peace on the island. He stood out in the crowded room, confident, quick, vocal and hard driving, clearly in control. He was now the big shot from St. John's, loved by some, despised by others. "Joey's Boy," was how some referred to him, those who had no time for Joey Smallwood, the upstart premier of the province. Joey, "the little fella from Gambo," who had wooed the people into giving away their country just a few years before and now he was after them again, this time, to give up their homes.

His old teacher looked across the room and took in the measure of Gerry Quinlan, noting the feeling of urgent impatience that surrounded the man. He had a job to do tonight, and a boat to catch tomorrow. Gerry knew the game, knew what he wanted.

"Now, is there anyone else would like to speak to this motion before we cast our vote?" It was an officious sounding call from the justice. There was a swell of voices in the crowd, which faded to a murmur, sporadic coughing, bodies shifted. It was time.

Matt Molloy's mind was on that night years ago and his bitter confrontation with Gerry Quinlan. The very notion that he could go off to New York and become an actor was ridiculous. How could he know about the loneliness and rigours of a big city like New York? Matt Molloy knew in his heart that he had been too harsh with his young student that night, and deep down he regretted it but he had never found the courage to admit it. He wondered now as he watched if, in fact, he had done him a service that day: if his advice, though harsh, had been sound. His eye caught the faded bronze knot of hair on the top of Peg's head across the room. It shone like a beacon amongst the patches of grey.

"Mr. Molloy, maybe you have something to add. Being an outsider an' all, you've been abroad and seen the world and at the same time know what we're about here. What do you think? Should we shut her down or what?"

He heard the word "outsider" and knew before he stood up that his opinion would count for nothing. He was just a decoy. He knew he shouldn't take the bait but he wasn't about to back away, not in front of Gerry Quinlan. He stood up reluctantly, aware of the deep silence in the room as he collected his thoughts. He was searching for truth.

"This island is a barren, isolated place," he began, "make no mistake about that." His tone was quiet and deferential, his eyes averted, not wanting to make contact with anyone in particular. "Even at the best of times life here is a challenge and you respond to that challenge by working hard." He shifted his feet, glad of the warmth coming from the belly of the woodstove. "Your life here has a strange, unrelenting rhythm. You know it, live with it and survive doing what you know best. In the new growth centres across the bay or in the city of St. John's that rhythm may not be too different from what you know, but make no mistake, it will be different. If you choose to leave, you have to understand that wherever you go, you simply may not fit in with the new order. That is all I have to say."

He sat down, glad of the partial concealment provided by the stove. He could hear some clapping but he had no way of telling if it was widespread. He wished he could leave now, quietly.

"Well, now, that's all very impressive." Like many of the island men, the speaker was short and powerfully built. He had a voice to match his bulk and a presence that demanded attention. Matt Molloy recognized him right away. Leo Power, another old student, bright enough, owner of the largest fishing boat in these parts. "Them's grand words from Mr. Molloy, yes, won'erful grand words." For a moment he stared at his boots and then turned a crafty eye on the crowd, taking time to eyeball certain people, making sure he had their attention. Then he straightened his back and pointed to where Matt Molloy sat by the stove. "But, tell me now, tell me this, what do he know about the likes of us? What do he know about makin' fish or bein' up to yer arse in debt before you ever gets to put yer boat in the water in the spring of the year and still in debt in the fall of the year no matter how good the catch. Now, I can take a swing at life, good as any man, and I'll tell ye this." He pointed his finger straight into the heart of the crowd. "If I has to jack up my house, put her aboard a raft and haul her across the bay, I'll do it, and I'll tell ye this much, I'll not be beatin' me brains out worryin' about whether I fits in with the crowd over there or not."

Wild cheers, shouting and arguing followed. That was the final word from the floor. A show of hands and it was over.

Peg looked about for Matt, thinking they could walk home together, but he had gone, so she made out across the path, happy for the first time about the whole situation. She knew now, for sure, what was best. They'd stay on, on the island, no matter what. The Byrnes too had made up their minds to stay and Pius Walsh. "He wasn't goin' nowhere," so he said. He had no need of a school or church, and the O'Briens down to the Gut, they were staying and there were a few more besides. She would make a nice cup of tea when she got in, stoke up the fire and tell Matt what she'd decided. Peg was delighted now that she knew what was best for them both. They'd manage, the two of them, like they'd always done.

There was no light on in the house when she came around the bend in the path. When she came through the door, he was at the kitchen table, sitting in the pitch dark, his head in his hands and not a stir out of him. Peg went straight for the lamp and lit it, paying no attention to him. Then she threw a few sticks in the stove and put on the kettle.

"Matt," she said, "I've made up my mind. I want to stay here on the island with you. This is where we belong."

"No, Peg," he said. "The reality is that you belong here. I don't. I realize that now. I suppose I always knew but didn't want to think about it." He continued, "You've been good to me, Peg, and I've been happy here. For that, I will be eternally grateful. I wanted to tell you that before I leave, but it's time I was off."

She couldn't believe her ears. She was willing to change her whole plans so they could spend their old age in peace and quiet in the place they both loved and all he could say was, "Thanks, I've been happy, but goodbye."

Peg turned on him then. "You don't care about me, Matt Molloy. You don't care about me or yourself or anybody else in the whole world. You'd be quite happy now after all these years to walk out that door and just leave me to find my own way. Well, you'd best go on then. Yes, go on out of it. My father told me years ago this would happen, told me to my face: 'He'll leave you on your own, Peg, out on the bawn.' Them's his very words. And you know somethin'? He was right. I should have listened to him."

Matt spun round in his chair, mad as a hornet, and shouted at her, "I do care for you, Peg."

She was shocked and so was he. She didn't think that was what he had in mind to say, but there it was: popped, like a cork from a bottle.

"There was an awkward minute between us then. He had never before raised his voice to me, but saying he 'cared for me' made me, well ..."

Her lower lip began to tremble but she covered it quickly, pausing before continuing. "But I knew what he said was true. I knew in my gut but hearing him say so was, well, it was what I needed to hear. When we finally got over the shock, he spoke first. 'It's not what I want to do or even what I'd like to do, but rather what I think is best for you. You want to go, I know that, and I'm in your way. I'm driving a wedge between you and the people around you and I don't want to do that. That's what I really believe but I never seem to be able to do or say the right thing.' I wanted to wrap him in my arms then, to hold him close to me 'til he understood how much I wanted to be with him always but ... he was sitting down and ..."

She started to giggle like a girl. "Anyway, I didn't. I just cupped his cheek in my hand and looked him straight in the eyes and said, 'I'm happy to hear you say that, Matt. That's all I need to hear. We must do what is best for us now. We'll stay, you and me together, and care for each other.' From then on, that was how it was between us. It's just how it was."

22

A shadowy figure was beginning to emerge from the dark boundaries that surrounded her grandfather and his arcane life. He was all around her now. Nora knew the look of him, could hear the deep resonance of his voice, could sense his detachment, feel his fear and uncertainty, knew of his passion. She could sense too a certain generosity of spirit but it was finely layered and fragile. But the heart and soul of the man remained elusive, shifting like a fog, at times thin and veiled, but mostly dense and impermeable.

She was unsure how she felt about this stranger who was her blood relative, her grandfather. She still had difficulty saying the word grandfather in relation to him, difficulty with the whole idea. It made demands on her that she was reluctant to meet. What if he should, by some miracle, walk in the door right there and then? Would she want to sit with him, tell him about the family he had left behind? Would she want to talk to him about Ireland, about the theatre, about teaching? Would she want to hold his hand, comfort an old man who wanted, above all else, to look upon his grandchild? She dropped her head into her hands. Everything was spinning, confused and muddled. She pushed hard on the hollow spaces at her temples. She felt no affection for the man, pity maybe, grudging admiration and, at times, shame.

We expect too much from family, she cautioned herself. A common bloodline does not necessarily produce people whom we trust, admire and love. Friends frequently fill those roles with greater understanding and sensitivity. She caught Peg's eye. Steadfast and true, here was the ultimate friend – loyal, generous, caring, understanding – what he had not been able to find in his family.

She took Peg's hand and squeezed it gently, saying nothing, allowing the warmth of her feelings to flow hand to hand. Their heads came together. "I hope he cared for you, Peg." There was a shadow of uncertainty there. Nora's grip tightened. "I hope he truly cared for you."

Peg fixed a steady gaze on Nora. "Yes, my dear, he was good to me and we cared for each other." Her voice was soft with contentment, but her eyes, still fixed steadfastly on Nora, said a whole lot more.

Nora searched, looking from one eye to the other, following an elusive shadow that hovered there all but invisible.

Peg never flinched but bright tears, rising to the surface from the deep veins of caring and want, began to form in the corner of each eye. They hung there on the brink, ready to flow but she held on, bravely forcing her eyes to remain wide. "There are things we hope for …" She took her time before trying again. "I ran out of time." She wiped her cheek with the back of her hand.

Nora could see it all now, wrapped up deep inside Peg Barry like a tight ball of string: the suffocating realization of lost time, lost opportunity, lost youth.

"I might have been your step-grandmother. That would be something now. Imagine." She laughed, the old twinkle back. "I'd have liked that."

"So would I." Then, after a moment's consideration, she added, "In a way, you are." They laughed.

"You must be tired, Peg."

"Yes, I am a bit but we'll finish off this bit of whiskey, girl. Let me have your glass." She poured half of what remained in the bottle into Nora's glass and the rest into her own. Added a splash of water from the jug and then passed it to Nora.

"Best thing we ever done, deciding to stay on the island. We were some happy, even though down the road I could have done with the services they were offering elsewhere." Peg looked at Nora. She was comfortable with his granddaughter. She could tell her all her long-held secrets, secrets she had never breathed to another soul. There had been some tense moments from time to time, flashes of anger behind those dark eyes but, always, Nora had held back and allowed her to continue and tell it like it was without interruption. Peg was thankful for that, thankful for the blessed simple comfort of having someone listen and not judge.

Now, seeing Nora there in the lamplight, looking more like her grandfather than ever, put Peg in mind of that night eight years ago when her old life had come to an end: everything she had known, her home, her way of life, her relationship with Matt.

She was jolted from her reverie by Nora's voice. "Most people moved away from the island then?"

"Yes, my dear. In the years following, it was happenin' all over the place."

"That must have been terrifying, seeing everyone leave and being left behind?"

"Well, I suppose I have to say it was." She ran her finger around the rim of the glass. "Sheila was gone, of course, and now Pat and Bride and the children were off, too. That was a hard day, the day they left. I went down on the wharf to see them go. I'll never forget the sight of it. Seein' the house, loaded up onto them big oil drums, just like it was a doll's house sittin' up there on the water, the curtains still on the windows, hitched up to John Mooney's boat and ready to be hauled to the other side. That took the heart right out of me. I'd seen other houses on their way, but somehow the sight of my poor sister's house, the room where she'd passed away givin' birth to Sheila, bobbin' about on the water and headed for Placentia, was more than I could bear. And worse again, all their belongings, piled on up the wharf, all the things that made up a warm comfortable home, lookin' now like they was fit for nothin' but the dump. When I saw that, in a way, I was some glad to be stayin'."

"So people took their houses with them across on the water?" Nora was dumbfounded. "I didn't know you could do that."

"Oh yes, some did, not everyone. They just rolled them down on the beach on logs and onto a raft and towed them across. There's times now I sees the refugees on the television, old people, little children, mothers with their babies clutched to their breasts headin' off down the road with their few things, and I thinks, That was us back then."

She looked at Nora, the shock of realization on her face. "Eventually when it came my turn to leave, I never did clear out the old place. I left it as it was, just took the few things I needed or couldn't part with, then pulled the door behind me and left. Thought I might go back for a spell come the nice weather, but I never did."

"And Matt?"

"Matt died home, on November 14, 1962." Her finger tapped the table top. We had a few wonderful years on the island after the crowd left. Those who stayed behind came closer together. Survival, I suppose. Times, it was a struggle but we always helped each other out, like in the old days. The biggest change I remember was people comin' to the house again. They were back and forth all the time. I liked that and I believe Matt did too, although he never did say. He was more comfortable, I think, with the few. We were all in the same boat. There was just no way we would have made it without each other. No way. When you're happy, girl, it makes a lot of things come together. Don't you think?"

Nora nodded. "But the isolation, the cold in the depths of winter, the dark, the work to keep wood cut, the fear of being far from help. It must have been terrible." She wrapped her arms tightly around her body.

"How did he die?" Nora suddenly asked. Then, in an attempt to take some of the bluntness out of her question, added, "My father just slipped away in his sleep at the age of sixty-two, just a few years before his coveted pension came due."

"It all happened so suddenly, one day he was the best kind, next day everything had changed." The tone of her voice dropped as she retreated into her world of memories. "He come out of his bedroom one day all wrapped up in his winter coat, the buttons all skew ways. 'Blessed Lord, what are you at?' I said. 'Look at the get-up on you. It's a beautiful day out.' Well, girl, he didn't know what I was talkin' about, but he let me help him off with the coat and we had a little laugh about it. But I thought it strange.

"By and by, there were other little things he'd do that was not like him. Like one day he opened the door to the back porch and said, 'I'm sure this used to be the outhouse.' I said, 'No, Matt, it's never been there. It's out back.' It was funny in a way and kind of nice to be having a laugh together, especially about personal things like that. But soon it wasn't funny no more. Times I was frightened. At night he'd usually read for a while by the fire. Always when he'd finish he'd close whatever book it was he was readin' and lay it on the shelf by the stove. This one night he was rummagin' about, tossin' things aside and makin' the biggest kind of fuss. His book was gone. I had taken it and hidden it away. He spoke quite harsh to me that night, not like himself, and when I passed him down the book from its usual spot, he never breathed a word of apology. He just sat down in the chair like nothin' had happened. What shocked me most that particular night was he hadn't the clue what to do with that book."

She looked at Nora and saw the look of disbelief on her face. "That's the truth. He turned it over and over, opened it and closed it. 'Here,' I said, turning it right way up and opening it at the right page. 'It's the poems you were readin' last night. Remember?' He was all right then. But now I knew for sure that the man I knew was slippin' away from me." Every word carried pain.

"That was the beginning of a long goodbye," she whispered.

Nora reached for her glass and over the rim stole a secretive glance at Peg, who was studying the diminished contents of her glass, swirling it slowly round and round. Then, she took a carefully measured sip.

"I was embarrassed to begin with, didn't tell anybody. I was hopin' it would all go away. But strange things began to happen all the time after that. Mostly, when people were about, he'd act almost normal. He had never been that talkative around others anyway so it wasn't that noticeable until one day Mary Anne Casey come by right excited.

She arrived in the kitchen panting, a letter clutched to her chest. "Peg, I got the finest kind of news today." Her breath came in short gasps as she fanned herself with the white envelope. "My daughter Agnes is goin' to have a baby." She finally got the words out. "They've waited nine years and here at last it's on the way. My dear, it was St. Jude, him an' me done it. We've been stormin' heaven these years, and finally we got through to the Almighty. I has great faith in St. Jude."

"Well, Mary Ann, that's wonderful news all together. Did you hear that, Matt? Mary Anne's daughter, you remember Agnes, the one in St. John's? She's to have a baby." Peg didn't wait for an answer.

"You sit down there now and take a spell and I'll make us a cup of tea to celebrate. You'll be goin' to St. John's then, by and by."

"Yes, but it's not for a while yet." She flopped down in the chair by the table. "When we was young, it was tryin' not to have them, we was. Right, Peg? What with one on the floor and one on the way most times."

Peg set the tea things on the table. She said nothing. Suddenly the woman realized her error. She leaned across the table. "I often thought," she whispered, "if you'd done the novena years back, things might have gone different for you." She gave Peg a knowing look, raised her eyebrows and gave a flick of her head in Matt's direction.

"You'll have tea, Matt?" Peg chose to ignore her visitor's comment but gave her a reassuring smile to show there were no hard feelings. "Sit in to the table now." She poured tea and set out plates of bread and jam.

"So when is the baby coming?"

"May month. I'll–"

The conversation stopped abruptly as both women turned to watch the activity at the other end of the table. Matt had tipped the slices of bread onto the table and had pulled the plate close to him. Slowly he picked up his mug and with great care began to pour the hot sweet tea onto the plate. When it was about half full he set down the mug, picked up the plate, carefully balancing it between widespread fingers, and brought it to his mouth. With a loud slurp the tea disappeared. The women stared. There was a soft tap as he set the plate down. He was pouring again, the trickling noise breaking the silence in the room. He worked carefully, setting down the mug, then, just as carefully, he picked up the plate and held it out to the woman on his left. She hesitated a moment, unsure, and then slowly reached for the brim-full plate. The tea slopped dangerously close to the edge. She steadied her hands and took a deep breath.

"Here's to the child," she said as she exhaled and brought the plate to her mouth.

Peg watched, wide-eyed.

When it was all gone, the woman set the plate down in front of Matt. "I'll tell Aggie we drank to the baby's health," she said.

At the other end of the table, Peg looked on like an unseen observer. A sudden realization swept over her like the touch of a warm breeze on a cool day. There was no shame, nothing to hide.

"That was a grand cup of tea, Peg. I'm some glad I was able to come by right away and tell the news. It couldn't wait."

"I'm glad you came too, Mary Anne. Good news is always welcome."

Mary Anne got up from the table then, said goodbye and left.

"It was a great relief to know that I didn't have to hide what was happening anymore, that I didn't have to face things on my own. Mary Anne was the best kind. She came by again the next day to tell me her grandfather had suffered the same thing years back when she was a child and she remembered quite well how it was. She was a great help to me in the months to come. It wasn't easy to open up just like that to an outsider but I couldn't have managed without her. I had never shared my business with anyone, especially with regards to Matt and me, never let them in our private life, but Mary Anne seemed to understand. She had the good sense to take things slowly, lettin' me find my own way. I was glad of that."

Peg, her eyes heavy with concern, looked at Nora. "It's a hard way to go, you know. You need people around you who care."

A car engine sounded in the distance and grew louder. A bright beam of light penetrated the thin blinds and briefly scanned the room as if seeking them out.

"That will be the crowd from the dance. They're headed home."

Nora looked at her watch: 12:30. Another car passed and another right behind. Music blared momentarily, someone yelled, a loud drunken yell. The car sped away and silence settled in again.

"I watched him slip back to his childhood. His garden became a playground. Days I saw a little boy playing in the mud, building castles, rapt in his own imaginings. He'd haul out the new carrots and turnip and then fill up the holes with water. It was terrible to watch. Other times he'd come in the kitchen and say, 'I'm off to school now,' and head off out the door. I was afraid for him to go out on his own, afraid he'd go too close to the cliffs. Times he couldn't find his way back. He seemed to have no sense. There was one time when I tried to stop him goin' off on his own, he turned and hit me hard. Knocked me right over, he did. I cut my head open on the door frame.

"I was about to give up after that but when Mary Anne come by and seen what had happened, she was full of wisdom. 'Peg girl, he does that because he's frustrated. He wants to go to school and no matter what you say it won't make no difference. What my mother would do with Poppy when he'd be like that is she'd say, "Very good then, let's go to school." Then she'd lead him off down the road or into the garden or wherever until he'd forgotten all about school.'

"Sometimes I could laugh at things he'd do and the things I'd do to keep him happy.

"One day I realized that he could recite a lot of the stuff he'd learned off in his head. So sometimes I'd start him off with a few words I knew and off he'd go like one of them tape recorders. He'd be happy as a clam then. I got so I'd have a line ready in my head, ready to distract him. Not everyone understood what I was at, especially Pat. There was one day in particular when he came across from Placentia to check on us."

Peg was in the yard hanging the washing on the line when Pat came around the corner of the house carrying a box of supplies.

"That's a fine load of washing you have there, Aunt Peg." He set down his load and then bent down to draw a heavy white sheet from the basin and throw it over the clothesline. "Matt should help with this. It's hard on you."

"Yes, he does normally but he's at the garden now and content so I won't bother him."

"How is he these days?"

"Oh, best kind. We manage, the two of us."

Pat stood next to her, helping to get the wet laundry on the line. When it was all done and neatly pegged she stepped back, and had he not been there to catch her, she would have tumbled to the ground. At arm's length, he took a good look at his aunt. "You look exhausted, Aunt Peg, and that dress looks like it could do with a wash and a button sewn on."

She looked down at her dress and was taken aback to see the front gaping open and the white flesh of her breast exposed.

"Come in the house now and we'll get you squared away," he said. Picking up the bags, they headed towards the back door. "Bride's got a job for the summer. She starts Monday," he called over his shoulder.

"Them few things should be dry by suppertime if the rain holds off. Maybe you could empty that water for me, Pat. Soon as I get clear of this, we'll have a cup of tea." It was as if she hadn't heard him.

Peg sat down. Her arms, heavy with exhaustion, rested on the table top.

"You can't continue like this," he said, beginning to clear up the remains of the washing. "He needs to see a doctor and so do you."

As he spoke, the back door opened and Matt Molloy stood there, the wet laundry clutched in his arms. He took a few steps into the kitchen, stumbled on a loose end, quickly flipped the dirty straggling end over his shoulder and furtively searched the room. He paid no attention to the two sets of incredulous eyes watching his every move. A few quick steps and he was across the room, the white sheet trailing the floor behind him. One last look around and he disappeared into his bedroom.

"Christ Almighty!" Pat said. "He's gone in the head."

Peg was on her feet, her open hand thrust forward, blocking what he was about to say. "Leave this to me. I know what to do."

She hurried towards Matt's bedroom door, knocked once and entered.

"But they're mine." The whiny voice came from behind the door.

"Yes, Matt, they're yours but we must dry them first. We'll hang them on the line in the sunshine and we'll dry them and then you can have them back."

There was a lengthy silence. Pat stood ready, tense.

"Let's see. What about … " Peg's voice was soft and cajoling. "*Friends, Romans, countrymen …* That's a good one. You remember that one?"

"*Lend me your ears. I come to bury Caesar not to praise him.*" The words were running off his tongue, strong at first and then petering off to a mumble.

Peg came through the door, the laundry in her arms. "Put that on the line for me, Pat. It's all right now."

"They're dirty."

"No matter, just get them on the line."

The mumbling continued from beyond the door.

Pat took the wet sheets in his arms. "Aunt Peg, he's not right in the top story. You know that, don't you?"

"He's sick, Pat, I know that. He just needs carin' for, that's all."

"That's not all, Aunt Peg, and you knows it. He needs a hospital. He needs puttin' away."

"Yes, into that hospital in St. John's! That's where they'd put him. I won't have it, Pat."

Behind the closed door they could hear him pacing the floor-boards, back and forth, back and forth, his mumbling punctuated by the odd shout.

Peg had seen the hospital in St John's. The Waterford Hospital they called it. She had walked by there once. It was just down the road from the sanatorium. In the spring of the year, when she was on the mend, oftentimes she'd go for walks to build up her strength to make ready for goin' home. It was a grim-looking place, she remembered. High brick walls with empty windows and not a soul to be seen about the place. "That's the loontic." Annie Walsh had grabbed her arm and steered her across the road. "It's where they puts them loontics to. Locks them up in the basement, they does. We'd best hang on to our wits, girl, or that's where we'll end up, too."

"It's you I'm concerned for, not him." Pat's voice startled her. "You're out here in the middle of nowhere." He dropped his voice. "Livin' with a friggin' lunatic."

She looked across at her nephew's dear earnest face. She loved Pat to pieces but she wished he wouldn't use that word. That was Annie Walsh's word and she didn't like it.

"Well, it's Matt I'm concerned with. I'll never allow them to take him away. Never! So don't keep on about it." She rubbed at the back of her hand. "I knows how to handle him. I'm gettin' better all the time and Mary Anne Casey, she–"

"Sh, sh, sh." Matt poked his head around the kitchen door, his finger to his lips. "Sh, sh, sh."

"Sh, sh." Peg brought her finger to her lip.

Quickly he darted to the big chair and sat down, quiet and content.

"See, he'll be all right now a while."

"Aunt Peg." Pat spoke in a low voice. "I've spoken to the doctor in Placentia. He explained to me how things will be later on. He'll come to be like a baby again. He'll need cleanin' and feedin' and he might even … Well, he might get out of hand."

"I know all that, Pat, but right now I can manage. I have good friends here and if things get to be too much, I'll say. But he's not goin' to that hospital and that's the end of it."

"I know what you're like. You get an idea in your head and there's no movin' you. But I'll be out every weekend so long as the weather's there, to check on you. There's things you'll be needin'. I'll look into that." He threw an exasperated look in Matt Molloy's direction and then headed outside to hang the sheets back up on the line.

"Pat was right. Things got to be a whole lot worse and it happened that quick I could hardly believe. 'Who are you?' he said to me one day. It hurt me terrible at the time. I remember thinkin', I'm nobody! It was like all the good had suddenly gone out of me. I don't know when I ever felt so lonely. Those days he'd slip in and out of my life, sometimes he'd be right here with me; more times he'd be back in Ireland or another place altogether. I couldn't go with him no more. But it was hard, girl, hard to watch, hard to keep going."

She looked down at her arthritic hands. "I wasn't so bad as I am now, but times I'd be that exhausted I'd fall in bed at night and not be able to sleep. When he could still get about, I'd bar the door at night, so he couldn't get out, but that wouldn't stop him roamin' around the house knockin' things over. Sometimes I'd get up and guide him back to bed but other times, I'd just lie there and listen and hope that God would soon see fit to bring it all to an end."

She looked at Nora, a long inquiring look. "By and by, he got the pneumonia and that took the good right out of him. He never got out of the bed after that."

"He don't look too good, Peg. His breathin' is shockin' bad. Maybe we should get the doctor to come from Placentia or maybe Father O'Reilly." Mary Anne looked from Peg to the wizened man in the bed.

"No, Mary Anne, we'll do none of that. He wouldn't want it. I'll give him a nice wash and a change of bed sheets and clothes and he'll do better then." Peg went to the kitchen and filled a basin with warm water and reached for the towel above the stove. She pressed it to her face. It was warm and full of the sweet smell of the outdoors. She smiled tiredly and tucked the towel under her arm.

"See that the clean sheets are put to warm," she called over her shoulder, and we'll need a few beach stones from the fire to warm the bed." She disappeared into the front room and closed the door. He lay on his back, inert, a thin grey man in striped flannel pyjamas, his eyes closed as if sleeping. She paused a moment to look at his skeletal image and turned to place the basin on the side table.

"Who are you?" The voice, surprisingly strong, startled her. It was like some hidden demon had awoken inside of him, had mustered up the strength to be hurtful. His eyelids slipped back in a smooth mechanical movement and she was looking into two eyeballs that were pale and moist like a clam. Peg could just as easily have asked the same question. There was so little left of the man she knew: bones covered with folds of slack yellow skin, dull lank hair, a mind sucked dry like a bone cleaned of its marrow.

"Good morning, Matt. It's me, Peg. How about a shave and a wash?"

His eyes rolled open but there was no reply.

She lathered the shaving brush like she had watched her father do so often. Early on, when Matt first took to his bed for good, she used to think about her father as she did this part of the job. He always hummed to himself as he shaved and usually burst into song when the job was done. It put her at ease and in a happy frame of mind to remember him. Now, sitting on the side of the bed, she thought only of Matt. She chatted to him as she scraped his hollow face and neck, telling him about the weather or any bit of news that was about and sometimes just making it up. His eyes followed her. She dampened the end of a small towel and wiped away the soapy remains, rinsed once more and then gently patted dry his damp hairline, mouth and neck. All the while he stared with blank eyes.

Bit by bit she followed her ritual: first one shoulder, then the other, his chest, thin arms, the long bony fingers of his hands. Only now, now that he was gone from her, could she touch him, look at him, feel the warm pulse of his body. He could no longer turn away. She continued, tucking the warm towels about his upper body while she washed his withered buttocks, his legs and genitals, carefully parting the slack folds of skin and wiping him clean. Her face remained serene, no flinching, no grimacing, no longing. It made no difference now; all she could do was care for him and make him comfortable. She was glad to do that.

When she had finished, she put on his fresh pyjamas. "There now, that feels better, I'll allow." There was no reply. At this point she liked to sit on the side of the bed for a spell, hold his hand and search his eyes, hoping to see that faint glimmer of recognition that told her he was still there. Sometimes she was rewarded with what seemed like a faint ray of light behind his eyes, the very beginnings of a smile or a slight pressure from his hand. These were the private intimate moments in her day when she could be close to him. Somehow in his need, something had changed between them. The touching of flesh to flesh, the salve of fresh clean water, the cleansing, had brought to her a new feeling of love and contentment, one that she would never have dreamed possible in the circumstances. It was a feeling at once powerful and gentle, a deep tenderness that had not been there before, and it filled her with a kind of happiness that needed no explanation, a happiness that would remain with her forever, warming her soul in years to come, making her firm in the knowledge that they were steadfastly bound to each other.

She leaned over and stroked his forehead and then called out to Mary Anne. Together they rolled him over and slipped the clean sheets onto the mattress and placed the hot beach stones wrapped in wool socks between the blankets but clear of his feet.

"I'll see to the sheets now while you get him something to eat." Mary Anne departed with the bundle under her arm.

It was a waste of time getting food for him. Peg knew that, but nonetheless she went to the kitchen and mixed up a couple of spoonfuls of the white powdery baby food that Pat had brought from Placentia. She took it in to him and sat on the bedside, spoon poised. "Just a small drop," she whispered, pressing the spoon to his lips. She watched silently as the thin gruel, mixed with a trickle of saliva, slid along his lips and ran from the corner of his mouth. She scooped the runny liquid onto the spoon. "Look," she said, tasting the sticky mess, "it's good." She brought the spoon back to his mouth. "You must eat, my darling," she whispered urgently, her eyes bright with tears. But he stared back at her with wide frightened eyes and finally she gave up and took the food back to the kitchen.

23

"*Those* days, Mary Anne was a wonderful friend to me. Every day she'd come by to help. She'd do the work about the house, mostly washin', and there was plenty of that, and I'd just tend to Matt. Pat came when he could. He laid in the wood for the winter that year and brought food and supplies from Placentia so we were well stocked up.

"Many times now, girl, I wonder why God sent him to me from halfways 'round the world. Did he mean to open a door for me so I could walk right through and have a different life? I stepped through the open door all right but there were many other doors I should have gone through instead of just standin' there listenin' and lookin' and wonderin' what might have been."

"What would you have done differently?" Nora asked.

"I don't know. Maybe tried to get him to come out of himself a bit more. To get over the feeling that he was an outsider. But you know something, Nora? Even when you belong to a place, you can still become an outsider. For years I cut myself off from everyone and sided with him. I should never have done that. You can't live like that. It's hard to understand but you know how it is sometimes: we just go along day to day and do whatever we can to make life manageable. I wish I had found a way to say right out in plain words what was deep in my heart. In a way I thought I was preserving what we had, bottling it away like you would a few turrs or a bit of fruit, the way it would last."

There was a long pause before she continued. "I was always afraid that if I pushed too hard he'd be gone and I'd not see him no more." She turned to look out across the water into the dark night. "When things turned bad with his health, it was a struggle then to keep going. It all became too much."

The wind was from the north. It savaged its way along the side of the wood-frame house, seeking out small cracks and sending icy chills into the makeshift bedroom that had been set up in the parlour. Peg stood in the grey light by the window, alone with her thoughts. In the garden the ground lay fallow, ragged and unkempt, thick with dying weeds and grass. Inside the fence, the mounds of the potato ridges were still visible, like small waves on the landscape. The past spring, she had put down a small patch of vegetables close enough to the house to see them through the winter, but had it not been for Mary Anne's husband, Pius, they would still be in the ground rotting away. Those days, not even a year past, Matt had worked alongside of her, like a child, helping for short spurts, sometimes being a nuisance, undoing what she had done, but more times he'd be off in a corner, busy doing other things. She had to be watchful, making sure he didn't roam. When the weather was fine it was so much easier to cope. She could recall then the warmth of the sun on her back as she stooped to the earth, and hear the wind tug at the endless rows of washing on the line

They would never plant the garden again. Those days were done; the weeds around the edges would take over and the long grass would come right to the door and grow strong and tall in the rich ground. Winter was just around the corner, and with Matt and the state he was in, she knew in her heart that she couldn't endure another January on the island. Yet each time Pat came she couldn't bring herself to make a decision.

The wind came hard against the house again and she thought she felt the floor shake beneath her feet. All her life she had hated the wind, feared the force that could in a minute whip up the sea into a frenzy of rage and fling her father, his boat, and the silvery cod fish he'd caught, high in the air and then send it all crashing back down into the cold black water. She sat now, transfixed by her old nightmare. "Take away the night," she had begged her father one time as they sat home curled up in his big chair while the storm battered the house. She had clung tightly to him, afraid that he might have to up and leave her, but he'd wrapped his great arms about her and held her all night close to his warm chest until the wind quieted and her little body relaxed into sleep. Peg wrapped herself now in her own arms and shivered.

A harsh raspy intake of breath sounded from the bed behind her and brought her back to reality with a start. She turned. A scrawny arm reached from beneath the blankets into the chilly air. She went to his side, taking his hand in both of hers. His eyes were closed, his face passive. She pressed the long fingers to her cheek; there was so little to hold on to anymore. Then without warning his eyes shot open. Wide and bright with fear, they stared at her long and hard. Terror hit the pit of her stomach. Something was happening, something she wanted but couldn't admit to. The hand gripped her fiercely. It was strong and unyielding.

The busy clanging of pots and pans came from the kitchen. Mary Anne was making such a racket.

She shivered again. It was cold, so cold … "The coldest room in the house," her mother always said. Then it came to her, a fire, yes, like Christmas time. She would light a fire in the old grate. No matter that the wood was supposed to last the winter. They would manage. Her heart was hammering inside her chest, making her breathless. A deep sense of urgency swept over her. She lifted the blankets to put the cold hand back in the warmth. The smell rose from beneath the covers. He needed changing again and he was cold.

She rushed to the door. "The fire, we must light the fire." Her voice was sharp.

Mary Anne straightened up from her position over the stove and looked at Peg. "A fire is a good idea," she said, accepting without question this sudden request.

Peg nodded, looking about her, uncertain what to do next. Her father's face came to her. If only he were here. He would know what to do. He'd have the fire in and lighted in no time. Suddenly she felt helpless and confused, unable to make a decision about a simple thing like lighting a fire.

Mary Anne was in the doorway, her arms laden with sticks. "Matches, Peg?" she called over her shoulder, stacking the dry wood with expert hands.

Peg, spurred into action, hurried to the kitchen and returned with matches. The fire leapt in the grate, warm, bright. Peg watched, transfixed. Black smoke puffed back into the room from the chimney.

"Crack the window, just a small bit. The chimney's cold, we needs a draft."

Peg sprang into action. The fire began to draw nicely and roar up the chimney.

"A few nice junks now and she'll be best kind." Mary Anne looked towards Peg and inclined her head towards the kitchen. Without a word, Peg hurried out of the bedroom and returned with an armful of logs and set them by the fire.

Mary Anne piled on the wood and, satisfied that the fire was going well, gave Peg the okay to close the window and then went to the bed. "There's a change needed again." She was gone to the kitchen before Peg could object.

Nobody cleaned and washed him but her. But like it or not, the job was underway and somehow Peg didn't have the will to stop it. Something had gone from her in those last few minutes, like her energy had suddenly drained away, running backwards through her veins and out into the floor beneath her feet. But it was more than that. It was a kind of resignation, a feeling deep down that it was over, that she could no longer protect him.

They worked together then, washing, cleaning, intent on his comfort. The fire blazed, the smell of fresh linen sweet in the room. His eyes were closed and he looked peaceful. When they had banked up the pillows and settled him comfortably, Mary Anne turned to Peg. "You need a cup of tea, girl. Now build up the fire and come in the kitchen."

Peg watched Mary Anne leave the room, the soiled sheets in her arms. It was all right, she decided, settling a junk on the blazing fire. It was just business that needed doing.

"I believe he has a like to die and it won't be too long," Mary Anne said gently over tea, with the assurance of someone who has witnessed the beginning and end of life on many occasions. "I'll stay and be with you while he's drawing a breath."

Peg's heart had ceased its pounding. The hot sweet tea had settled her as it always did. "Thank you, Mary Anne, I believe you are right, but I'd rather be alone tonight, if you don't mind. I think I can manage now. Maybe you'd come by in the morning."

Mary Anne looked at her friend. "Peg," she began, but seemed to lose the words that were on the tip of her tongue. She tried again. "I knows how you are, you has your own ideas and you knows what you wants. I've learned that over the past few years so I'm not going to argue with you." She tapped her mug with her fingernails, making a little tinkling sound like pennies dropping in a jar. "Time was, I thought you was a bit up on yourself, but I knows better now. You are a good, kind woman, no doubt about it, and strong too. I've wanted to tell you that, Peg, but didn't know how. So there it is. Anyway, if that's what you wants, girl, then it's fine with me." She stood to go. "There's a nice bit of rabbit stew on the stove for your supper. Mind you eat now. You're goin' needin' your strength for what's to come. I'll see you in the mornin'."

"That night I kept the fire going in the room and the lamp burning. Nice it was, not at all like someone was dyin'. I felt content. Can you believe that?" She cast a sideways glance at Nora. "It's true, yes, I was content. I had done the best I could by Matt and now it was time. I piled the wood high on the fire and made it blaze and roar up the chimney and I did the same in the kitchen. I'd have no more need of the junks piled up outside, no need to spare the lamp oil. I sat by his bed the whole night and I'd only stir to tend the fire or make a cup of tea. Around three o'clock I began to nod off, so to keep myself awake I had the idea that maybe I could read to him, you know like we used do together nights."

"What a lovely idea, Peg." Nora, to her surprise, was feeling quite emotional. "What did you read?"

"He had given me a little book of poems one time. He got it to Dicks and Company in St. John's. It was a collection of sonnets by different poets, all decorated inside with delicate, pale coloured vines and wildflowers. It was there by my bed when I got back from the hospital. That's where I still keep it. That was what I decided to read to him." She began to fidget. "I thought it was a lovely idea too at the time, but once I started, it seemed to kind of … put me over the edge and suddenly made me realize what was happening: this was the end. I was struggling, the beautiful words touching a sore spot inside of me when the next thing, my God in heaven, didn't he rise up from in the bed and call out clear as a bell, 'Peg' and then fell back on the pillows and was gone."

Peg looked across at Nora. "He called my name," she said simply.

24

The doorbell jangled. Nora stood on the doorstep of the presbytery, uncertain, wishing now that she had declined the priest's invitation to come by again. She wanted to be off on the water with Pat.

The door opened. "Back again?" the housekeeper's voice sang out, cutting off Nora's planned opener. "Father is in the parlour waiting for you." She jerked her head in the direction of the door on the left.

"Thank you." Nora strode past into the hall, stood by the parlour door and waited for the housekeeper to show her in. She nodded her head in thanks and walked purposefully into the room. In her mind, the old priest had taken on the role of an adversary, but now as she entered the hot stuffy room, she saw an old man struggling to get to his feet to greet her.

"Please," she murmured, indicating that he should stay seated, and quickly took the chair across from him as she had done the day before. The housekeeper disappeared and the door closed quietly. Nora listened for the retreat of footsteps but heard nothing. There would be no tea today and Nora was glad.

"Lovely day today. You've had a fine spell of weather. Mary tells me you even managed to get to the garden party."

"Yes, I did but I didn't see her there. It's been a great visit."

"You have come all this way, Miss Molloy, to find out about your grandfather, and I've been thinking that maybe I could have been more helpful yesterday. However, you know how it is. One has to be so careful, especially if one is a priest."

Over the rim of his heavy glasses, the pale watery eyes looked earnest.

"What is it you would like to know? I may be able to fill in some of the gaps for you." The glasses slipped forward as he dipped his head still more to observe his visitor.

It was a game, Nora decided, a continuous game of cat and mouse, of dodging in and out of hiding places, showing yourself briefly, then taking off again to yet another hiding spot. She turned away. Was he just a lonely old man with neither chit nor child to warm his old age, someone who wanted to keep his visitor here as long as possible for the chat? Or was he a cunning old fox, looking to find out what she had learned, smart enough to know what he wanted and cute enough to get it? Why can't he just say what he has to say and let her be gone? It was her turn and he was waiting.

"I have spoken with a lot of people who knew him, including yourself, and I think have learned most of what there is to be learned about his life here, unless of course you have something more to add. I know there are circumstances but–"

"Do you know that he betrayed his father, not intentionally of course, but, let us say, inadvertently caused his death?"

Nora straightened, became alert like an animal sensing danger. "What do you mean?"

"When he was a small boy, only five or six years old, I believe, his father Joseph Molloy got himself in a bit of trouble. He was a fine man by all accounts, literate, a leader, active within the Fenian

KATE EVANS

231

Movement in the fight for independence." His eyes searched her startled eyes for a look that might indicate that he should continue.

"Yes. I mean, no." She was confused, couldn't think what to say.

"It was the time of The Land League in Ireland, late 1800s. It seems Matt's father was right in there, with the great leader at the time, Charles Stuart Parnell, and his followers. There was an important rent agreement in place, between tenants and landlords. As I recall, it was called The Land Act. Rents were controlled, the amount being worked out in accordance with the value of the crops produced. This agreement was to put an end to the terrible repression and cruelty associated with evictions."

He leaned back in his chair and tapped his lips with his steepled fingers. "That was fine while the crops were good but when things turned bad the old problem sprung up again. The people couldn't pay their rents and the threat of evictions loomed again. Well, it seems that at that time Joseph Molloy led the fight in his area to restore justice. It turned out to be a bitter and violent time. The upshot of it was that a landlord in the area was murdered and his house torched one night. They came looking for Joseph Molloy the next day."

"They're here," he said to his wife as he walked into the kitchen. "You'll leave me to do the talking." Then he went straight to the fireplace, reached into the thatch in the corner and withdrew a gun. In one quick movement he lifted the lid off the kettle, where it hung above the fire, dropped it into the steaming water and replaced the lid. Then he turned to the boy. "Shsh ... You hear me, Matt, not a word." He raised his finger to his lips. "Now go to your mother, there's a good ladeen." He brought his finger to his lips again, making a soft shshing sound, and winked reassuringly at the boy. He was stoking the fire when they kicked open the door.

They watched, petrified, as their kitchen was torn apart. Frustrated and angry, the intruders turned on Joseph Molloy. The first kick behind his knee brought him down. The next was to the side of his head and everything began to swim.

"The back room, turn it out."

The child ran to his mother, grabbing her around the leg, peeping terrified from behind her skirts. The kettle began to boil, steam driving the lid to an urgent rat tat tat. The lid bounced and hopped madly, demanding attention. In a flash the boy broke away from his mother and ran to stand with his back to the rattling kettle in his childish attempt to help.

"So, what is our little man hiding?" Coarse cloth brushed his face as he was shoved aside.

The old priest moved uncomfortably in his chair. "They took the father away that day and that was the last they saw of him alive. Later that night, his body was taken from the side of a ditch, a bullet through his head."

Nora stared at the priest. How could he know all this? If Matt had told anyone of his ordeal it would have been Peg. She was certain. Could Peg have known and not told her?

The sunlight struggled to penetrate the heavy lace on the windows. She thought how nice it would be to walk over into the spacious bay of the window and draw back the curtains, watch the excitement as the light danced and played with the dust motes, and then open the window wide to the fresh air and the living noise of the town. She fell back against the hard upright chair, seeing in her mind the tiny kitchen, the big open hearth with its smoky black fire irons and the fat-bellied kettle, flames to its bottom, holding within the fate of a family.

Betrayed! She sat up alarmed. Was that the word the priest had used? Betrayed. He was talking about a child. "Who told you this?" Her voice was razor thin.

The priest didn't move and for a moment she thought he hadn't heard. Then, he shifted slightly, pulled himself upwards and gradually settled back into the same position. "My dear child." He adjusted the glasses on his nose. "As a priest of God, I have an obligation to my parishioners. When we place someone in a position of trust, they have to be of exceptional moral character. We have to run a check and it was no different with Mr. Molloy." He cleared his throat. "I have connections in Ireland, from my days over there in the seminary, so I was in a position to put out a few discreet feelers. It's no trouble to find what you are looking for when you know where to look." He peered at her. How neatly he had tied up the package to suit his own plans.

"Father O'Reilly." She held his gaze. "Did he know that you had delved into his past, that you had checked him out?"

He dismissed her query, quite obviously sure of the righteousness of his action. "No, no point to that," he said. "It was not necessary to disclose that."

There was no embarrassment in that matter-of-fact look, no discomfort. His two big inward-pointing feet lay motionless on the worn rug. They seemed ridiculously large today, cumbersome and awkward, incapable of dancing. It occurred to her that he almost certainly knew something of her grandmother.

"Do you, by any chance, know what became of my grandmother, his wife?"

"Yes." He stretched the word out as if reluctant to continue and then took a deep breath. "During the Troubles in the twenties when the Black and Tans were about the country terrorizing innocent people, they set upon the poor woman one night and burnt the roof from over her head for no reason, it seems, other than

WHERE OLD *Ghosts* MEET

234

that she was a bit of a recluse and they decided she had something to hide. She lost everything that night. The boy, your father, was with her."

Nora's head nodded in agreement.

"I'm told she was never the same after that. There was nowhere for her to go but back to her brother's place or the County Home. She went to her brother. It seems from then on the poor soul cried day and night. One day she took a shovel to the house and smashed every window and then started on the inside; anything that was breakable, she destroyed. She was taken off to the mental hospital and never came back. She died there, I'm afraid."

"And my father, her son?" Nora could barely get the words out.

"He was away at school when she was taken away. He never came back to the uncle's house. He stayed on at the school during the holidays. There were always the few youngsters who had nowhere to go. Then he joined the seminary, but of course, like his father, he left before ordination. But, my dear, I want to tell you this and I know it to be a fact: your father visited his mother once a month at the hospital until the day she died."

Nora pushed her fist into her stomach to suppress a feeling of nausea. The space felt hollowed out, sour and barren. She needed to get back to her car. "I must go." She pushed herself to her feet. The sudden movement made her feel light-headed.

"Please. Stay." The priest struggled from the depths of his armchair.

She offered her hand. "Thank you." Her voice was quiet.

"I'm sorry, my dear." He took her hand. "But I thought you would want to know."

"It's okay, thank you. I have to meet someone. Thank you." She hurried from the room into the hall, fumbled with the latch on the front door but couldn't get it open.

"Let me do that. It's a bit stiff. We could do with a new lock." He moved forward and in a moment had the door open. She stepped eagerly into the sunshine, reaching for the handrail on the steps to steady herself. At the bottom she turned briefly. His hand was raised as if in blessing.

Before getting into the car she glanced back again. The door to the presbytery was already closed.

25

It lifted Nora's spirits to see Pat, his broad stocky frame and smiling face waiting for her aboard his boat at the wharf. She knew him now to be a kind and considerate man who was protective of his elderly aunt and she liked that.

"Careful now, let me have your hand." The boat lurched as she stepped on board.

She felt a surge of excitement. Berry Island was now deeply entrenched in her imagination. She had a strange longing to see the place, to smell the grass, to walk the paths that she had travelled with Peg as she told her story, but most of all she wanted to go from room to room in the house and put it all into perspective. This was where she felt it would finally come together for her.

"Are you good on the water?" He eyed her up and down as if somehow the set of her body would tell him what he needed to know.

"Yes, fine, I think, so long as it's not too rough."

"She's lookin' best kind for today. Keep an eye where you're headed and you'll be fine."

Nora looked about her as he busied himself with the ropes. It was a smallish craft with a cabin up front to house the wheel and engine, homemade by the looks of the finish.

"She's sturdy enough," he said, as if he had sensed her uncertainty.

She nodded.

The engine leaped to life, the water churning noisily, sending a flock of seagulls into sudden and angry departure. The boat pulled away and headed out towards the black tip of the headland. The wind tugged at her hair and filled her thin blouse with a blustery chill. She remembered how cold the water had been on her feet and shivered. The boat surged forward as he shifted gear.

"There's a jacket there. You'll be needin' that when we get beyond the headland."

She reached eagerly for the red plaid jacket on the hook behind her. It was way too big and the sleeves hung below her hands but it was cozy and warm and kept out the biting wind. She pulled the collar up and wrapped the jacket snugly around her body. The boat sped forward, pitching and dipping on the waves as it moved into top gear. She grabbed the rail and braced herself. She had never been on the open sea in a small craft before and it was a little frightening. She had a fleeting image of her grandfather and his first foray into the world of fishing on the waters of the cold North Atlantic. She felt his misery: no suitable clothing, raw and inexperienced, the men likely having a bit of sport at his expense, delighted to show this townie how a real man makes a living. She gathered up her shoulders protectively, burying her nose in the pocket of warmth that rose from inside the jacket. She could smell the heavy odour of work.

Her eyes met Pat's and he flicked his head backward, a question. Was everything all right?

She nodded.

"You've had a fine time with Aunt Peg." His voice boomed above the noise of the engine. "She's taken quite the liking to you."

Nora smiled. "She's a wonderful woman."

"You'll be writing to her then from time to time?"

"Yes, I'll be writing to her and I'll be back. For a short visit," she added, mocking him.

"Maybe find yourself a good Newfoundlander? I have a young fella to St. John's, not married, finest kind. Be perfect for you."

Nora laughed. Now there was a thought. The Molloys settling down in Newfoundland again, and with the same crew!

"Now wouldn't that be somethin'?" He was reading her mind.

"Pat, you know she has a lot of books and stamps belonging to Matt."

"Yes, I suppose I do. Brought them all from the island, didn't I? Bloody ridiculous, I thought at the time. But you know now, there's no arguing with Aunt Peg."

"They are valuable. And she insists that I have them."

"That's what he wanted, I believe."

"So she says."

"Then that's it. Got nothin' to do with me, so long as you don't want them packed up again and sent to Montreal. I had enough of that."

"No, I'll arrange that."

"I believe she loved him," he said suddenly out of the blue, "though she never did say." He looked across at her for confirmation.

"You think?" She looked away then so he couldn't see her lips move. "They loved each other," she whispered.

"You don't say much. As I recall, it was hard to get the word out of him too. Like a gull on a rock he was, a real loner. Most he ever said to me, apart from when I was in school, was one day I was over to Aunt Peg's. He said, 'Learnin' to read is the most important thing you'll ever do in your whole life.' I didn't believe him at the time. Learnin' to fish, read the weather, handle the boat, that's what was important to me then. But I kept me mouth shut."

"Was he right?"

"Well, girl, I know there's truth to it for sure, but I don't know that it's more important than learnin' to make a livin'."

They were beyond the headland now and on the open sea. The boat rolled and dipped more violently, but while it was a bit unnerving, it was also exhilarating.

"I'm going outside on deck for a while."

"Mind you hold that rail. You're not used to the roll."

She staggered to the rail, grabbing it tightly. The coast was far behind them now and she watched silently as the black streak of land and cliff gradually disappeared into the ocean. Parting from Peg had been difficult for Nora. She had developed a quiet but intense admiration for the gentle woman, who had taken her, with honest and endearing openness, through the depth and breadth of her life, sharing her most private and tender moments, her fears and anxieties, her simple need to love and be loved.

Nora watched as the water churned, boiling and frothing convulsively as it formed a perfect "V" in the wake of the boat. In the distance it dissipated and disappeared. For a long time she stood there, mesmerized by the constant motion, recalling bits and pieces of events related to the past few days. It would take weeks, even months or years, before she would be able to process it all and come to terms with what she had heard. Right now she couldn't make up her mind if she admired the man in any way or even if she liked him. Her grip tightened as the boat pitched. She could certainly understand his rejection of the water; it was cold and inhospitable, constantly shifting, unpredictable and treacherous. She turned away and tottered back to the comparative safety of the cabin. Pat, at the wheel, was silent, scanning the horizon.

"All right?" He turned to look at her, concerned.

"Yes, I'm fine. Just thinking, you know."

"You'll be anxious to see the old house. It's lookin' bad these days. Been picked over. Furniture stolen and the like."

"Who would do the like of that?"

"Oh, youngsters out pokin' about, nothin' better to do. Sometimes people from away lookin' for old stuff. Once a house is left empty, it don't take long for it to fall apart. I'll drop you to the wharf and you can follow the path around to Peg's place. The graveyard is up over the hill. Nothing would do her, when Mr. Molloy died, but to have him buried right there on the island. I had to go dig a hole in the middle of November and the ground half froze, right on the spot she chose. Then she wanted a white painted rail all around it, and if that wasn't enough, a special stone was ordered from St. John's with some lines or other that he liked cut right onto the stone. You'll see it above in the graveyard. In time it was all done as she wanted. He was to have a decent marker and that was all there was to it. I suppose she wanted it there in case, down the road when she was gone, the likes of you was to come lookin' for the place he was buried."

"You're a good man, Pat. Peg is lucky to have you." She fixed him with a straight honest look. "I'm grateful also. Thank you. I'm glad to know he didn't leave the world alone and abandoned."

He nodded and said no more but continued to scan the horizon. "There she is." He was pointing.

"Where?"

"That way," he said, "at two o'clock."

She followed his gaze to the dark spot on the horizon. Like a mirage, the grey-black mound grew bigger and bigger. Nora stood, eyes glued to the spot, eager for the first sight of the place that had once been Peg's home. The outline was becoming sharper; rocky headlands jutted out into the ocean, forming small coves and inlets. She could distinguish now the white shaley angles of the cliff face and the scrubby thatch of green firs on the crown of the hill. White spray drenched the pock-marked coastline, leaping into the air and collapsing into a frenzy of froth and white foam. Birds screamed and soared away to safe places amongst the cracks and crevices. The boat headed for a wide opening between two headlands. Suddenly the houses appeared, strung like jagged ornaments around the wide neck of the cove.

"I'm going outside again," she said, her excitement mounting.

The houses drifted by, one by one. Some, looking gloomy and dilapidated, leaned heavily to one side, while others stood erect, refusing to succumb to wind and weather, steadfastly retaining a quiet dignity. She was thinking about him, fifty years ago coming through the same way. He probably stood aboard a ferry boat scanning the shoreline as she did now, a small package tucked away carefully in his jacket pocket, a gift to deliver from a soldier husband. Now, that was something she could admire, she admitted with a certain degree of pleasure: to come such a long way in order to follow through on a promise. That was admirable.

A tap at the window made her turn. Pat was pointing to the left. He poked his head around the door. "There she is."

She could barely hear him above the noise of the engine. She followed his pointing finger to a simple square two-story house with peeling white clapboard. "The white one?" she mouthed, pointing, looking to Pat for confirmation.

He nodded.

She stared at the house passing in front of her eyes. The green trim on the windows and about the door was still visible. It looked solid and neat. Emotion welled up inside of her. She shut her eyes, momentarily unsure what she was feeling. This was it, the home where Peg and her grandfather had lived, the place Peg had finally abandoned out of sheer necessity. She turned eagerly to Pat in the wheel-house. He winked, jerking his head slightly. When she looked again the house had slipped past.

The throttle on the engine shifted and the boat slowed down. They were coming alongside of what was left of a wharf.

Nora watched him leap ashore and tie up.

"Mind your step." He grabbed her hand as she stepped off the boat. "You'll be okay while I'm gone?" He searched her face. "I'll be by again in a couple of hours." Without waiting for an answer he continued, "You can walk all the way round either way, to the point or up and over the top." His arm swept about the cove.

"Where's the gulch?"

An inquiring look crossed his eyes and he hesitated just a moment before answering. "Just keep on goin' away from the cemetery across the cliff. You can't miss it. Be careful. It's a rough spot."

"Great."

"Here's a lunch Bride made for you, case you gets hungry. The restaurant here's closed down!" He grinned and passed her a paper bag.

"Thanks, Pat." She reached over and took the bag. "I'll see you in a couple of hours." She checked her watch. "I'll be watching for you."

He stepped back on board, surefooted and confident, gave her a wave and was off, swinging out in a wide arc and heading for the open sea. The steady throb of the engine carried across the water. She followed the boat's progress until it was no more than a speck and was gone. She was alone. In the sudden quiet she could hear the water lapping on the pylons below her feet. She looked down and with a start she realized that she was standing on a rotting platform of broken boards and gaping holes. She jumped down onto the stony beach and picked her way carefully up a grassy slope where she decided to sit for a while, maybe get a feel for the place before taking the path out along the arm.

She spread Pat's jacket on the grass and unpacked the lunch he had given her. The sight of food made her realize that she was starving and she tucked into the meat sandwich with gusto. She drew her knees close to her chest as she munched and stared at the desolation across the water. Empty windows, like plucked-out eye sockets, stared back at her. Everything seemed more dilapidated, less romantic now that she was at close quarters. She tried to picture the place full of life, people working, children playing and laughing, the smell of the fish.

She spotted a rough-looking shack a little way along the beach and decided to take a look. Perched on top of long spindly stilts, it had been a neat little structure at one time, but now it was tipping slightly to one side and the door hung open on one hinge. She didn't dare trust her weight on the wooden platform, but inside she could see the remains of a rusty potbelly stove, a scrap of frayed rope dangling from a nail, and close to the stove a few upturned crates. The only hint of colour was a piece of an orange plastic float lying by the door.

She turned away and headed towards the path that led to Peg's house. It was barely visible now, just a beaten-down track that was partly overgrown. The grass on either side grew long and silky and swayed gently in the breeze off the water. She ran her fingers along the heads of the tall buttercups and stooped to smell the spiky pink clover tips and inspect the clumps of tiny star-like flowers that she couldn't identify. She pulled at a long stalk of grass, nibbling on the pale succulent end. She passed one house and then another and another, noticing the perfect symmetry of some houses, windows equally spaced, doorway neatly centred. Others were more haphazard in style, built, she suspected, more for utility and without much thought for style. She stopped to look at small details like a pretty pattern around a doorway, carefully carved by someone with a love of the beautiful as well as the practical, detailed mouldings around windows and doors, a fragment of faded cotton flapping by a broken window, a clump of tall yellow daisies nestled by a faded blue doorway. She tried to imagine who might have lived there, perhaps someone she'd met: Foxy, who had danced her round and round with great glee at the garden party, or Mary Anne or Gerry Quinlan?

Farther along, the old schoolhouse had keeled over completely. Two faded pinkish walls leaning precariously inward and braced by a solitary beam were all that remained. It stood on a rise, back from the main path, conspicuous by its colour. Someone had made a valiant effort to try to keep the old school on its feet.

Behind the school she picked up the path that led to the graveyard. Her heart raced as she hurried forward, taking long purposeful strides. Up ahead, like a mouthful of crooked and broken teeth, the grey-white headstones poked out of the hillside. It was an exposed spot with only meagre shelter from wind and weather provided by a few trees that hung together for support like ragged beggars. In this place sheltered hollows were reserved for the comfort of the living. She waded through the long grass, eager to see his name. There were so many: Mallaley, Tobin, O'Reilly.

John Quinlan
of
Waterford, Ireland
1853 - 1901
and
His loving wife
Mary Margaret
1856 - 1906
Requistat Im Pace

She went from one to another, reading the words, tributes to lives lived, hands clasped in prayer. This was me, I was here, important. Remembered.

McGrath
1864 - 1895
Gone but not forgotten

The same names were repeated over and over, men and women, their sons and daughters, the first people to inhabit this tiny isolated island and their descendants.

She stopped by a sprawling wild rose bush thick with bright pink roses and heavy with a rich sweet perfume. As she stood there she spotted the remains of the white rail farther up on the hill. It stood apart from the other graves, commanding a larger space and a substantial headstone. Now that she had found it she felt suddenly shy, reluctant to approach.

Matthew Molloy
Late of
Roscommon
Ireland
Died November 14, 1962
R.I.P.

Seeing his name, her name, in black letters neatly carved, shocked her. She read it again. There it was for the record, simple and to the point, his marker saying he had been here.

Nora reached down and drew back the long grass from around the base of the stone and read, as carefully as a child might, faltering over partly obscured letters.

He shall not hear the bittern cry
In the wild sky, where he is lain,
Nor voices of the sweeter birds
Above the wailing of the rain.

She knew these lines, knew them backwards, as did every school child in Ireland. She finished the lines, reciting them aloud:

Nor shall he know when loud March blows
Thro' slanting snows her fanfare shrill,
Blowing to flame the golden cup
Of many an upset daffodil.

A young poet, Francis Ledwidge, had jotted down these lines while working as a labourer on a building site in London. In the end he had lost his life on the battlefield at Flanders. This poem had been a favourite with her father. It was the one he would recite in his more mellow moments, his party piece. She felt overcome by a deep sadness, aching feelings of opportunities missed, people lost and forgotten.

Nora let the grass slip back into place. She stood silent at the foot of the grave but could find no words to say, so she blessed herself quickly, muttered a short prayer and turned away. As she passed the rose bush the sweet perfume again caught her attention. She stopped and on an impulse plucked a pink rose from its thorny branch, ran back to the grave, gently drew back the long grass and laid the flower by the poet's words, then turned and hurried off back down the hill. She didn't stop until she reached Peg's old house.

It was beautifully situated in a snug, sheltered hollow with the ground running down to a small inlet. Now that she was close up, the house appeared to list slightly to one side, and several of the windows were shattered, but other than that it seemed to be in better condition than many of the others. She felt a rush of excitement and, after a moment's hesitation, stepped off the path, lifting her feet high, grabbing at tufts of long grass for support. The ground was uneven and she stumbled. Poking about with her foot she discovered rutted mounds and realized she was standing in what used to be the garden. The ridges under her feet were his potato furrows. Pictures flooded her mind, bits and pieces of a past life. She reached into the long grass, separating the stalks, hoping for a better look at what once was. She wanted to feel the soil, let it run between her fingers, but a tight skin of grass and weed had grown over the mounds, sealing them tightly. They would remain like that for years to come, visible to the observant eye in the spring of the year when the grass was young and low to the ground.

Her fingers touched something rough and stringy. She pulled and a length of grey rope came away from the grass. She was about to drop it when she saw a solitary wooden clothespin dangling limply from one end. She unhooked the wooden pin, pinched it open and closed. How had Peg ever managed those last few months? She slipped it into her pocket and held it tightly in her fist.

The house now became solid and real. She could touch the rough dry texture of the white wooden clapboard, pick at the flaking paint on the doorpost, and see the carefully fitted mouldings that had at one time made this an attractive house. The glass in one window, the one to the right, was still intact. A sun-bleached statue of the Virgin Mary stood in the window, looking forlornly to the outdoors. The door was slightly ajar, as if someone was already within. She hesitated, aware of the uncanny quietness which hung about the place. The door refused to open any farther. She lifted up the handle and leaned into the wood. It gave way and she was standing in the hallway. She had expected to find a semblance of Peg's old home but there was only desolation. The kitchen to the left was empty except for the old stove that had been ripped from the wall, dragged halfway across the room and now lay tipped over in the middle of the floor. The remains of the metal stovepipe dangled from a hole in the chimney. She stepped cautiously through the doorway onto the worn linoleum that still lay smooth and tight to the floorboards. A picture of the Sacred Heart, exactly the same one that had hung in the kitchen at home in Ireland, hung on the wall askew, the glass shattered. A rosary dangled on a nail alongside. Nora walked across the room, reached up and straightened the picture. The face staring at her looked more dejected than ever.

Fresh air from the broken window swept across the room like a silent breath. She reached for a small tin box on the window ledge and pried it open. Tea, the faint smell trapped for years, still remained. She tried to imagine the kitchen as it had been: Matt's chair, the smooth wooden table with the dark shiny groove, the old lamp. Around her feet years and years of activity showed on the worn linoleum.

The door across the hall was closed. The front room. She stopped for a moment and then headed up over the stairs. The treads groaned with each step. She moved stealthily, her eyes alert for danger. All about her the light, the walls, the air, all had a grey pallor, like death. Standing on the landing she felt the slope in the floor where the house was listing. A storm or two and she'd buckle at the knees and come down just like the others. Nora peeped in each room but, like the kitchen, they were stripped almost bare. She thanked God that Peg had had the good sense not to come back. She crept back down the stairs, holding tightly to the wobbly rail, anxious to be safe on the ground floor again.

"Still shut off," she said aloud as she approached the closed door. All of a sudden she felt giddy and childish. "Well, Matt Molloy," she continued, "you are about to be confronted by your granddaughter." She knocked lightly, her ear to the door, mocking the silence. She knocked again, louder this time, insistent. She put her ear to the door again. *Open the door, Richard.* The words of the song came to her. She was singing in a whisper, *Open the door and let me in.* Then angry at her timidness she sang out, *Open the door, Matthew, Matthew, why don't you o—pen the door.*

She heard the words echo about the house, climb the stairs, bounce off the walls, float out the front door and into the garden. She laughed out loud and took hold of the doorknob. "Ready or not," she called, "here I come."

Slowly she turned the handle and peeped mischievously around the door. Her little charade ended abruptly. The blank wall of silence came right at her. It mocked her high spirits and made her feel ridiculous. She straightened up and stepped inside. There was a different feel to this room. The window was still intact and the thin wisps of curtain were drawn together so it was dim and dusty and the air heavy and stale. Moving cautiously she looked about. An iron bedstead stood in the corner. She jumped as an empty soup can rolled drunkenly across the floor and came to a clanging halt by an empty beer carton. Dead bottles lay strewn on the floor, several poked out from beneath the iron bedstead, one lay on the filthy mattress and a couple more lay in the corner by the window. Someone had camped out here in the past. She picked up a bottle and sniffed. It was bone dry.

She moved to the window and pulled aside the dusty curtain. The tiny enclosure was filled with trapped sunshine. A whole world existed in this secret place. A nest of cobwebs, like stringy hammocks, hung in the corners cradling years of dirt. All about, the dust swarmed in tiny constellations. The Virgin Mary stood guard over all. Nora picked up the end of the curtain, rubbed at the dirt on the windowpane and peered through the smudgy circle. She could see where her feet had made a path to the door.

The sunlight improved the room but the silence was still unsettling. She had a strange feeling that things were staring right back at her, the bed, the walls, the overturned chair in the corner. He had died in this room in the comfort of fresh sheets, the warmth of a crackling fire, and with his dying breath he had spoken Peg's name. In the mad confusion of his mind he had set her apart.

Nora walked over and straightened the broken chair and set it securely on its legs.

It was the old newspapers pasted to the wall behind the chair that first caught her attention. She crouched low, searching for a date or maybe a headline. There were several layers of wallpaper, all torn and puffy with dampness. Suddenly she had the feeling that she was being watched. She spun around, terrified. She could have sworn there was someone there. Her breath came in tight gasps; her eyes, wide with fright, searched the room. Unnerved, she brought her attention back to the wall and began to peel away the layers. Before she even got down to the bare wall she just knew that underneath all the layers, she would find faded water lilies. He was by her shoulder, watching, guiding her; she could feel his presence. She traced the outline of the big flat leaf and then the petals of the lily with her fingertips. "Okay. It's okay now."

She stood then and without looking left or right she turned and hurried from the room, pulling the door quietly behind her.

At the top of the hill she stood for a moment and looked back. It was no longer Peg's house; he had taken over. He was alone again, isolated and cut off. She wondered if that was in fact what he wanted all along. Solitude. In that moment she knew she never wanted to come back here again. The gulch and the berry patch were no longer important. She wanted to be gone. She would be sitting, waiting, when Pat's boat came alongside the wharf.

"All done, girl?" he called, reaching for her hand as she stepped down into the boat.

"All done, Pat. It's a beautiful spot and a great lunch," she added, anxious to show her gratitude for the time and effort he had taken. "A great place to have grown up."

"Looks great on a day like today. Everything looks great when the sun's shining." He revved the engine and swung the boat back out to the middle of the cove. "But truth is, it was a hard bloody place to live. Aunt Peg and the old people, they just like to remember the good times. Everything was the best kind back then, best kind of fishin', best kind of life. But, girl, that's how it is, we like to remember the good times. Right? Memories are not always real."

She followed the route of the path as the shoreline drifted by. There was the house again, silent and deserted, another headstone to the past. She felt for the clothespin in her pocket and held it as she watched the white frame house slip by. "Give this to Peg from me," she said, handing him the clothespin. "I took it from her clothesline by the house. Don't forget, will you?"

"If that's what you want." He looked at her askance.

She moved to the doorway of the wheelhouse for a last glimpse. Suddenly, quite clearly in the front-room window, she saw a light. "Look, Pat, look!" She was shouting, her hand waving madly to get his attention. "There's someone there. There's a light in the window."

He looked over his shoulder and laughed. "It's the sun shining on the glass, girl, a reflection, no more than that."

Acknowledgements

My paternal grandfather walked away from his small farm in the West of Ireland and left his wife and young family to fend for themselves. I never knew him, nor, for some unknown reason, did I ever meet or know my grandmother. I have borrowed these facts from my family history but the rest of the story is fiction. Any similarities to living people are entirely coincidental.

I am deeply grateful to Stan Tobin and the late John Whelan for sharing with me their deeply felt love for the Cape Shore of Newfoundland and their memories of growing up there. Thank you also to Mrs. Mary Anne Councel, for her vivid and wonderful stories about living on the islands in Placentia Bay, one of which, with her permission, is included in this novel. I am grateful also to Dr. Eithne Knowling and Dr. Bill Kennedy for their valuable guidance and assistance. To Ed Furlong and Marjory Johns for sharing with me their very personal experience with Alzheimer's disease, a big thank you. I spent several wonderful afternoons with Dr. Martin Howley at Memorial University Library, looking at and talking about the collection of rare and treasured Irish books. His passion for and knowledge of the collection inspired and delighted me. I also received very good advice and help from Prof. Kevin B. Nowlan, now retired, of University College Dublin, as to what I should seek out amongst the collection of rare books.

My thanks also go to several people who, in different ways, have given generously of their time to assist me: Dr. Allison Feder, Sheila Redmond, Dr. Noel Shuell, the late Dr. Aly O'Brien, Susan Pahl, and Loreto Hyde Doyle. Thank you to Lisa Moore, who read an early draft of the manuscript and provided insightful feedback and suggestions, and, at the time, much needed encouragement. To the members of The Writers' Guild, I owe a deep debt of gratitude for their constant support and valuable criticism of the work in progress. I especially want to thank Georgina Queller for her valuable help and her friendship and for giving me that final nudge to the finish line.

I am deeply grateful to Annamarie Beckel, my editor, for her insight and for her understanding of where I wanted to go with this novel and for skilfully and patiently showing me the way. To all the staff at Breakwater, thank you. What a great crew to work with!

Lastly I must thank my family for their loving support, and especially my husband, Tony, for always being there.

PHOTOGRAPH BY SHARON SMITH

Born in County Sligo, Ireland, Kate Evans now lives with her husband Tony in St. John's, Newfoundland. She is a teacher of English as a Second Language and has taught in Dublin, London, Montreal, and Bangkok. She started her writing career doing feature articles for the newspaper, drawing for her material on her passion for travel and the theatre. She has also written several radio scripts and has published a short story in *Ireland of the Welcomes*. *Where Old Ghosts Meet* is her first novel.